Deemed 'the father of the scientific d____ **Austin Freeman** had a long and distingu____ a writer of detective fiction. He was born ____ _____, the son of a tailor who went on to train as a pharmacist. After graduating as a surgeon at the Middlesex Hospital Medical College, Freeman taught for a while and joined the colonial service, offering his skills as an assistant surgeon along the Gold Coast of Africa. He became embroiled in a diplomatic mission when a British expeditionary party was sent to investigate the activities of the French. Through his tact and formidable intelligence, a massacre was narrowly avoided. His future was assured in the colonial service. However, after becoming ill with blackwater fever, Freeman was sent back to England to recover and, finding his finances precarious, embarked on a career as acting physician in Holloway Prison. In desperation, he turned to writing and went on to dominate the world of British detective fiction, taking pride in testing different criminal techniques. So keen were his powers as a writer that part of one of his best novels was written in a bomb shelter.

The Stoneware Monkey

R Austin Freeman

HOUSE OF
STRATUS

This edition published in 2001 by House of Stratus, an imprint of Stratus Books Ltd., 21 Beeching Park, Kelly Bray, Cornwall, PL17 8QS, UK.

www.houseofstratus.com

Typeset, printed and bound by House of Stratus.

A catalogue record for this book is available from the British Library and the Library of Congress.

ISBN 0-7551-0379-3

CONTENTS

Book I
Narrated by James Oldfield, MD

Book II
Narrated by Christopher Jervis, MD

To
MY FRIEND
WP WATT
IN COMMEMORATION OF MANY YEARS
OF HAPPY AND HARMONIOUS
COLLABORATION

BOOK I

Narrated by James Oldfield, MD

CHAPTER ONE

Hue and Cry

The profession of medicine has a good many drawbacks in the way of interrupted meals, disturbed nights and long and strenuous working hours. But it has its compensations. For a doctor's life is seldom a dull life. Compared, for instance, with that of a civil servant or a bank official, it abounds in variety of experience and surroundings, to say nothing of the intrinsic interest of the work in its professional aspects. And then it may happen at any moment that the medical practitioner's duties may lead him into the very heart of a drama or a tragedy or bring him into intimate contact with crime.

Not that the incident which I am about to describe was, in the first place, directly connected with my professional duties. The initial experience might have befallen anyone. But it was my medical status that enlarged and completed that experience.

It was about nine o'clock on a warm September night that I was cycling at an easy pace along a by-road towards the town, or village, of Newingstead, in which I was temporarily domiciled as the *locum tenens* of a certain Dr Wilson. I had been out, on an emergency call, to a small village about three miles distant and had taken my bicycle instead of the car for the sake of the exercise; and having ridden out at the speed that the occasion seemed to demand, was now making a leisurely return, enjoying the peaceful quiet of the by-way and even finding the darkness restful with a good head-light to show the way and a rear-light to secure me from collisions from behind.

At a turn of the lane, a few twinkling lights seen dimly through spaces in the hedgerow told me that I was nearing my destination. A little reluctant to exchange the quiet of the countryside for the light and bustle of the town, I dismounted, and, leaning my bicycle against a gate, brought out my pipe and was just dipping into my pocket for my tobacco pouch when I heard what sounded to me like the call of a police whistle.

I let go the pouch and put away my pipe as I strained my ears to listen. The sound had come from no great distance, but I had not been able exactly to locate it. The cart-track from the gate, I knew, skirted a small wood, from which a footpath joined it, and the sound had seemed to come from that direction. But the wood was invisible in the darkness, though I could judge its position by a group of ricks, the nearest of which loomed vaguely out of the murk.

I had switched off the lamps of my machine and was just considering the expediency of walking up the cart-track to explore, when the unmistakable shriek of a police whistle rang out, considerably nearer than the last and much shorter, and was succeeded by the sound of voices – apparently angry voices – accompanied by obscure noises as of bodies bursting through the undergrowth of the wood, from the direction of which the sounds now clearly proceeded. On this I climbed over the gate and started up the cart-track at a quick pace, treading as silently as I could and keeping a bright look-out. The track led through the group of ricks, the great shapes of which loomed up one after another, looking strangely gigantic in the obscurity, and near the last of them I passed a farm wagon and was disposed to examine it with my pocket-lamp, but then judged it to be more prudent not to show a light. So I pushed on with the lamp in my hand, peering intently into the darkness and listening for any further sounds.

But there were none. The silence of the countryside – now no longer restful, but awesome and sinister – was deepened rather than broken by the faint sounds that belonged to it; the half-audible "skreek" of a bat, the faint murmur of leaves, and far away, the fantastic cry of an owl.

Presently I was able to make out the wood as a vague shape of deeper darkness and then I came on the little footpath that meandered away towards it. Deciding that this was the right direction, I turned on to it and followed it – not without difficulty, for it was but a narrow track through the grass – until I found myself entering the black shadows of the wood. Here I paused for a moment to listen while I peered into the impenetrable darkness ahead. But no sounds came to my ear save the hushed whisper of the trees. Whatever movement there had been was now stilled; and as I resumed my advance towards the wood I began to ask myself uneasily what this strange and sudden stillness might portend. But I had not gone more than a score of paces and was just entering the wood when the question was answered. Quite suddenly, almost at my feet, I saw the prostrate figure of a man.

Instantly, I switched on my lamp, and, as its light fell on him it told the substance of the tragic story in a single flash. He was the constable whose whistle I had heard – it was still hanging loose at the end of its chain. He was bareheaded and at the first glance I thought he was dead; but when I knelt down by his side I saw that he was still breathing, and I now noticed a small trickle of blood issuing from an invisible wound above his ear. Very carefully I sought the wound by a light touch of my finger, and, immediately, became aware of a soft area of the scalp which further cautious and delicate palpation showed to be a depression in the skull.

I felt his pulse – a typical brain-compression pulse – and examined his eyes; but there was no doubt as to his condition. The dent in the skull was compressing his brain and probably the compression was being increased from moment to moment by internal bleeding. The question was, what was to be done? I could do nothing for him here, but yet I could hardly leave him to go in search of help. It was a horrible dilemma; for whatever could be done for him would need to be done quickly, and the sands of his life were running out while I knelt helplessly at his side.

Suddenly I bethought me of his whistle. The sound of it had brought me to the spot and it must surely bring others. Picking it up, I put it to my lips and blew a loud and prolonged blast, and, after a few moments' pause, another and yet another. The harsh, strident screech, breaking in on the deathly stillness of the wood and setting the sleeping birds astir, seemed to strike my over-strung nerves a palpable blow. It was positive pain to me to raise that hideous din, but there was nothing else to do. I must keep it up until it should be heard and should attract someone to this remote and solitary place.

It took effect sooner than I had expected; for I was in the act of raising the whistle once more to my lips when I heard sounds from within the wood as of someone trampling through the undergrowth. I threw the light of my lamp in that direction, but took the precaution to stand up until I should have seen who and what the newcomer might be. Almost immediately there appeared a light from the wood which flashed out and then disappeared as if a lantern were being carried among tree trunks. Then it became continuous and was evidently turned full on me as the newcomer ran out of the wood and advanced towards me. For a few moments I was quite dazzled by the glare of his lamp, but as he came nearer, my lamp lighted him up and I then saw that he was a police constable. Apparently he had just observed the figure lying at my feet, for he suddenly quickened his pace and arrived so much out of breath that, for a moment or two, he was unable to speak, but stood with the light of his lantern cast on his unconscious comrade, breathing hard and staring down at him with amazement and horror.

"God save us!" he muttered at length. "What the devil has been happening? Who blew that whistle?"

"I did," I replied, upon which he nodded, and then, once more throwing his light on me, and casting a searching glance at me, demanded:

"And who are you, and how do you come to be here?"

I explained the position very briefly and added that it was urgently necessary that the injured man should be got to the hospital as quickly as possible.

"He isn't dead, then?" said he. "And you say you are a doctor. Can't you do anything for him?"

"Not here," I answered. "He has got a deep depressed fracture of the skull. If anything can be done, it will have to be done at the hospital; and he will have to be moved very gently. We shall want an ambulance. Could you go and fetch one? My bicycle is down by the gate."

He considered for a few moments. Apparently he was in somewhat of a dilemma, for he replied:

"I oughtn't to go away from here with that devil probably lurking in the wood. And you oughtn't to leave this poor chap. But there was another man coming along close behind me. He should be here any minute if he hasn't lost his way. Perhaps I'd better go back a bit and look for him."

He threw the beam from his lantern into the opening of the wood and was just starting to retrace his steps, when there sounded faintly from that direction the voice of someone apparently hailing us.

"Is that you, Mr Kempster?" the constable roared.

Apparently it was, though I could not make out the words of the reply, for a minute or so later a man emerged from the wood and approached us at a quick walk. But Mr Kempster, like the constable, was a good deal the worse for his exertions, and, for a time, was able only to stand panting with his hand to his side while he gazed in consternation at the prostrate form on the ground.

"Can you ride a bicycle, Mr Kempster?" the constable asked.

Mr Kempster managed to gasp out that he could, though he wasn't much of a rider.

"Well," said the constable, "we want an ambulance to take this poor fellow to the hospital. Could you take the doctor's bicycle and run along to the police station and just tell them what has happened?"

"Where is the bicycle?" asked Kempster.

"It is leaning against the gate at the bottom of the cart-track," I replied, adding, "You can have my lamp to find your way and I will see you down the path to the place where it joins the track."

He agreed, not unwillingly, I thought, having no great liking for the neighbourhood, so I handed him my lamp and conducted him along the path to its junction with the cart-track, when I returned to the place where the constable was kneeling by his comrade, examining him by the light of his lantern.

"I can't make this out," said he as I came up. "He wasn't taken unawares. There seems to have been a considerable scrap. His truncheon's gone. The fellow must have managed to snatch it out of his hand, but I can't imagine how that can have happened. It would take a pretty hefty customer to get a constable's truncheon out of his fist, especially as that's just what he'd be on his guard against."

"He seems to have been a powerful ruffian," said I, "judging by the character of the injury. He must have struck a tremendous blow. The skull is stove in like an egg-shell."

"Blighter!" muttered the constable. Then, after a pause, he asked: "Do you think he is going to die, Doctor?"

"I am afraid his chances are not very good," I replied, "and the longer we have to wait for that ambulance, the worse they will be."

"Well," he rejoined, "if Mr Kempster hustles along, we shan't have very long to wait. They won't waste any time at the station."

He stood up and swept the beam of his lamp around, first towards the wood and then in the direction of the ricks. Suddenly he uttered an indignant snort and exclaimed, angrily:

"Well, I'm damned! Here's Mr Kempster coming back." He kept the light of his lantern on the approaching figure, and, as it came within range, he roared out: "What's the matter, sir? We thought you'd be half way there."

Mr Kempster hurried up, breathing hard and looking decidedly resentful of the constable's tone.

"There is no bicycle there," he said, sulkily. "Somebody must have made off with it. I searched all about there but there was not a sign of it."

The constable cursed as a well-trained constable ought not to curse.

"But that's put the lid on it," he concluded. "This murderous devil must have seen you come up, Doctor, and as soon as you were out of sight, he must have got on your machine and cleared out. I suppose you had a head-light."

"I had both head and rear light," I replied, "but I switched them both off before I started up the cart-track. But, of course, if he was anywhere near – hiding behind one of those ricks, for instance – he would have seen my lights when I came up to the gate."

"Yes," the constable agreed, gloomily, "it was a bit of luck for him. And now he's got clean away; got away for good and all unless he has left some sort of traces."

Mr Kempster uttered a groan. "If he has slipped through your fingers," he exclaimed indignantly, "there's about ten thousand pounds' worth of my property gone with him. Do you realize that?"

"I do, now you've told me," replied the constable, adding unsympathetically, "and it's bad luck for you; but still, you know, you are better off than my poor mate here who was trying to get it back for you. But we mustn't stop here talking. If the man has gone, there is no use in my staying here. I'll just run back the way I came and report at the station. You may as well wait here with the doctor until I come back with the ambulance."

But Mr Kempster had had enough of the adventure.

"There is no use in my waiting here," said he, handing me my pocket lamp. "I'll walk back through the wood with you and then get along home and see exactly what that scoundrel has taken."

The constable made no secret of his disapproval of this course, but he did not actually put it into words. With a brief farewell to me, he turned the light of his lantern on the entrance to the wood and set off at a pace that kept his companion at a brisk trot. And as the light faded among the trees and the sound of their footsteps died away in the distance, I found myself once more alone with my patient, encompassed by the darkness and wrapped in a silence which was broken only by an occasional soft snore from the unconscious man.

It seemed to me that hours elapsed after the departure of the constable; hours of weary expectation and anxiety. I possessed myself of my patient's lantern and by its light examined him from time to time. Naturally, there was no improvement; indeed, each time that I felt his pulse it was with a faint surprise to find it still beating. I knew that, actually, his condition must be getting worse with every minute that passed, and it became more and more doubtful whether he would reach the hospital alive.

Then my thoughts strayed towards my bicycle and the unknown robber. We had taken it for granted that the latter had escaped on the machine, and in all probability he had. Yet it was possible that the cycle might have been stolen by some tramp or casual wayfarer and that the robber might still be lurking in the neighbourhood. However, that possibility did not disturb me, since he could have no object in attacking me. I was more concerned about the loss of my bicycle.

From the robber my reflections drifted to the robbed. Who and what was Mr Kempster? And what sort of property was it that the thief had made off with? There are not many things worth ten thousand pounds which can be carried away in the pocket. Probably the booty consisted of something in the nature of jewellery. But I was not much interested. The value of property, and especially of such trivial property as jewellery, counts for little compared with that of a human life. My momentarily wandering attention quickly came back to the man lying motionless at my feet, whose life hung so unsteadily in the balance.

At last my seemingly interminable vigil came to an end. From the road below came the distinctive clang of an ambulance bell, and lights winked over the unseen hedgerow. Then the glare from a pair of powerful headlamps came across the field, throwing up the ricks in sharp silhouette, and telling me that the ambulance was passing in through the gate. I watched the lights growing brighter from moment to moment; saw them vanish behind the ricks and presently emerge as the vehicle advanced up the cart-track and at length turned on to the footpath.

It drew up eventually within a few paces of the spot where the injured man was lying, and immediately there descended from it a number of men, including a police inspector and the constable who had gone with Kempster. The former greeted me civilly, and, looking down on his subordinate with deep concern, asked me a few questions while a couple of uniformed men brought out a stretcher and set it down by the patient. I helped them to lift him on to the stretcher and to convey the latter to its place in the ambulance. Then I got in myself, and while the vehicle was being turned round, the inspector came to take a last look at the patient.

"I am not coming back with you, Doctor," said he. "I have got a squad of men with some powerful lamps to search the wood."

"But," said I, "the man has almost certainly gone off on my bicycle."

"I know," said he. "But we are not looking for him. It's the poor fellow's truncheon that I want. If the thief managed to snatch it away from him, there are pretty certain to be fingerprints on it. At any rate, I hope so, for it's our only chance of identifying the man."

With this, as the ambulance was now ready to start, he turned away; and as we moved off towards the cart-track, I saw him, with the constable and three plain-clothes men advancing towards the wood which, by the combined effects of all their lamps, was illuminated almost to the brightness of daylight.

Once out on the road, the smoothly running ambulance made short work of the distance to the hospital. But yet the journey had not been short enough. For when the stretcher had been borne into the casualty-room and placed on the table, the first anxious glance showed that the feebly flickering light had gone out. In vain the visiting surgeon – who had been summoned by telephone – felt the pulse and listened to the heart. Poor Constable Murray – such, I learned, was his name – had taken his last turn of duty.

"A bad business," said the surgeon, putting away his stethoscope and passing his fingers lightly over the depression in the dead man's skull. "But I doubt whether we could have done much for him even if he had come in alive. It was a devil of a blow. The man was a fool to hit so hard, for now he'll have to face a charge of wilful murder – that is, if they catch him. I hope they will."

"I hope so, too," said I, "but I doubt whether they will. He seems to have found my bicycle and gone off on it, and I gather that nobody saw him near enough to recognize him."

"H'm," grunted the surgeon, "that's unfortunate; and bad luck for you, too, though I expect you will get your cycle back. Meanwhile, can I give you a lift in my car?"

I accepted the offer gladly, and, after a last look at the dead constable, we went out together to return to our respective homes.

CHAPTER TWO

The Inquest

It was on the fourth day after my adventure that I received the summons to attend the inquest – which had been kept back to enable the police to collect such evidence as was available – and in due course presented myself at the little Town Hall in which the inquiry was to be held. The preliminaries had already been disposed of when I arrived, but I was in time to hear the coroner's opening address to the jury. It was quite short, and amounted to little more than the announcement of his intention to take the evidence in its chronological order; a very sensible proceeding, as it seemed to me, whereby the history of the tragedy would evolve naturally from the depositions of the witnesses. Of these, the first was Mr Arthur Kempster, who, by the coroner's direction, began with a narrative of the events known to him.

"I am a diamond merchant, having business premises in Hatton Garden and a private residence at The Hawthorns, Newingstead. On Friday, the 16th of September, I returned from a trip to Holland and came direct from Harwich to The Hawthorns. At Amsterdam I purchased a parcel of diamonds and I had them in a paper packet in my inside waistcoat-pocket when I arrived home, which I did just about dinner time. After dinner, I went to my study to examine the diamonds and to check their weight on the special balance which I keep for that purpose. When I had finished weighing them and had looked them over, one by one, I put away the balance and looked about for the lens which I use to examine stones as to their cutting. But I couldn't find the lens. Then I had a faint recollection of having used it in the dining-room, which adjoins the study, and I went to that room to see if I might have left it there. And I had. I found it after a very short search and went back with it to the study. But when I went to the table on which I had put the diamonds, to my amazement I found that they had vanished. As nobody could possibly have come into the study by the door, I looked at the window; and then I saw that it was open, whereas it had been shut when I went to the dining-room.

"I immediately rushed out through the dining-room to the front door, and, as I came out of it I saw a man walking quickly down the drive. He was nearly at the bottom of it when I ran out, and, as soon as he heard me, he darted round the corner and disappeared. I ran down the drive as fast as I could go, and, when I came out into the road, I could see him some distance ahead, running furiously in the direction of the country. I followed him as fast as I could, but I could see that he was gaining on me. Then, as I came to a side turning – Bascombe Avenue – I saw a policeman approaching along it and quite near. So I hailed him and gave the alarm; and when he ran up, I told him, very briefly, what had happened; and, as the thief was still in sight, he ran off in pursuit. I followed as well as I could, but I was already out of breath and couldn't nearly keep up with him. But I saw the thief make off along the country road and get over a gate nearly opposite Clay Wood; and the policeman, who seemed to be gaining on the fugitive, also got over the gate, and I lost sight of them both.

"It seemed to me that it was useless to try to follow them, so I turned back towards the town to see if I could get any further assistance. Then, on the main road, I met Police Constable Webb and told him what had happened, and we started off together to the place where the thief had disappeared. We got over the gate, crossed a field, and entered the wood. But there we rather lost ourselves as we had missed the path. We heard a police whistle sounding from the wood while we were crossing the field; and we heard another shorter one, just after we had entered. But we couldn't make out clearly the direction the sounds had come from, and we still couldn't find the path.

"Then, after a considerable time, we heard three long blasts of a whistle and at the same moment we saw a glimmer of light; so we ran towards the light – at least the constable did, for I was too blown to run any farther – and at last I found the path and came out of the wood and saw Dr Oldfield standing by deceased, who was lying on the ground. Constable Webb suggested that I should take Dr Oldfield's bicycle and ride to the police station, and the Doctor gave me his pocket-lamp to light me down the cart-track to a gate where he had left the bicycle. But when I got to the gate, there was no sign of any bicycle, so I returned and reported to the constable, who then decided to go, himself, to the station, and we went back together through the wood. When we got back to the field he ran on ahead and I went back to my house."

"When you went to the dining-room," said the coroner, "how long were you absent from the study?"

"About two minutes, I should say. Certainly not more than three."

"You say that the study window was closed when you went out of the room. Was it fastened?"

"No. It was open at the top. I opened it when I came in after dinner, as it was a warm night and the room seemed rather close."

"Was the blind drawn?"

"There is no blind; only a pair of heavy curtains. They were drawn when I came into the room, but I had to pull them apart to open the window and I may not have drawn them close afterwards; in fact, I don't think I did."

"Do you think that anyone passing outside could have seen into the room?"

"Yes. The study is on the ground floor – perhaps a couple of feet above the level of the ground – and the window sill would be about the height of a man's shoulder, so that a man standing outside could easily look into the room."

"Does the window face the drive?"

"No. It looks on the alley that leads to the back premises."

"You, apparently, did not hear the sound of the window sash being raised?"

"No, but I shouldn't, in the dining-room. The sash slides up easily, and I have all the sash pulleys of my windows kept oiled to prevent them from squeaking."

"Were the diamonds in an accessible position?"

"Yes, quite. They were lying, all together, on a square of black velvet on the table."

"Were they of any considerable value?"

"They were indeed. The whole parcel would be worth about ten thousand pounds. There were fifteen of them, and they were all very exceptional stones."

"Would you be able to recognize them if them could be traced?"

"I could easily identify the complete parcel, and I think I could identify the individual stones. I weighed each one separately and the whole group together, and I made certain notes about them of which I have given a copy to the police."

"Was anything taken besides the diamonds?"

"Nothing, not even the paper. The thief must have just grabbed up the stones and put them loose in his pocket."

This completed Mr Kempster's evidence. Some of the jury would have liked more detailed particulars of the diamonds, but the coroner reminded them, gently, that the inquiry was concerned, not with the robbery, but with the death of Constable Alfred Murray. As there were no other questions, the depositions were read and signed and the witness was released.

Following the chronological sequence, I succeeded Mr Kempster, and, like him, opened my evidence with a narrative statement. But I need not repeat this, or the examination that amplified it, as I have already told the story of my connection with the case. Nor need I record Constable Webb's evidence, which was mainly a repetition of Kempster's. When the constable had retired, the name of Dr James Tansley was called and the surgeon whom I had met at the hospital came forward.

"You have made an examination of the body of deceased," said the coroner when the preliminary questions had been answered. "Will you tell us what conditions you found?"

"On external examination," the witness replied, "I found a deep depression in the skull two and a quarter inches in diameter starting from a point an inch and a half above the left ear, and a contused wound an inch and three-quarters in length. The wound and the depressed fracture of the skull appeared to have been both produced by a heavy blow from some blunt instrument. There was no sign of more than one blow. On removing the cap of the skull I found that the inner table – that is, the hard inner layer of the skull – had been shattered and portions of it driven into the substance of the brain, causing severe lacerations. It had also injured one or two arteries and completely divided one, with the result that extensive bleeding had occurred between the skull and the brain, and this will have produced great pressure on the surface of the brain."

"What should you say was the cause of death?"

"The immediate cause of death was laceration and compression of the brain, but, of course, the ultimate cause was the blow on the head which produced those injuries."

"It is a mere formality, I suppose, to ask whether the injury could have been self-inflicted?"

"Yes. It is quite impossible that the blow could have been struck by deceased himself."

This was the substance of the doctor's evidence. When it was concluded and the witness had been released, the name of Inspector Charles Roberts was called, and that officer took his place by the table. Like the preceding witnesses, he began, at the coroner's invitation, with a general statement.

"On receiving Constable Webb's report, as the Chief Constable was absent, I ordered the sergeant to get out the ambulance and I collected a search party to go with it. When we arrived at the spot where the deceased was lying, I saw him transferred to the ambulance under the doctor's supervision, and, when it had gone, I took my party into the wood. Each member of the party was provided with a powerful lamp, so that we had a good light to work by.

"We saw no sign of anyone hiding in the wood, but near the path we found deceased's helmet. It was uninjured and had probably been knocked off by a branch of a tree. We searched especially for deceased's truncheon and eventually found it quite near to the place where deceased had been lying. I picked it up by the wrist strap at the end of the handle and carried it in that way until we reached the station, when I examined it carefully, and could see that there were several fingerprints on it. I did not attempt to develop the prints, but hung up the truncheon by its strap in a cupboard, which I locked. On the following morning I delivered the key of the cupboard to the Chief Constable when I made my report."

"Did you find any traces of the fugitive?"

"No. We went down to the gate and found there marks on the earth where the bicycle had stood; and we could see where it had been wheeled off on to the road. But we were unable to make out any visible tracks on the road itself."

"Has the bicycle been traced since then?"

"Yes. Two days after the robbery it was found hidden in a cart shed near the London Road, about four miles from Clay Wood towards London. I went over it carefully with developing powder to see if there were any fingerprints on it, but, although there were plenty of finger-marks, they were only smears and quite unidentifiable."

This was the sum of the inspector's evidence; and, as there were no questions, the officer was released and was succeeded by Chief Constable Herbert Parker, who took up and continued the inspector's account of the dead constable's truncheon.

"The key of the cupboard at the police station was delivered to me by Inspector Roberts as he has deposed. I unlocked the cupboard and took out the truncheon, which I examined in a good light with the aid of a magnifying lens. I could see that there were, on the barrel of the truncheon, several fingerprints; and by their position and grouping, I judged that they had been made by the thief when he snatched the trucheon out of deceased's hand. They were quite distinct on the polished surface, but not sufficiently so to photograph without development; and I did not attempt to develop them because I thought that, having regard to their importance, it would be better to hand the truncheon intact to the experts at Scotland Yard. Accordingly, I packed the truncheon in such a way that the marked surfaces should be protected from any contact, and took it up to the Fingerprint Department at Scotland Yard, where I delivered it to the Chief Inspector, who examined it and developed the fingerprints with a suitable powder.

"It was then seen that there were four decipherable prints, evidently those of a left hand; one was a thumbprint and was perfectly clear, and the others, of the first three fingers, though less perfect, were quite recognizable. As soon as they had been developed, they were photographed; and when the photographs were ready, they were handed to the expert searchers, who took them to the place where the collections are kept and went through the files with them. The result of the search was to make it certain that no such fingerprints were in any of the files; neither in those of the main collection nor in those containing single fingerprints."

"And what does that amount to?"

"It amounts to this: that, since these fingerprints are not in the principal files – those containing the complete sets taken by prison officers – it is certain that this man has never been convicted; and, since they are not in the single fingerprint files, there is no evidence that he has ever been connected with any crime. In short – so far as the fingerprints are concerned – this man is not known to the police."

"That is very unfortunate," said the coroner. "It would seem as if there were practically no chance of ever bringing the crime home to him."

"I wouldn't say that," the Chief Constable replied. "His fingerprints are now in the files of Scotland Yard, so that if ever he should get into trouble of any kind and have his fingerprints taken, he will certainly be identified and brought to trial. And then there is a very fair chance that the diamonds may be traced and the identity of the thief disclosed."

"Well, I hope it may be so," said the coroner. "But, for the purposes of this inquiry, the important fact is that the identity of the man who killed deceased is at present unknown. Is there anything more that you have to tell us?"

"There is one other point," the officer replied. "When we came to examine the truncheon after it had been photographed, we found on its end distinct traces of blood and two hairs. The hairs have been preserved with the truncheon, and I have sent up to Scotland Yard several hairs and a sample of blood from the body of deceased."

"That may be useful as verification," said the coroner, "though there can be no doubt as to how deceased met his death. But, as a final question, have you, by the light of your experience of crime, formed any ideas as to how this affair happened and what sort of person the criminal is likely to have been?"

"As to the criminal, my impression – which is shared by my fellow officers – is that he was not a regular hand. The whole affair is suggestive of the amateur. The man has no criminal record, he was obviously unarmed, and there was no occasion for any skill or experience. It looks as if some casual stranger, probably a tramp, had strayed into the premises and was prowling round the house when he came to a lighted window, and, looking in between the curtains, saw Mr Kempster weighing the diamonds and inspecting them on the black velvet. Then Mr Kempster went out of the room, and there was the chance of a lifetime for a sneak thief. The man simply slid up the window, climbed in, grabbed up the diamonds, dropped out of the window, and made off. Anyone could have done it. That is the unsatisfactory aspect of the case from the police point of view. On the other hand, if he is an amateur who doesn't know the ropes, he will probably get into difficulties when he tries to dispose of the diamonds."

The coroner agreed to this probability but was not greatly interested. And, as he had now got all the available evidence relevant to the subject of the inquiry, he dismissed the Chief Constable and proceeded, briefly and concisely, to sum up.

"There is little," he began, "that I need say to you, members of the jury. You have heard the evidence, and the evidence tells the whole sad story. I do not suppose that you will have any doubt that the gallant officer whose tragic and untimely death is the subject of this inquiry, was killed by the runaway thief. But I have to point out to you that if that is your decision, you are legally bound to find a verdict of wilful murder against that unknown man. The law is quite clear on that subject. If any person, while engaged in committing a felony, and in furtherance of such felony, kills, or directly causes, the death of any other person, he is guilty of wilful murder, whether he did or did not intend to kill that person.

"Now, there is no evidence that the fugitive desired or intended to kill the constable. But he dealt him a blow which might have killed him and which, in fact, did kill him; and the fugitive was, at the time, engaged in committing a felony. Therefore, he is guilty of wilful murder. That is all, I think, that I need say."

The jury had apparently already made up their minds on the subject, for, after but the briefest whispered consultation with them, the foreman announced that they had agreed on their verdict.

"We find," he continued as the coroner took up his pen, "that deceased was murdered in Clay Wood by the unknown man who entered Mr Kempster's house to commit a robbery."

The coroner nodded. "Yes," he said, "I am in entire agreement with you and I shall record a verdict of wilful murder against that unknown man; and I am sure you will concur with me in expressing our deepest sympathy with the family of this gallant officer whose life was sacrificed in the performance of a dangerous duty."

Thus, gloomily enough, ended the adventure that had brought me, for the first time, into intimate contact with serious crime. At least, it appeared to me that the adventure was at an end and that I had heard the last of the tragedy and of the sinister, shadowy figure that must have passed so near to me on the margin of the wood. It was a natural belief, since I had played but a super's part in the drama and seemed to be concerned with it no more, and since my connection with Newingstead and its inhabitants would cease when my principal, Dr Wilson, should return from his holiday.

But it was, nevertheless, a mistaken belief, as will appear at a later stage of this narrative.

CHAPTER THREE

Peter Gannet

A problem that has occasionally exercised my mind is that of the deterioration of London streets. Why do they always deteriorate and never improve? The change seems to be governed by some mysterious law. Constantly we meet with streets, once fashionable but now squalid, whose spacious houses have fallen from the estate of mansions, tenanted by the rich and great, to that of mere tenements giving shelter to all grades of the poverty-stricken, from the shabby-genteel to the definitely submerged; streets where the vanished coaches have given place to the coster's barrow and the van of the yelling coal-vendor. But never, in my experience, does one encounter a street that has undergone a change in the reverse direction; that has evolved from obscurity to fashion, from the shabby to the modish.

The reflection is suggested to me by the neighbourhood in which I had recently taken up my abode, on the expiration of my engagement at Newingstead. Not that Osnaburgh Street, Marylebone, could fairly be described as squalid. On the contrary, it is a highly respectable street. Nevertheless, its tall, flat-faced houses with their spacious rooms and dignified doorways are evidently survivors from a more opulent past, and the whole neighbourhood shows traces of the curious subsidence that I have referred to.

23

The occasion of my coming to Osnaburgh Street was the purchase by me of a "death vacancy"; very properly so described; for there was no doubt of the decease of my predecessor, and the fact of the vacancy became clearly established as I sat, day after day, the undisturbed and solitary occupant of the consulting-room, incredulously turning over the pages of the old ledgers and wondering whether the names inscribed therein might perchance appertain to mythical persons, or whether those patients could, with one accord, have followed the late incumbent to his destination in Heaven or Gehenna.

Yet there were occasional calls or messages, at first from casual strangers or newcomers to the district; but presently, by introduction and recommendation, the vacancy grew into a visible "nucleus", which, expanding by slow degrees, seemed to promise an actual practice in the not too far distant future. The hours of solitary meditation in the consulting-room began more frequently to be shortened by welcome interruptions, and my brisk, business-like walks through the streets to have some purpose other than mere geographical exploration.

Principally, my little practice grew, as I have said, by recommendation. My patients seemed to like me and mentioned the fact to their friends; and thus it was that I made the acquaintance of Peter Gannet. I remember the occasion very clearly, though it seemed so insignificant at the time. It was a gloomy December morning, some three months after my departure from Newingstead, when I set forth on my "round" (of one patient), taking a short cut to Jacob Street, Hampstead Road, through the by-streets behind Cumberland Market, and contrasting the drab little thoroughfares with the pleasant lanes around Newingstead. Jacob Street was another instance of the "law of decay" which I have mentioned. Now at the undeniably shabby-genteel stage, it had formerly been the chosen resort of famous and distinguished artists. But its glory was not utterly departed; for, as several of the houses had commodious studios attached to them, the population still included a leavening of artists, though of a more humble and unpretentious type. The husband of my patient, Mrs Jenkins, was a monumental mason, and from the bedroom window I could see him in the small yard below, chipping away at a rather florid marble headstone.

The introduction came when I had finished my leisurely visit and was about to depart.

"Before you go, Doctor," said Mrs Jenkins, "I must give you a message from my neighbour, Mrs Gannet. She sent her maid in this morning to say that her husband is not very well, and that she would be glad if you would just drop in and have a look at him. She knows that you are attending me, and they've got no doctor of their own. It's next door but one; Number 12."

I thanked her for the introduction, and, having wished her "good morning," let myself out of the house and proceeded to Number 12, approaching it slowly to take a preliminary glance at the premises. The result of the inspection was satisfactory as an index to the quality of my new patient, for the house was in better repair than most of its neighbours, and the bright brass knocker and door-knob and the whitened doorstep suggested a household rather above the general Jacob Street level. At the side of the house was a wide, two-leaved gate with a wicket at which I glanced inquisitively. It seemed to be the entrance to a yard or factory, adapted to the passage of trucks or vans, but it clearly belonged to the house, for a bell-pull on the jamb of the gate had underneath it a small brass plate bearing the inscription, "P Gannet".

The door was opened in response to my knock by a lanky girl of about eighteen with long legs, a short skirt, and something on her head which resembled a pudding cloth. When I had revealed my identity, she conducted me along a tiled hall to a door, which she opened, and, having announced me by name, washed her hands of me and retired down the kitchen stairs.

The occupant of the room, a woman of about thirty-five, rose as I entered and laid down some needlework on a side-table.

"Am I addressing Mrs Gannet?" I asked.

"Yes," she replied. "I am Mrs Gannet. I suppose Mrs Jenkins gave you my message?"

"Yes. She tells me – which I am sorry to hear – that your husband is not very well."

"He is not at all well," said she, "though I don't think it is anything that matters very much, you know."

"I expect it matters to him," I suggested.

"I suppose it does," she agreed. "At any rate, he seems rather sorry for himself. He is sitting up in his bedroom at present. Shall I show you the way? I think he is rather anxious to see you."

I held the door open for her, and, when she passed out, I followed her up the stairs, rapidly sorting out my first impressions. Mrs Gannet was a rather tall, slender woman with light-brown hair and slightly chilly blue eyes. She was decidedly good-looking, but yet I did not find her prepossessing. Comely as her face undoubtedly was, it was not – at least, to me – a pleasant face. There was a tinge of petulance in its expression, a faint suggestion of unamiability. And I did not like the tone in which she had referred to her husband.

Her introduction of me was as laconic as that of her maid. She opened the bedroom door and, standing at the threshold, announced: "Here's the doctor." Then, as I entered, she shut me in and departed.

"Well, Doctor," said the patient, "I'm glad to see you. Pull up a chair to the fire and take off your overcoat."

I drew a chair up to the fire gladly enough, but I did not adopt the other suggestion; for already I had learned by experience that the doctor who takes off his overcoat is lost. Forthwith he becomes a visitor and his difficulties in making his escape are multiplied indefinitely.

"So you are not feeling very well," said I, by way of opening the proceedings.

"I'm feeling devilish ill," he replied. "I don't suppose it's anything serious, but it's deuced unpleasant. Little Mary in trouble, you know."

I didn't know, not having heard the expression before, and I looked at him inquiringly, and probably rather vacantly.

"Little Mary," he repeated. "Tummy. Belly-ache, to put it bluntly."

"Ha!" said I, with sudden comprehension. "You are suffering from abdominal pain. Is it bad?"

"Is it ever good?" he demanded, with a sour grin.

"It certainly is never pleasant," I admitted. "But is the pain severe?"

"Sometimes," he replied. "It seems to come and go – Whoo!"

A change of facial expression indicated that, just now, it had come. Accordingly, I suspended the conversation until conditions should be more favourable, and, meanwhile, inspected my patient with sympathetic interest. He was not as good-looking as his wife, and his appearance was not improved by a rather deep scar which cut across his right eyebrow, but he made a better impression; a strongly built man, though not large, so far as I could judge, seeing him sitting huddled in his easy chair, of a medium complexion and decidedly lean. He wore his hair rather long and had a well-shaped moustache and a Vandyke beard. Indeed, his appearance in general was distinctly Vandykish, with his brown velveteen jacket, his open, deep-pointed collar, and the loose bow with drooping ends which served as a necktie. I also noted that his eyes looked red and irritable like those of a long-sighted person who is in need of spectacles.

"Phoo!" he exclaimed after a spell of silence. "That was a bit of a twister, but it's better now. Going to have a lucid interval, I suppose."

Thereupon I resumed the conversation, which, however, I need not report in detail. I had plenty of time and could afford to encourage him to enlarge on his symptoms, the possible causes of his illness, and his usual habits and mode of life. And, as he talked, I looked about me, bearing in mind the advice of my teacher, Dr Thorndyke, to observe and take note of a patient's surroundings as a possible guide to his personality. In particular I inspected the mantelpiece which confronted me, and considered the objects on it in their possible bearings on my patient's habits and life-history.

They were rather curious objects, examples of pottery of a singularly uncouth and barbaric type which I set down as the gleanings gathered in the course of travel in distant lands among primitive and aboriginal peoples. There were several bowls and jars, massive, rude and unshapely, of a coarse material like a primitive stoneware, and, presiding over the whole collection, a crudely modelled effigy of similar material, apparently the artless representation of some forest deity, or, perhaps a portrait of an aboriginal man. The childish crudity of execution carried my thoughts to Darkest Africa or the Ethnographical galleries of the British Museum, or to those sham primitive sculptures which have recently appeared on some of the public buildings in London. I looked again at Mr Gannet and wondered whether his present trouble might be the aftermath of some tropical illness contracted in the forests or jungles where he had collected these strange, and not very attractive, curios.

Fortunately, however, I did not put my thoughts into words, but, in pursuance of another of Dr Thorndyke's precepts to "let the patient do most of the talking", listened attentively while Mr Gannet poured out the tale of his troubles. For, presently, he remarked after a pause:

"And it isn't only the discomfort. It's such a confounded hindrance. I want to get on with my work."

"By the way, what is your work?" I asked.

"I am a potter," he replied.

"A potter!" I repeated. "I didn't know that there were any pottery works in London – except, of course, Doultons."

"I am not attached to any pottery works," said he. "I am an artist potter, an individual worker. The pieces that I make are what is usually called studio pottery. Those are some of my works on the mantelpiece."

In the vulgar phrase, you could have knocked me down with a feather. For the moment I was bereft of speech, and could only sit like a fool, gazing round-eyed and agape at these amazing products of the potter's art, while Gannet observed me gravely, and, I thought, with slight disfavour.

"Possibly," he remarked, "you find them a little over-simplified."

It was not the expression that I should have used, but I grasped at it eagerly.

"I think I had that feeling at the first glance," I replied; "that and the – er – the impression that perhaps – ha – in the matter of precision and – er – symmetry – that is, to an entirely inexpert eye – er – "

"Exactly!" he interrupted. "Precision and symmetry are what the inexpert eye looks for. But they are not what the artist seeks. Mechanical accuracy he can leave to the ungifted toiler who tends a machine."

"I suppose that is so," I agreed. "And the" – I was about to say "image" but hastily corrected the word to "statuette" – "that is your work, too?"

"The figurine," he corrected; "yes, that is my work. I was rather pleased with it when I had it finished. And apparently I was justified, for it was extremely well received. The art critics were quite enthusiastic, and I sold two replicas of it for fifty guineas each."

"That was very satisfactory," said I. "It is a good thing to have material reward as well as glory. Did you give it any descriptive title?"

"No," he replied. "I am not like those anecdote painters who must have a title for their pictures. I just called it 'Figurine of a monkey'."

"Of a – oh, yes. Of a monkey. Exactly!"

I stood up the better to examine it and then discovered that its posterior aspect bore something like a coil of garden hose, evidently representing a tail. So it obviously was a monkey and not a woodland god. The tail established the diagnosis; even as, in those sculptures that I have mentioned, the absence of a tail demonstrates their human character.

"And I suppose," said I, "you always sign your works?"

"Certainly," he replied. "Each piece bears my signature and a serial number; and, of course, the number of copies of a single piece is rigidly limited. You will see the signature on the base."

With infinite care and tenderness I lifted the precious figurine and inverted it to examine the base, which I found to be covered with a thick layer of opaque white glaze, rather out of character with the rough grey body but excellent for displaying the signature. The latter was in thin blue lines as if executed with a pen and consisted of something resembling a bird, supported by the letters "PG" and, underneath, "Op. 571. A."

"The goose is, I suppose," said I, "your sign manual or personal mark – it is a goose, isn't it?"

"No," he replied, a little testily. "It's a gannet."

"Of course it is," I agreed, hastily. "How dull of me not to recognize your rebus, though a gannet is not unlike a goose."

He admitted this, and watched me narrowly as I replaced the masterpiece on the little square of cloth which protected it from contact with the marble shelf. Then it occurred to me that I had, perhaps, stayed long enough, and, as I buttoned my overcoat, I reverted to professional matters with a few parting remarks.

"Well, Mr Gannet, you needn't be uneasy about yourself. I shall send you some medicine which I think will soon put you right. But if you have much pain, you had better try some hot fomentations or a hot water bottle – a rubber one, of course; and you would probably be more comfortable lying down."

"It's more comfortable sitting by the fire," he objected; and, as it appeared that he was the best judge of his own comfort, I said no more, but having shaken hands, took my departure.

As I was descending the stairs I met a man coming up, a big man who wore a monocle and was carrying a glass jug. He stopped for a moment when he came abreast, and explained:

"I am just taking the invalid some barley-water. I suppose that is all right. He asked for it."

"Certainly," I replied. "A most suitable drink for a sick person."

"I'll tell him so," said he, and, with this, we went our respective ways.

When I reached the hall, I found the dining-room door open, and, as Mrs Gannet was visible within, I entered to make my report and give a few directions; to which she listened attentively though with no great appearance of concern. But she promised to see that the patient should take his medicine regularly, and to keep him supplied with hot-water bottles, "though," she added, "I don't expect that he will use them. He is not a very tractable invalid."

"Well, Mrs Gannet," said I, pulling on my gloves, "we must be patient. Pain is apt to make people irritable. I shall hope to find him better tomorrow. Good morning!"

At intervals during the day my thoughts reverted to my new patient, but not, I fear, in the way that they should have done. For it was not his abdomen – which was my proper concern – that occupied my attention, but his queer pottery and, above all, the unspeakable monkey. My reflections oscillated between frank incredulity and an admission of the possibility that these pseudo-barbaric works might possess some subtle quality that I had failed to detect. Yet I was not without some qualifications for forming a judgment, for mine was a distinctly artistic family. Both my parents could draw, and my maternal uncle was a figure-painter of some position who, in addition to his pictures, executed small, unpretentious sculptures in terra-cotta and bronze; and I had managed, when I was a student, to spare an evening a week to attend a life-class. So I, at least, could draw, and knew what the human figure was like; and, when I compared my uncle's graceful, delicately-finished little statuettes with Gannet's uncouth effigy, it seemed beyond belief that this latter could have any artistic quality whatever.

Yet it doesn't do to be too cocksure. It is always possible that one may be mistaken. But yet, again, it doesn't do to be too humble and credulous; for the simple, credulous man is the natural prey of the quack and the impostor. And the quack and the impostor flourish in our midst. The post-war twentieth century seems to be the golden age of "bunk".

So my reflections went about and about and brought me to no positive conclusion; and meanwhile, poor Peter Gannet's abdomen received less attention than it deserved. I assumed that a dose or two of bismuth and soda, with that fine old medicament, once so over-rated and now rather under-valued – compound tincture of cardamoms – would relieve the colicky pains and set the patient on the road to recovery; and, having dispatched the mixture, dismissed the medical aspects of the case from my mind.

But the infallible mixture failed to produce the expected effect, for, when I called on the following morning, the patient's condition was unchanged. Which was disappointing (especially to him), but not disturbing. There was no suspicion of anything serious; no fever, and no physical signs suggestive of appendicitis or any other grave condition. I was not anxious about him, nor was he anxious about himself, though slightly outspoken on the subject of the infallible mixture, which I promised to replace by something more effectual, repeating my recommendations as to hot-water bottles or fomentations.

The new treatment, however, proved no better than the old. At my third visit I found my patient in bed, still complaining of pain and in a state of deep depression. But even now, though the man looked definitely ill, neither exhaustive questioning nor physical examination threw any light either on the cause or the exact nature of his condition. Obviously he was suffering from severe gastro-intestinal catarrh. But why he was suffering from it, and why no treatment gave him any relief, were mysteries on which I pondered anxiously as I walked home from Jacob Street, greatly out of conceit with myself and inclined to commiserate the man who had the misfortune to be my patient.

CHAPTER FOUR

Dr Thorndyke takes a Hand

It was on the sixth day of my attendance on Mr Gannet that my vague but increasing anxiety suddenly became acute. As I sat down by the bedside and looked at the drawn, haggard, red-eyed face that confronted me over the bedclothes, I was seized by something approaching panic. And not without reason. For the man was obviously ill – very ill – and was getting worse from day to day; and I had to admit – and did admit to myself – that I was completely in the dark as to what was really the matter with him. My diagnosis of gastro-enteritis was, in effect, no diagnosis at all. It was little more than a statement of the symptoms; and the utter failure of the ordinary empirical treatment convinced me that there was some essential element in the case which had completely eluded me.

It was highly disturbing. A young, newly established practitioner cannot afford to make a hash of a case at the very outset of his career, as I clearly realized, though, to do myself justice, I must say that this was not the consideration that was uppermost in my mind. What really troubled me was the feeling that I had failed in my duty towards my patient and in ordinary professional competence. My heart was wrung by the obvious suffering of the quiet, uncomplaining man who looked to me so pathetically for help and relief – and looked in vain. And then there was the further, profoundly disquieting consideration that the man was now very seriously ill and that if he did not improve, his condition would presently become actually dangerous.

"Well, Mr Gannet," I said, "we don't seem to be making much progress. I am afraid you will have to remain in bed for the present."

"There's no question about that, Doctor," said he, "because I can't get out; at least I can't stand properly if I do. My legs seem to have gone on strike and there is something queer about my feet; sort of pins and needles, and a dead kind of feeling, as if they had got a coat of varnish over them."

"But," I exclaimed, concealing as well as I could my consternation at this fresh complication, "you haven't mentioned this to me before."

"I hadn't noticed it until yesterday," he replied, "though I have been having cramps in my calves for some days. But the fact is that the pain in my gizzard occupies my attention pretty completely. It may have been coming on before I noticed it. What do you suppose it is?"

To this question I gave no direct answer. For I was not supposing at all. To me the new symptoms conveyed nothing more than fresh and convincing evidence that I was completely out of my depth. Nevertheless, I made a careful examination which established the fact that there was an appreciable loss of sensibility in the feet and some abnormal conditions of the nerves of the legs. Why there should be I had not the foggiest idea, nor did I make any great efforts to unravel the mystery; for these new developments brought to a definite decision a half-formed intention that I had been harbouring for the last day or two.

I would seek the advice of some more experienced practitioner. That was necessary as a matter of common honesty, to say nothing of humanity. But I had hesitated to suggest a second opinion, since that would not only have involved the frank admission that I was gravelled – an impolitic proceeding in the case of a young doctor – but it would have put the expense of the consultant's fee on the patient; whereas I felt that, since the need for the consultation arose from my own incompetence, the expense should fall upon me.

"What do you think, Doctor, of my going into a nursing home?" he asked, as I resumed my seat by the bed.

I rather caught at the suggestion, for it seemed to make my plan easier to carry out.

"There is something to be said for a nursing home," I replied. "You would be able to have more constant and skilled attention."

"That is what I was thinking," said he, "and I shouldn't be such a damned nuisance to my wife."

"Yes," I agreed, "there's something in that. I will think about your idea and make a few inquiries; and I will look in again later in the day and let you know the result."

With this I rose, and, having shaken his hand, took my departure, closing the door audibly and descending the stairs with a slightly heavy tread to give notice of my approach to the hall. When I arrived there, however, I found no sign of Mrs Gannet and the dining-room door was shut; and, glancing towards the hat-rack on which my hat was awaiting me, I noted another hat upon an adjoining peg and surmised that it possibly accounted for the lady's non-appearance. I had seen that hat before. It was a somewhat dandified velour hat which I recognized as appertaining to a certain Mr Boles – the man whom I had met on the stairs at my first visit and had seen once or twice since; a big, swaggering, rather good-looking young man with a noisy, bullying manner and a tendency to undue familiarity. I had disliked him at sight. I resented his familiarity, I suspected his monocle of a merely ornamental function, and I viewed with faint disapproval his relations with Mrs Gannet – though, to be sure, they were some sort of cousins, as I had understood from Gannet, and he obviously knew all about their friendship.

So it was no affair of mine. But, still, the presence of that hat gave me pause. It is awkward to break in on a tête-à-tête. However, my difficulty was solved by Boles himself, who opened the dining-room door a short distance, thrust out his head, and surveyed me through his monocle – or perhaps with the less-obstructed eye.

"Thought I heard you sneaking down, Doc," said he. "How's the sufferer? Aren't you coming in to give us the news?"

I should have liked to pull his nose. But a doctor must learn early to control his temper – especially in the case of a man of Boles' size. As he held the door open, I walked in and made my bow to Mrs Gannet, who returned my greeting without putting down her needlework. Then I delivered my report, briefly and rather vaguely, and opened the subject of the nursing home. Instantly Boles began to raise objections.

"Why on earth should he go to a nursing home?" he demanded. "He is comfortable enough here. And think of the expense."

"It was his own suggestion," said I, "and I don't think it a bad one."

"No," said Mrs Gannet. "Not at all. He would get better attention there than I can give him."

There followed something like a wrangle between the two, to which I listened impassively, inwardly assessing their respective motives. Obviously the lady favoured the prospect of getting the invalid off her hands, while as to Boles, his opposition was due to mere contrariety; to an instinctive impulse to object to anything that I might propose.

Of course, the lady had her way – and I had intended to have mine in any case. So, when the argument had petered out, I took my leave with a promise to return some time later to report progress.

As I turned away from the house, I rapidly considered the position. I had no further visits to make, so, for the present, my time was my own; and as my immediate purpose was to seek the counsel of some more experienced colleague, and as my hospital was the most likely place in which to obtain such counsel, I steered a course for the nearest bus route by which I could travel to its neighbourhood. There, having boarded the appropriate omnibus, I was presently delivered at the end of the quiet street in which St Margaret's Hospital is situated.

It seemed but a few months since I had reluctantly shaken from my feet the dust of that admirable institution and its pleasant, friendly medical school; and now, as I turned into the familiar street, I looked about me with a certain wistfulness as I recalled the years of interesting study and companionship that I had spent here as I slowly evolved from a raw freshman to a fully qualified practitioner. And as, approaching the hospital, I observed a tall figure emerge from the gate and advance towards me, the sight brought back to me one of the most engrossing aspects of my life as a student. For the tall man was Dr John Thorndyke, the lecturer on Medical Jurisprudence, perhaps the most brilliant and the most popular member of the teaching staff.

As we approached, Dr Thorndyke greeted me with a genial smile, and held out his hand.

"This, I think," said he, "is the first time we have met since you fluttered out of the nest."

"We used to call it the incubator," I remarked.

"I think 'nest' sounds more dignified," he rejoined. "There is something rather embryonic about an incubator. And how do you like general practice?"

"Oh, well enough," I replied. "Of course, it isn't as thrilling as hospital practice – though mine happens, at the moment, to be a bit more full of thrills than I care for."

"That sounds as if you were having some unpleasant experiences."

"I am," said I. "The fact is that I am up a tree. That is why I am here. I am going to the hospital to see if one of the older hands can give me some sort of tip."

"Very wise of you, Oldfield," Thorndyke commented. "Would it seem impertinent if I were to ask what sort of tree it is that you are marooned in?"

"Not at all, sir," I replied warmly. "It is very kind of you to ask. My difficulty is that I have got a rather serious case, and I am fairly gravelled in the matter of diagnosis. It seems to be a pretty acute case of gastro-enteritis, but why the fellow should have got it and why none of my treatment should make any impression on it, I can't imagine at all."

Dr Thorndyke's kindly interest in an old pupil seemed to sharpen into one more definitely professional.

"The term 'gastro-enteritis'," said he, "covers a good many different conditions. Perhaps a detailed description of the symptoms would be better as a basis for discussion."

Thus encouraged, I plunged eagerly into a minute description of poor Gannet's symptoms – the abdominal pain, the obstinate and distressing nausea and physical and mental depression – with some account of my futile efforts to relieve them; to all of which Dr Thorndyke listened with profound attention. When I had finished, he reflected for a few moments and then asked:

"And that is all, is it? Nothing but the abdominal trouble? No neuritic symptoms, for instance?"

"Yes, by Jove, there are!" I exclaimed. "I forgot to mention them. He has severe cramp in his calves and there is quite distinct numbness of the feet with loss of power in the legs; in fact, he is hardly able to stand, at least so he tells me."

Dr Thorndyke nodded, and, after a short pause, asked:

"And as to the eyes. Anything unusual about them?"

"Well," I replied, "they are rather red and watery, but he put that down to reading in a bad light; and then he seems to have a slight cold in his head."

"You haven't said anything about the secretions," Dr Thorndyke remarked. "I suppose you made all the routine tests?"

"Oh, yes," I replied. "Most carefully. But there was nothing in the least abnormal; no albumen, no sugar, nothing out of the ordinary."

"I take it," said Thorndyke, "that it did not occur to you to try Marsh's test?"

"Marsh's test!" I repeated, gazing at him in dismay. "Good Lord, no! The idea never entered my thick head. And you think it may actually be a case of arsenic poisoning?"

"It is certainly a possibility," he replied. "The complex of symptoms that you have described is entirely consistent with arsenic poisoning, and it doesn't appear to me to be consistent with anything else."

I was thunderstruck. But yet no sooner was the suggestion made than its obviousness seemed to stare me in the face.

"Of course!" I exclaimed. "It is almost a typical case. And to think that I never spotted it, after attending all your lectures, too! I am a fool. I am not fit to hold a diploma."

"Nonsense, Oldfield," said Thorndyke, "you are not exceptional. The general practitioner nearly always misses a case of poisoning. Quite naturally. His daily experience is concerned with disease, and, as the effects of a poison simulate disease, he is almost inevitably misled. He has, by habit, acquired an unconscious bias towards what we may call normal illness; whereas an outsider, like myself, coming to the case with an open mind, or even with a bias towards the abnormal, is on the look-out for suspicious symptoms. But we mustn't rush to conclusions. The first thing is to establish the presence or absence of arsenic. That would be a good deal easier if we had him in hospital, but I suppose there would be some difficulty – "

"There would be no difficulty at all, sir," said I. "He has asked me to arrange for him to go to a nursing home."

"Has he?" said Thorndyke. "That almost seems a little significant; I mean that there is a slight suggestion of some suspicions on his own part. But what would you like to do? Will you make the test yourself, and carry on, or would you like me to come along with you and have a look at the patient?"

"It would be an enormous relief to me if you would see him, sir," I replied, "and it is awfully good of you to – "

"Not at all," said Thorndyke. "The question has to be settled, and settled without delay. In a poisoning case, the time factor may be vital. And if we should bring in a true bill, he should be got out of that house at once. But you understand, Oldfield, that I come as your friend. My visit has no financial implications."

I was disposed to protest, but he refused to discuss the matter, pointing out that no second opinion had been asked for by the patient. "But," he added, "we may want some reagents. I had better run back to the hospital and get my research case, which I had left to be called for, and see that it contains all that we are likely to need."

He turned and retraced his steps to the hospital where he entered the gateway, leaving me to saunter up and down the forecourt. In a few minutes he came out, carrying what looked like a small suitcase covered with green Willesden canvas, and, as there happened to be a disengaged taxi at the main entrance, where it had just set down a passenger, Thorndyke chartered it forthwith; and when I had given the driver the necessary directions, I followed my senior into the interior of the vehicle and slammed the door.

During the journey Dr Thorndyke put a few discreet questions respecting the Gannet household, to which I returned correspondingly discreet answers. Indeed, I knew very little about the three persons – or four, including Boles – of whom it consisted, and I did not think it proper to eke out my slender knowledge with surmises. Accordingly I kept strictly to the facts actually known to me, leaving him to make his own inferences.

"Do you know who prepares Gannet's food?" he asked.

"To the best of my belief," I replied, "Mrs Gannet does all the cooking. The maid is only a girl. But I am pretty sure that Mrs Gannet prepares the invalid food, in fact, she told me that she did. There isn't much of it, as you may imagine."

"What is Gannet's business or profession?"

"I understand that he is a potter; an artist potter. He seems to specialize in some sort of stoneware. There are one or two pieces of his in the bedroom."

"And where does he work?"

"He has a studio at the back of the house; quite a big place, I believe, though I haven't seen it. But it seems to be bigger than he needs, as he lets Boles occupy part of it. I don't quite know what Boles does, but I fancy it is something in the goldsmithing and enamelling line."

Here, as the taxi turned from Euston Road into Hampstead Road, Thorndyke glanced out of the window and asked:

"Did I hear you mention Jacob Street to the driver?"

"Yes, that is where he lives. Rather a seedy-looking street. You don't know it, I suppose?"

"It happens that I do," he replied. "There are several studios in it, relics of the days when it was a more fashionable neighbourhood. I knew the occupant of one of the studios. But here we are, I think, at our destination."

As the taxi drew up at the house, he got out and paid the cabman while I knocked at the door and rang the bell. Almost immediately, the door was opened by Mrs Gannet herself, who looked at me with some surprise and with still more at my companion. I hastened to anticipate questions by a tactful explanation.

"I've had a bit of luck, Mrs Gannet. I met Dr Thorndyke, one of my teachers at the hospital, and when I mentioned to him that I had a case which was not progressing very satisfactorily, he very kindly offered to come and see the patient and give me the benefit of his great experience."

"I hope we shall all benefit from Dr Thorndyke's kindness," said Mrs Gannet, with a smile and a bow to Thorndyke, "and most of all my poor husband. He has been a model of patience, but it has been a weary and painful business for him. You know the way up to his room."

While we were speaking, the dining-room door opened softly and Boles' head appeared in the space, adorned with the inevitable eyeglass through which he inspected Thorndyke critically and was not, himself, entirely unobserved by the latter. But the mutual inspection was brief, for I immediately led the way up the stairs and was closely followed by my senior.

As we entered the sick room after a perfunctory knock at the door, the patient raised himself in bed and looked at us in evident surprise. But he asked no question, merely turning to me interrogatively; whereupon I proceeded at once concisely to explain the position.

"It is very good of Dr Thorndyke," said Gannet, "and I am most grateful and pleased to see him, for I don't seem to be making much progress. In fact, I seem to be getting worse."

"You certainly don't look very flourishing," said Thorndyke, "and I see that you haven't taken your arrowroot, or whatever it is."

"No," said Gannet. "I tried to take some, but I couldn't keep it down. Even the barley-water doesn't seem to agree with me, though I am parched with thirst. Mr Boles gave me a glassful when he brought it up with the arrowroot, but I've been uncomfortable ever since. Yet you'd think that there couldn't be much harm in barley-water."

While the patient was speaking, Thorndyke looked at him thoughtfully as if appraising his general appearance, particularly observing the drawn, anxious face and the red and watery eyes. Then he deposited his research case on the table, and, remarking that the latter was rather in the way, carried it, with my assistance, away from the bedside over the window, and, in place of it, drew up a couple of chairs. Having fetched a writing-pad from the research case, he sat down, and, without preamble, began a detailed interrogation with reference to the symptoms and course of the illness, writing down the answers in shorthand and noting all the dates. The examination elicited the statement that there had been fluctuations in the severity of the condition, a slight improvement being followed by a sudden relapse. It also transpired that the relapses, on each occasion, had occurred shortly after taking food or a considerable drink. "It seems," Gannet concluded dismally, "as if starvation was the only possible way of avoiding pain."

I had heard all this before, but it was only now, when the significant facts were assembled by Thorndyke's skilful interrogation, that I could realize their unmistakable meaning. Thus set out, they furnished a typical picture of arsenic poisoning. And so with the brief but thorough physical examination. The objective signs might have been taken from a text-book case.

"Well, Doctor," said Gannet, as Thorndyke stood up and looked down at him gravely, "what do you think of me?"

"I think," replied Thorndyke, "that you are very seriously ill, and that you require the kind of treatment and attention that you cannot possibly get here. You ought to be in a hospital or a nursing home, and you ought to be removed there without delay."

"I rather suspected that myself," said Gannet; "in fact, the doctor was considering some such arrangement. I'm quite willing."

"Then," said Thorndyke, "if you agree, I can give you a private ward or a cubicle at St Margaret's Hospital; and, as the matter is urgent, I propose that we take you there at once. Could you bear the journey in a cab?"

"Oh, yes," replied Gannet, with something almost like eagerness, "if there is a chance of some relief at the end of it."

"I think we shall soon be able to make you more comfortable," said Thorndyke. "But you had better just look him over, Oldfield, to make sure that he is fit to travel."

As I got my stethoscope to listen to the patient's heart, Thorndyke walked over to the table, apparently to put away his writing-pad. But that was not his only purpose. For, as I stooped over the patient with the stethoscope at my ears, I could see him (though the patient could not), carefully transferring some arrowroot from the bowl to a wide-mouthed jar. When he had filled it and put in the rubber stopper, he filled another jar from the jug of barley-water and then quietly closed the research case.

Now I understood why he had moved the table away from the bed to a position in which it was out of the range of the patient's vision. Of course, the specimens of food and drink could not have been taken in Gannet's presence without an explanation, which we were not in a position to give; for, although neither of us had much doubt on the subject, still the actual presence of arsenic had yet to be proved.

"Well, Oldfield," said Thorndyke, "do you think he is strong enough to make the journey?"

"Quite," I replied, "if he can put up with the discomfort of travelling in a taxi."

As to this, Gannet was quite confident, being evidently keen on the change of residence.

"Then," said Thorndyke, "perhaps you will run down and explain matters to Mrs Gannet; and it would be just as well to send out for a cab at once. I suppose Madame is not likely to raise objections?"

"No," I replied. "She has already agreed to his going to a nursing home; and if she finds our methods rather abrupt, I must make her understand that the case is urgent."

The interview, however, went quite smoothly so far as the lady was concerned, though Boles was disposed to be obstructive.

"Do you mean that you are going to cart him off to the hospital now?" he demanded.

"That is what Dr Thorndyke proposes," I replied.

"But why?" he protested. "You say that there is no question of an operation. Then why is he being bustled off in this way?"

"I think," said I, "if you will excuse me, I had better see about that cab"; and I made a move towards the hall, whereupon Mrs Gannet intervened, a little impatiently.

"Now, don't waste time, Fred. Run along and get a taxi while I go up with the doctor and make Peter ready for the journey."

On this Boles rather sulkily swaggered out into the hall, and without another word, snatched down the velour hat, jammed it on his head, and departed on his quest, slamming the street door after him. As the door closed Mrs Gannet turned towards the staircase and began to ascend, and I followed, passing her on the landing to open the bedroom door.

When we entered the room we found Thorndyke standing opposite the mantelpiece apparently inspecting the stoneware image; but he turned, and, bowing to the lady, suavely apologized for our rather hurried proceedings.

"There is no need to send any clothes with him," said he, "as he will have to remain in bed for the present. A warm dressing-gown and one or two blankets or rugs will do for the journey."

"Yes," she replied. "Rugs, I think, will be more presentable than blankets." Then, turning to her husband she asked: "Is there anything that you will want to take with you, Peter?"

"Nothing by my attaché case," he replied. "That contains all that I am likely to want, excepting the book that I am reading. You might put that in, too. It is on the small table."

When this had been done, Mrs Gannet proceeded to make the few preparations that were necessary while Thorndyke resumed his study of the pottery on the mantelpiece. The patient was assisted to rise and sit on the edge of the bed while he was inducted into a thick dressing-gown, warm woollen socks and a pair of bedroom slippers.

"I think we are all ready now," said Mrs Gannet. Then, as there seemed to be a pause in the proceedings, she took the opportunity to address a question to Thorndyke.

"Have you come to any conclusion," she asked, "as to what it is exactly that my husband is suffering from?"

"I think," Thorndyke replied, "that we shall be able to be more definite when we have had him under observation for a day or two."

The lady looked a little unsatisfied with this answer – which, certainly, was rather evasive – as, indeed, the patient also seemed to note. But here the conversation was interrupted, providentially, by the arrival of Boles to announce that the cab was waiting.

"And now, old chap," said he, "the question is, how are we going to get you down to it?"

That problem, however, presented no difficulty, for when the patient had been wrapped in the rugs, Thorndyke and I carried him, by the approved ambulance method, down the stairs and deposited him in the taxi, while Boles and Mrs Gannet brought up the rear of the procession, the latter carrying the invaluable attaché case. A more formidable problem was that of finding room in the taxi for two additional large men; but we managed to squeeze in, and, amidst valedictory hand-wavings from the two figures on the doorstep, the cab started on its journey.

It seemed that Thorndyke must have given some instructions at the hospital, for our arrival appeared to be not unexpected. A wheeled chair was quickly procured, and in this the patient was trundled, under Thorndyke's direction, through a maze of corridors to the little private ward on the ground floor which had been allotted to him. Here we found a nurse putting the finishing touches to its appointments, and presently the sister from the adjacent ward came to superintend the establishment of the new patient. We stayed only long enough to see Gannet comfortably settled in bed, and then took leave of him; and in the corridor outside we parted after a few words of explanation.

"I am just going across to the chemical laboratories," said Thorndyke, "to hand Professor Woodfield a couple of samples for analysis. I shall manage to see Gannet tomorrow morning, and I suppose you will look in on him from time to time."

"Yes," I replied. "If I may, I will call and see him tomorrow."

"But of course you may," said he. "He is still your patient. If there is anything to report – from Woodfield, I mean – I will leave a note for you with Sister. And now I must be off."

We shook hands and went our respective ways; and as I looked back at the tall figure striding away down the corridor, research case in hand, I speculated on the report that Professor Woodfield would furnish on a sample of arrowroot and another of barley-water.

CHAPTER FIVE

A True Bill

Impelled by my anxiety to clear up the obscurities of the Gannet case, I dispatched the only important visit on my list as early on the following morning as I decently could and then hurried off to the hospital, in the hope that I might be in time to catch Thorndyke before he left. And it turned out that I had timed my visit fortunately, for, as I passed in at the main entrance, I saw his name on the attendance board and learned from the hall porter that he had gone across to the school. Thither, accordingly, I directed my steps, but, as I was crossing the garden, I met him coming from the direction of the laboratories and turned to walk back with him.

"Any news yet?" I asked.

"Yes," he replied. "I have just seen Woodfield and had his report. Of the two samples of food that I gave him for analysis, one – some of the arrowroot that you saw – contained no arsenic. The other – a specimen of the barley-water – contained three-quarters of a grain of arsenic in the five fluid ounces of my sample. So, assuming that this jug held twenty fluid ounces, it would have contained about three grains of arsenic – that is, of arsenious acid."

"My word!" I exclaimed. "Why, that is a fatal dose, isn't it?"

"It is a possibly fatal dose," he replied. "A two-grain dose has been known to cause death, but the effects of arsenic are very erratic. Still, we may fairly say that if he had drunk the whole jugful, the chances are that it would have killed him."

I shuddered to think of the narrow escape that he – and I – had had. Only just in time had we – or rather Thorndyke – got him away from that house.

"Well," I said, "the detection of arsenic in the barley-water settles any doubts that we might have had. It establishes the fact of arsenic poisoning."

"Not quite," Thorndyke dissented. "But we have established the fact by clinical tests. Woodfield and the House Physician have ascertained the presence of arsenic in the patient's body. The quantity was quite small; smaller than I should have expected, judging by the symptoms. But arsenic is eliminated pretty quickly; so we may infer that some days have elapsed since the last considerable dose was taken."

"Yes," said I, "and you were just in time to save him from the next considerable dose, which would probably have been the last. By the way, what are our responsibilities in this affair? I mean, ought we to communicate with the police?"

"No," he replied, very decidedly. "We have neither the duty nor the right to meddle in a case such as this, where the patient is a responsible adult in full control of his actions and his surroundings. Our duty is to inform him of the facts which are known to us and to leave him to take such measures as he may think fit."

That, in effect, is what we did when we had made the ordinary inquiries as to the patient's condition – which by the way, was markedly improved.

"Yes," Gannet said, cheerfully, "I am worlds better; and it isn't from the effects of the medicine, because I haven't had any. I seem to be recovering of my own accord. Queer, isn't it? Or perhaps it isn't. Have you two gentlemen come to any conclusion as to what is really the matter with me?"

"Yes," Thorndyke replied in a matter-of-fact tone. "We have ascertained that your illness was due to arsenic poisoning."

Gannet sat up in bed and stared from one to the other of us with dropped jaw and an expression of the utmost astonishment and horror.

"Arsenic poisoning!" he repeated, incredulously. "I can't believe it. Are you sure that there isn't some mistake? It seems impossible."

"It usually does," Thorndyke replied drily. "But there is no mistake. It is just a matter of chemical analysis, which can be sworn to and proved, if necessary, in a court of law. Arsenic has been recovered from your own body and also from a sample of barley-water that I brought away for analysis."

"Oh!" said Gannet, "so it was in the barley-water. I suppose you didn't examine the arrowroot?"

"I brought away a sample of it," replied Thorndyke, "and it was examined, but there was no arsenic in it."

"Ha!" said Gannet. "So it was the barley-water. I thought there was something wrong with that stuff. But arsenic! This is a regular facer! What do you think I ought to do about it, Doctor?"

"It is difficult for us to advise you, Mr Gannet," Thorndyke replied. "We know no more than that you have been taking poisonous doses of arsenic. As to the circumstances in which you came to take that poison, you know more than we do. If any person knowingly administered that poison to you, he, or she, committed a very serious crime; and if you know who that person is, it would be proper for you to inform the police."

"But I don't," said Gannet. "There are only three persons who could have given me the arsenic, and I can't suspect any of them. There is the servant maid. She wouldn't have given it to me. If she had wanted to poison anybody, it would have been her mistress. They don't get on very well, whereas the girl and I are on quite amiable terms. Then there is my wife. Well, of course, she is outside the picture altogether. And then there is Mr Boles. He often brought up my food and drink, so he had the opportunity; but I couldn't entertain the idea of his having tried to poison me. I would as soon suspect the Doctor – who had a better opportunity than any of them." He paused to grin at me, and then summed up the position. "So, you see, there is nobody whom I could suspect, and perhaps there isn't any poisoner at all. Isn't it possible that the stuff might have got into my food by accident?"

"I wouldn't say that it is actually impossible," Thorndyke replied, "but the improbability is so great that it is hardly worth considering."

"Well," said Gannet, "I don't feel like confiding in the police and possibly stirring up trouble for an innocent party."

"In that," said Thorndyke, "I think you are right. If you know of no reason for suspecting anybody, you have nothing to tell the police. But I must impress on you, Mr Gannet, the realities of your position. It is practically certain that some person has tried to poison you, and you will have to be very thoroughly on your guard against any further attempts."

"But what can I do?" Gannet protested. "You agree that it is of no use to go to the police and raise a scandal. But what else is there?"

"The first precaution that you should take," replied Thorndyke, "would be to tell your wife all that you know, and advise her to pass on the information to Mr Boles – unless you prefer to tell him yourself – and to anyone else whom she thinks fit to inform. The fact that the poisoning has been detected will be a strong deterrent against any further attempts, and Mrs Gannet will be on the alert to see that there are no opportunities. Then you will be wise to take no food or drink in your own house which is not shared by someone else; and, perhaps, as an extra precaution, it might be as well to exchange your present maid for another."

"Yes," Gannet agreed, with a grin, "there will be no difficulty about that when my wife hears about the arsenic. She'll send the girl packing at an hour's notice."

"Then," said Thorndyke, "I think we have said all that there is to say. I am glad to see you looking so much better, and, if you continue to improve at the same rate, we shall be able to send you out in a few days to get back to your pottery."

With this he took leave of the patient, and I went out with him in case he should have anything further to say to me; but it was not until we had passed out of the main entrance and the porter had duly noted his departure, that he broke the silence. Then, as we crossed the courtyard, he asked:

"What did you make of Gannet's statement as to the possible suspects?"

"Not very much," I replied; "but I rather had the feeling that he was holding something back."

"He didn't hold it back very far," Thorndyke commented with a smile. "I gathered that he viewed Mr Boles with profound suspicion and that he was not unwilling that we should share that suspicion. By the way, are you keeping notes of this case?"

I had to admit that I had nothing beyond the entries in the day-book.

"That won't do," said he. "You may not have heard the last of this case. If there should, in the future, be any further developments, you ought not to be dependent on your memory alone. I advise you to write out now, while the facts are fresh, a detailed account of the case, with all the dates and full particulars of the persons who were in any way connected with the affair. I will send you a certified copy of Woodfield's analysis, and I should be interested to see your memoranda of the case to compare with my own notes."

"I don't suppose you will learn much from mine," said I.

"They will be bad notes if I don't," said he. "But the point is that if anything should hereafter happen to Gannet – anything, I mean, involving an inquest or a criminal charge – you and I would be called, or would volunteer, as witnesses, and our evidence ought to agree. Hence the desirability of comparing notes now when we can discuss any disagreements."

Our conversation had brought us to the cross-roads; and here, as our ways led in opposite directions, we halted for a few final words and then parted, Thorndyke pursuing his journey on foot and I waiting at the bus-stop for my omnibus.

During Gannet's stay in hospital I paid him one or two visits, noting his steady improvement and copying into my notebook the entries on his case-sheet. But his recovery was quite uneventful, and, after a few days, I struck him off my visiting-list, deciding to await his return home to wind up the case.

But in the interval I became aware that he had, at least in one particular, acted on Thorndyke's advice. The fact was conveyed to me by Mrs Gannet, who appeared one evening, in a very disturbed state, in my consulting-room. I guessed at once what her mission was, but there was not much need for guessing as she came to the point at once.

"I have been to see Peter this afternoon," said she, "and he has given me a most terrible shock. He told me – quite seriously – that his illness was really not an illness at all, but that his condition was due to poison. He says that somebody had been putting arsenic into his food, and he quotes you and Dr Thorndyke as his authorities for this statement. Is he off his head or did you really tell him this story?"

"It is perfectly true, Mrs Gannet," I replied.

"But it can't be," she protested. "It is perfectly monstrous. There is nobody who could have had either the means or the motive. I prepared all his food with my own hands and I took it up to him, myself. The maid never came near it – though I have sent her away all the same – and even if she had had the opportunity, she had no reason for trying to poison Peter. She was really quite a decent girl and she and he were on perfectly good terms. But the whole thing is impossible – fantastic. Dr Thorndyke must have made some extraordinary mistake."

"I assure you, Mrs Gannet," said I, "that no mistake has been made. It is just a matter of chemical analysis. Arsenic is nasty stuff, but it has one virtue; it can be identified easily and with certainty. When Dr Thorndyke saw your husband, he at once suspected arsenic poisoning, so he took away with him two samples of the food – one of arrowroot and one of barley-water – for analysis. They were examined by an eminent analyst and he found in the barley-water quite a considerable quantity of arsenic – the whole jugful will have contained enough to cause death. You see, there is no doubt. There was the arsenic, in the barley-water. It was extracted and weighed, and the exact amount is known; and the arsenic, itself, has been kept and can be produced in evidence if necessary."

Mrs Gannet was deeply impressed – indeed, for the moment she appeared quite overwhelmed, for she stood speechless, gazing at me in the utmost consternation. At length she asked, almost in a whisper:

"And the arrowroot? I took that up to him, myself."

"There was no arsenic in the arrowroot," I replied; and it seemed to me that she was a little relieved by my answer, though she still looked scared and bewildered. I could judge what was passing in her mind, for I realized that she remembered – as I did – who had carried the barley-water up to the sick room. But whatever she thought, she said nothing, and the interview presently came to an end after a few questions as to her husband's prospects of complete recovery, and an urgent request that I should come and see him when he returned from the hospital.

That visit, however, proved unnecessary, for the first intimation that I received of Gannet's discharge from hospital was furnished by his bodily presence in my waiting-room. I had opened the communicating door in response to the "ting" of the bell ("Please ring and enter") and behold! there he was with velveteen jacket and Vandyke beard, all complete. I looked at him with the momentary surprise that doctors and nurses often experience on seeing a patient for the first time in his ordinary habiliments and surroundings; contrasting this big, upstanding, energetic-looking man with the miserable, shrunken wretch who used to peer at me so pitifully from under the bedclothes.

"Come to report, sir," said he, with a mock naval salute, "and to let you see what a fine job you and your colleagues have made of me."

I shook hands with him and ushered him through into the consulting-room, still pleasantly surprised at the completeness of his recovery.

"You didn't expect to see me looking so well," said he.

"No," I admitted. "I was afraid you would feel the effects for some time."

"So did I," said he, "and in a sense I do. I am still aware that I have got a stomach; but, apart from that dyspeptic feeling, I am as well as I ever was. I am eternally grateful to you and Dr Thorndyke. You caught me on the hop just in time. Another few days and I suspect it would have been a case of *Hic jacet*. But what a rum affair it was. I can make nothing of it. Can you? Apparently it couldn't have been an accident."

"No," I replied. "If the whole household had been poisoned, we might have suspected an accident, but the continued poisoning of one person could hardly have been accidental. We are forced to the conclusion that the poison was administered knowingly and intentionally by some person."

"I suppose we are," he agreed. "But what person? It's a regular corker. There are only three, and two of them are impossible. As to Boles, it is a fact that he brought up that jug of barley-water and he poured out half a tumblerful and gave it me to drink. And he has brought me up barley-water on several other occasions. But I really can't suspect Boles. It seems ridiculous."

"It is not for me to suggest any suspicions," said I. "But the facts that you mention are rather striking. Are there any other facts? What about your relations with Boles? There is nothing, I suppose, to suggest a motive?"

"Not a motive for poisoning me," he replied. "It is a fact that Boles and I are not as good friends as we used to be. We don't hit it off very well nowadays, though we remain, in a sort of way, partners. But I suspect that Boles would have cut it and gone off some time ago if it had not been for my wife. She and he have always been the best of friends – they are distant cousins of some kind – and I think they are quite attached to each other. So Boles goes on working in my studio for the sake of keeping in touch with her. At least, that is how I size things up."

It seemed to me that this was rather like an affirmative answer to my question, and perhaps it appeared so to him. But it was a somewhat delicate matter and neither of us pursued it any farther. Instead, I changed the subject and asked:

"What do you propose to do about it?"

"I don't propose to do anything," he replied. "What could I do? Of course, I shall keep my weather eyelid lifting, but I don't suppose anything further will happen now that you and Dr Thorndyke have let the cat so thoroughly out of the bag. I shall just go on working in my studio in the same old way, and I shall make no difference whatever in my relations with Boles. No reason why I should as I really don't suspect him."

"Your studio is somewhere at the back of the house, isn't it?" I asked.

"At the side," he replied, "across the yard. Come along one day and see it," he added cordially, "and I will unfold the whole art and mystery of making pottery. Come whenever you like and as soon as you can. I think you will find the show interesting."

As he issued this invitation (which I accepted gladly) he rose and picked up his hat; and we walked out together to the street door and said farewell on the doorstep.

CHAPTER SIX

Shadows in the Studio

Peter Gannet's invitation to me to visit his studio and see him at work was to develop consequences that I could not then have foreseen; nor shall I hint at them now, since it is the purpose of this narrative to trace the course of events in the order in which they occurred. I merely mention the consequences to excuse the apparent triviality of this part of my story.

At my first visit I was admitted by Mrs Gannet, to whom I explained that this was a friendly call and not a professional visit. Nevertheless, I loitered awhile to hear her account of her husband and to give a few words of advice. Then she conducted me along the hall to a side door which opened on a paved yard, in which the only salient object was a large, galvanized dust-bin. Crossing this, we came to a door which was furnished with a large, grotesque, bronze knocker and bore in dingy white lettering the word "Studio". Mrs Gannet executed a characteristic rat-tat on the knocker, and, without waiting for an answer, opened the door and invited me to enter; which I did, and found myself in a dark space, the front of which was formed by a heavy black curtain. As Mrs Gannet had shut the door behind me, I was plunged in complete obscurity, but, groping at the curtain, I presently drew its end aside and then stepped out into the light of the studio.

"Excuse my not getting up," said Gannet, who was seated at a large bench, "and also not shaking hands. Reasons obvious," and in explanation he held up a hand that was plastered with moist clay. "I am glad to see you, Doctor," he continued, adding, "Get that stool from Boles' bench and set it alongside mine."

I fetched the stool and placed it beside his at the bench, and, having seated myself, proceeded to make my observations. And very interesting observations they were, for everything that met my eye — the place itself, and everything in it — was an occasion of surprise. The whole establishment was on an unexpected scale. The studio, a great barn of a place, evidently, by its immense north window, designed and built as such, would have accommodated a sculptor specializing in colossal statues. The kiln looked big enough for a small factory; and the various accessories — a smaller kiln, a muffle furnace, a couple of grinding mills, a large iron mortar with a heavy pestle, and some other appliances — seemed out of proportion to what I supposed to be the actual output.

But the most surprising object was the artist himself, considered in connection with his present occupation. Dressed correctly for the part in an elegant gown or smock of blue linen, and wearing a black velvet skullcap, "The Master" was, as I have said, seated at the bench, working at the beginnings of a rather large bowl. I watched him for a while in silent astonishment, for the method of work used by this "Master Craftsman" was that which I had been accustomed to associate with the kindergarten. It was true that the latter had simply adopted, as suitable for children, the methods of ancient and primitive people, but these seemed hardly appropriate to a professional potter. However, such as the method was, he seemed to be quite at home with it and to work neatly and skilfully; and I was interested to note how little he appeared to be incommoded by a stiff joint in the middle of the right hand. Perhaps I might as well briefly describe the process.

On the large bench before him was a stout, square board, like a cook's pastry board, and, on this was a plaster "bat", or slab, the upper surface of which had a dome-like projection (now hidden) to impart the necessary hollow to the bottom of the bowl. This latter (I am now speaking from subsequent experience) was made by coiling a roll, or cord, of clay into a circular disc, somewhat like a Catherine Wheel, and then rubbing the coils together with the finger to produce a flat plate. When the bottom was finished and cut true, the sides of the bowl were built up in the same way. At the side of the pastry board was an earthenware pan in which was a quantity of the clay cord, looking rather like a coil of gas tubing, and from this the artist picked out a length, laid it on top of the completed part of the side, and, having carried it round the circumference, pinched it off and then pressed it down, lightly, and rubbed and stroked it with the finger and a wooden modelling tool until it was completely united to the part below.

"Why do you pinch it off?" I inquired. "Why not coil it up continuously?"

"Because," he explained, "if you built a bowl by just coiling the clay cord round and round without a break, it would be higher one side than the other. So I pinch it off when I have completed a circle; and you notice that I begin the next tier in a different place, so that the joins don't come over each other. If they did, there would be a mark right up the side of the bowl."

"Yes," I agreed. "I see that, though it hadn't occurred to me. But do you always work in this way?"

"With the clay coils?" said he. "No. This is the quick method and the least trouble. But for more important pieces, to which I seek to impart the more personal and emotional qualities and at the same time to express the highest degree of plasticity, I dispense with the coil and work, as a sculptor does, with simple pellets of clay."

"But," said I, "what about the wheel? I see you have one, and it looks quite a high-class machine. Don't you throw any of your work on it?"

He looked at me solemnly, almost reproachfully, as he replied:

"Never. The machine I leave to the machinist; to the mass-producer and the factory. I don't work for Woolworth's or the crockery shops. I am not concerned with speed of production or quantity of output or mechanical regularity of form. Those things appertain to trade. I, in my simple way, am an artist, and though my work is but simple pottery, I strive to infuse into it qualities that are spiritual, to make it express my own soul and personality. The clay is to me, as it was to other and greater masters of the medium – such as Della Robbia and Donatello – the instrument of emotional utterance."

To this I had nothing to say. It would not have been polite to give expression to my views, which were that his claims seemed to be extravagantly disproportionate to his achievements. But I was profoundly puzzled, and became more so as I watched him; for it appeared to me that what he was doing was not beyond my own powers, at least with a little practice, and I found myself half-unconsciously balancing the three obvious possibilities but unable to reach a conclusion.

Could it be that Gannet was a mere impostor, a pretender to artistic gifts that were purely fictitious? Or was he, like those mentally unbalanced "modernists" who honestly believe their crude and childish daubings to be great masterpieces, simply suffering from a delusion? Or was it possible that his uncouth, barbaric bowls and jars did really possess some subtle aesthetic qualities that I had failed to perceive merely from a lack of the necessary special sensibility? Modesty compelled me to admit the latter possibility. There are plenty of people to whom the beauties of nature or art convey nothing, and it might be that I was one of them.

My speculations were presently cut short by a thundering flourish on the knocker, at which Gannet started with a muttered curse. Then the door burst open and Mr Frederick Boles swaggered into the studio humming a tune.

"I wish you wouldn't make that damned row when you come in, Boles," Gannet exclaimed, irritably.

He cast an angry glance at his partner, or tenant, to which the latter responded with a provocative grin.

"Sorry, dear boy," said he. "I'm always forgetting the delicate state of your nerves. And here's the doctor. How de do, Doc? Hope you find your patient pretty well. Hm? None the worse for all that arsenic that they tell me you put into his medicine? Haha!"

He bestowed on me an impudent stare through his eye-glass, removed the latter to execute a solemn wink, and then replaced it; after which, as I received his attentions quite impassively (though I should have liked to kick him), he turned away and swaggered across to the part of the studio which appeared to be his own domain, followed by a glance of deep dislike from Gannet which fairly expressed my own sentiments. Mr Boles was not a prepossessing person.

Nevertheless, I watched his proceedings with some interest, being a little curious as to the kind of industry that he carried on; and presently, smothering my distaste – for I was determined not to quarrel with him – I strolled across to observe him at close quarters. He was seated on a rough, box-like stool, similar to the one which I had borrowed, at an ordinary jeweller's bench fitted with a gas blowpipe and a tin tray in place of the usual sheep-skin. At the moment he was engaged in cutting with an engraving tool a number of shallow pits in a flattened gold object which might have been a sketchy model of a plaice or turbot. I watched him for some time, a little mystified as to the result aimed at, for the little pits seemed, themselves, to have no determinate shape, nor could I make out any plan in their arrangement. At length I ventured on a cautious inquiry.

"Those little hollows, I suppose, form the pattern on this – er – object?"

"Don't call it an object, Doc," he protested. "It's a pendant, or it will be when it is finished; and those hollows will form the pattern – or more properly, the surface enrichment – when they are filled with enamel."

"Oh, they are to be filled with enamel," said I, "and the spots of enamel will make the pattern. But I don't quite see what the pattern represents."

"Represents!" he repeated, indignantly, fixing his monocle (which he did not use while working) to emphasize the reproachful stare that he turned on me. "It doesn't represent anything. I'm not a photographer. The enamel spots will just form a symphony of harmonious, gem-like colour with a golden accompaniment. You don't want representation on a jewel. That can be left to the poster artist. What I aim at is harmony – rhythm – the concords of abstract colour. Do you follow me?"

"I think I do," said I. It was an outrageous untruth, for his explanation sounded like mere meaningless jargon. "But," I added, "probably I shall understand better when I have seen the finished work."

"I can show you a finished piece of the same kind now," said he; and, laying down his work and the scorper, he went to the small cupboard in which he kept his materials and produced from it a small brooch which he placed in my hand and requested me to consider as "a study in polychromatic harmony".

It was certainly a cheerful and pleasant-looking object but strangely devoid of workmanship (though I noticed, on turning it over, that the pin and catch seemed to be quite competently finished); a simple elliptical tablet of gold covered with irregular-shaped spots of many-coloured enamel distributed over the surface in apparently accidental groups. The effect was as if drops of wax from a number of coloured candles had fallen on it.

"You see," said Boles, "how each of these spots of colour harmonizes and contrasts with all the others and reinforces them."

"Yes, I see that," I replied, "but I don't see why you should not have grouped the spots into some sort of pattern."

Boles shook his head. "No," said he, "that would never do. The intrusion of form would have destroyed the natural rhythm of contrasting colour. The two things must be kept separate. Gannet is concerned with abstract form mainly uncomplicated with colour. My concern is with abstract colour liberated from form."

I made shift to appear as if this explanation conveyed some meaning to me and returned the brooch with a few appreciative comments. But I was completely fogged; so much so that I presently took the opportunity to steal away in order that I might turn matters over in my mind.

It was quite a curious problem. What was it that was really going on in that studio? There was a singular air of unreality about the industries that were carried on there. Gannet, with his archaic pottery, had been difficult enough to accept as a genuine artist; but Boles was even more incredible. And, different as the two men were in all other respects, they were strangely alike in their special activities. Both talked what sounded like inflated, pretentious nonsense. Both assumed the airs of artists and virtuosi. And yet each of them appeared to be occupied with work which – to my eye – showed no sign of anything more than the simplest technical skill, and nothing that I could recognize as artistic ability.

Yet I had to admit that the deficiency might be in my own powers of perception. The curious phase of art known as "modernism" made me aware of a widespread taste for pictures and sculpture of a pseudo-barbaric or primitive type; and the comments of the art critics on some of those works were not so very unlike the stuff that I had heard from Boles and Gannet. So perhaps these queer productions were actually what they professed to be, and I was just a Philistine who couldn't recognize a work of art when I saw it.

But there was one practical question that rather puzzled me. What became of these wares? Admittedly, neither of these men worked for the retail shops. Then how did they dispose of their works, and who bought them? Both men were provided with means and appliances on a quite considerable scale and it was to be presumed that their output corresponded to the means of production; moreover, both were apparently obtaining a livelihood by their respective industries. Somewhere there must be a demand for primitive pottery and barbaric jewellery. But where was it? I decided – though it was none of my business – to make a few cautious inquiries.

Another matter, of more legitimate interest to me, was that of the relations of these two men. Ostensibly they were friends, comrades, fellow workers, and, in a sense, partners. But real friends they certainly were not. That had been frankly admitted by Gannet; and even if it had not been, his dislike of Boles was manifest and hardly dissembled. And, of course, it was natural enough if he suspected Boles of having tried to poison him, to say nothing of the rather doubtful relations of that gentleman with Mrs Gannet. Indeed, I could not understand why, if he harboured this suspicion – of which Thorndyke seemed to entertain no doubt – he should have allowed the association to continue.

But if Gannet's sentiments towards Boles were unmistakable, the converse was by no means true. Boles' manners were not agreeable. They were coarse and vulgar – excepting when he was talking "high-brow" – and inclined to be rude. But though he was a bounder he was not consciously uncivil, and – so far as I could at present judge – he showed no signs of unfriendliness towards Gannet. The dislike appeared to be all on the one side.

Yet there must have been something more than met the eye. For, if it was the fact – and I felt convinced that it was – that Boles had made a deliberate, cold-blooded attempt to poison Gannet, that attempt implied a motive which, to put it mildly, could not have been a benevolent one.

These various problems combined to make the studio a focus of profound interest to me, and, as my practice, at this period, was productive principally of leisure, I spent a good deal of my time there; more, indeed, than I should if Gannet had not made it so plain that my visits were acceptable. Sometimes I wondered whether it was my society that he enjoyed, or whether it might have been that my frequenting the studio gave him some sort of feeling of security. It might easily have been so, for, whenever I found him alone, I took the opportunity to satisfy myself that all was well with him. At any rate, he seemed always glad to see me, and, for my part, I found the various activities of the two workers interesting to watch, quite independently of the curious problems arising out of their very odd relations.

By degrees my status changed from that of a mere spectator to something like that of a co-worker. There were many odd jobs to be done requiring no special skill and in these I was able to "lend a hand". For instance, there was the preparation of the "grog" – why so called I never learned, for it was a most unconvivial material, being simply a powder made by pounding the fragments of spoiled or defective earthenware or broken saggers and used to temper the clay to prevent it from cracking in the fire. The broken pots or saggers were pounded in a great iron mortar until they were reduced to small fragments when the latter were transferred to the grog mill and ground to powder. Then the powder was passed through a series of sieves, each marked with the number of meshes to the inch, and the different grades of powder – coarse, medium and fine – stored in their appropriate bins.

Then there was the plaster work. Both men used plaster, and I was very glad to learn the technique of mixing, pouring and trimming. Occasionally, Gannet would make a plaster mould of a successful bowl or jar (much to my surprise, for it seemed totally opposed to his professed principles) and "squeeze" one or two replicas; a process in which I assisted until I became quite proficient. I helped Boles to fire his queer-looking enamel plaques and to cast his uncouth gold ornaments and took over some of the pickling and polishing operations. And then, finally, there was the kiln, which interested me most of all. It was a coal-fired kiln and required a great deal of attention both before and during the firing. The preparation of the kiln Gannet attended to, himself, but I stood by and watched his methods; observed the way in which he stacked the pieces, bedded in ground flint or bone-ash – he mostly used bone-ash – in the "saggers" (fireclay cases or covers to protect the pieces from the flames) and at length closed the opening of the kiln with slabs of fireclay.

But when the actual firing began, we were all kept busy. Even Boles left his work to help in feeding the fires, raking out the ashes and clearing the hearths, leaving Gannet free to control the draught and modify the fire to the required intensity. I was never able to observe the entire process from start to finish, for, even at this time, my practice called for some attention; but I was present on one occasion at the opening of the kiln – forty-eight hours after the lighting of the fires – and noted the care with which Gannet tested the temperature of the pieces before bringing them out into the cool air.

One day when I was watching him as he built up a wide-mouthed jar from a rough drawing – an extraordinarily rough drawing, very unskilfully executed, as I thought – which lay on the bench beside him, he made a new suggestion.

"Why shouldn't you try your hand at a bit of pottery, Doctor?" said he. "Just a simple piece. The actual building isn't difficult and you've seen how I do it. Get some of the stoneware body out of the bin and see what sort of a job you can make of it."

I was not very enthusiastic about built pottery, for, recently I had purchased a little treatise on the potter's art and had been particularly thrilled by the directions for "throwing" on the wheel. I mentioned the fact to Gannet, but he gave me no encouragement. For some reason he seemed to have an invincible prejudice against the potter's wheel.

"It's all right for commercial purposes," said he; "for speed and quantity. But there's no soul in the mechanical stuff. Building is the artist's method; the skilled hand translating thought directly into form."

I did not contest the matter. With a regretful glance at the wheel, standing idle in its corner, I fetched a supply of the mixed clay from the bin and proceeded to roll it into cords on the board that was kept for the purpose. But it occurred to me as an odd circumstance that, hating the wheel as he appeared to, he should have provided himself with one.

"I didn't buy the thing," he explained, when I propounded the question. "I took over this studio as a going concern from the executors of the previous tenant. He was a more or less commercial potter and his outfit suited his work. It doesn't suit mine. I don't want the wheel or that big mixing mill and I would

65

sooner have had a smaller, gas-fired kiln. But the place was in going order and I got it dirt cheap with the outfit included, so I took it as it was and made the best of it."

My first attempt, a simple bowl, was no great success, being distinctly unsymmetrical and lop-sided. But Gannet seemed to think quite well of it – apparently for these very qualities – and even offered to fire it. However, it did not satisfy me, and, eventually I crumpled it up and returned it to the clay-bin, whence, after remoistening, it emerged to be rolled out into fresh coils of cord. For I was now definitely embarked on the industry. The work had proved more interesting than I had expected, and, as usually happens in the case of any art, the interest increased as the difficulties began to be understood and technical skill developed and grew.

"That's right, Doctor," said Gannet. "Keep it up and go on trying; and remember that the studio is yours whenever you like to use it, whether I am here or not." (As a matter of fact, he frequently was not, for both he and Boles took a good many days off, and – rather oddly, I thought – their absences often coincided.) "And you needn't trouble to come in through the house. There is a spare key of the wicket which you may as well have. I'll give it to you now."

He took a couple of keys from his pocket and handed me one, whereby I became, in a sense, a joint tenant of the studio. It was an insignificant circumstance, and yet, as so often happens, it developed unforeseen consequences, one of which was a little adventure for the triviality of which I offer no apology since it, in its turn, had further consequences not entirely irrelevant to this history.

It happened that on the very first occasion on which I made use of the key, I found the studio vacant; and the condition of the benches suggested that both my fellow tenants were taking a day off. On the bench that I used was a half-finished pot, covered with damp cloths. I removed these and fetched a fresh supply of moist clay from the bin with the intention of going on with the work, when the wheel happened to catch my eye; and instantly I was assailed by a great temptation. Here was an ideal opportunity to satisfy my ambition; to try my prentice hand with this delightful toy, which, to me, embodied the real romance of the potter's art.

I went over to the wheel and looked at it hungrily. I gave it a tentative spin and tried working the treadle, and, finding it rather stiff, fetched Boles' oil-can and applied a drop of oil to the pivots. Then I drew up a stool and took a few minutes' practice with the treadle until I was able to keep up a steady rotation. It seemed quite easy to me, as I was accustomed to riding a bicycle, and I was so far encouraged that I decided to try my skill as a thrower. Placing a basin of water beside the wheel, I brought the supply of clay from the bench, and, working it into the form of a large dumpling, slapped it down on the damped hard-wood disc and, having wetted my hands, started the rotation with a vigorous spin.

The start was not a perfect success, as I failed to centre the clay ball correctly and put on too much speed, with the result that the clay flew off and hit me in the stomach. However, I collected it from my lap, replaced it on the wheel-head, and made a fresh start with more care and caution. It was not so easy as it had appeared. Attending to the clay, I was apt to forget the treadle, and then the wheel stopped; and when I concentrated on the treadle, strange things happened to the clay. Still, by degrees, I got the "hang" of the process, recalling the instructions in my handbook and trying to practise the methods therein prescribed.

It was a fascinating game. There was something almost magical in the behaviour of the revolving clay. It seemed, almost of its own accord, to assume the most unexpected shapes. A light pressure of the wet hands and it rose into the form of a column, a cylinder or a cone. A gentle touch from above turned it miraculously into a ball; and a little pressure of the thumbs on the middle of the ball hollowed it out and transformed it into a bowl. It was wonderful and most delightful. And all the transformations had the charm of unexpectedness. The shapes that came were not designed by me;

they simply came of themselves, and an inadvertent touch instantly changed them into something different and equally surprising.

For more than an hour I continued, with ecstatic pleasure and growing facility, to play this incomparable game. By that time, however, signs of bodily fatigue began to make themselves felt, for it was a pretty strenuous occupation, and it occurred to me that I had better get something done. I had just made a shallow bowl (or, rather, it had made itself), and, as I took it gently between my hands, it rose, narrowed itself, and assumed the form of a squat jar with slightly in-turned mouth. I looked at it with pleased surprise. It was really quite an elegant shape and it seemed a pity to spoil it by any further manipulation. So I decided to let well alone and treat it as a finished piece.

When I took my foot off the treadle and let the wheel run down, some new features came into view. The jar at rest was rather different from the jar spinning. Its surface was scored all over with spiral traces of "the potter's thumb", which stamped it glaringly as a thrown piece. This would not quite answer my purpose; which was to practise a playful fraud on Peter Gannet by foisting the jar on him as a build piece. The telltale spirals would have to be eliminated and other, deceptive, markings substituted.

Accordingly, I attacked it cautiously with a modelling tool and a piece of damp sponge, stroking it lightly in vertical lines and keeping an eye on one of Gannet's own jars, until all traces of the wheel had been obliterated and the jar might fairly have passed for a hand-built piece. Of course, a glance at the inside, which I did not dare to touch, would have discovered the fraud, but I took the chance that the interior would not be examined.

The next problem was the decoration. Gannet's usual method – following the tradition of primitive and barbaric ornament – was either to impress an encircling cord into the soft clay or to execute simple thumb-nail patterns. He did not actually use his thumb-nail for this purpose. A bone mustard-spoon produced the same effect and was more convenient. Accordingly I adopted the mustard-spoon, with which I carried a sort of rude *guilloche* round the jar, varied by symmetrically placed dents, made with the end of my clinical thermometer. Finally, becoming ambitious for something more distinctive, I produced my latch-key, and, having made a few experiments on a piece of waste clay, found it quite admirable as a unit of pattern, especially if combined with the thermometer. A circle of key-impressions radiating from a central thermometer dent produced a simple but interesting rosette, which could be further developed by a circle of dents between the key-marks. It was really quite effective, and I was so pleased with it that I proceeded to enrich my masterpiece with four such rosettes, placing them as symmetrically as I could (not that the symmetry would matter to Gannet) on the bulging sides below the thumb-nail ornament.

When I had finished the decoration and tidied it up with the modelling-tool I stood back and looked at my work, not only with satisfaction but with some surprise. For, rough and crude as it was, it appeared, to my possibly indulgent eye, quite a pleasant little pot; and, comparing it with the row of Gannet's works which were drying on the shelf, I asked myself once again what could be the alleged subtle qualities imparted by the hand of the master.

Having made a vacancy on the shelf by moving one of Gannet's pieces from the middle to the end, I embarked on the perilous task of detaching my jar from the wheel-head. The instrument that I employed was a thin wire, with a wooden handle at each end, which we used for cutting slices of clay; a dangerous tool, for a false stroke would have cut the bottom off my jar. But Providence, which – sometimes – watches over the activities of the tyro, guided my hand, and, and, at last the wire emerged safely, leaving the jar free of the surface to which it had been stuck. With infinite care and tenderness – for it was still quite soft – I lifted it with both hands and carried it across to the shelf, when I deposited it safely in the vacant space. Then I cleaned up the wheel, obliterating all traces of my unlawful proceedings, threw my half-finished built piece back into the clay-bin, and departed, chuckling over the surprise that awaited Gannet when he should come to inspect the pieces that were drying on the shelf.

As events turned out, my very mild joke fell quite flat, so far as I was concerned, for I missed the dénouement. A sudden outbreak of measles at a local school kept me so busy that my visits to the studio had to be suspended for a time, and when, at last, I was able to make an afternoon call, the circumstances were such as to occupy my attention in a more serious and less agreeable manner. As this episode was, later, to develop a special significance, I shall venture to describe it in some detail.

On this occasion, I did not let myself in, as usual, by the wicket, for, at the end of Jacob Street I overtook Mrs Gannet and we walked together to the house, which I entered with her. It seemed that she had some question to ask her husband, and, when I had opened the side door, she came out to walk with me across the yard to the studio. Suddenly, as we drew near to the latter, I became aware of a singular uproar within; a clattering and banging, as if the furniture were being thrust about and stools overturned, mingled with the sound of obviously angry voices. Mrs Gannet stopped abruptly and clutched my arm.

"Oh, dear!" she exclaimed, "there are those two men quarrelling again. It is dreadful. I do wish Mr Boles would move to another workshop. If they can't agree, why don't they separate?"

"They don't hit it off very well, then?" I suggested, listening attentively and conscious of a somewhat unfortunate expression – for they seemed to be hitting it off rather too well.

"No," she replied, "especially since – you know. Peter thinks Mr Boles gave him the stuff, which is ridiculous, and Mr Boles – I think I won't go in now," and with this she turned about and retreated to the house, leaving me standing near the studio door, doubtful whether I had better enter boldly or follow the lady's discreet example and leave the two men to settle their business.

It was very embarrassing. If I went in, I could not pretend to be unaware of the disturbance. On the other hand, I did not like to retreat when my intervention might be desirable. Thus I stood hesitating between considerations of delicacy and expediency until a furious shout in Boles' voice settled the question.

"You're asking for it, you know!" he roared; whereupon, flinging delicacy to the winds, I rapped on the door with my knuckles and entered.

I had opened the door deliberately and rather noisily and I now stood for a few moments in the dark lobby behind the curtain while I closed it after me in the same deliberate manner to give time for any necessary adjustments. Sounds of quick movement from within suggested that these were being made, and, when I drew aside the curtain and stepped in, the two men were on opposite sides of the studio. Gannet was in the act of buttoning a very crumpled collar and Boles was standing by his bench, on which lay a raising hammer that had a suspicious appearance of having been hastily put down there. Both men were obviously agitated: Boles, purple-faced, wild-eyed and furiously angry; Gannet, breathless, pale, and venomous.

I greeted them in a matter-of-fact tone as if I had noticed nothing unusual, and went on to excuse and explain the suspension of my visits. But it was a poor pretence, for there were the overturned stools and there was Boles, scowling savagely and still trembling visibly, and there was that formidable-looking hammer, the appearance of which suggested that I had entered only just in time.

Gannet was the first to recover himself, though even Boles managed to growl out a sulky greeting, and when I had picked up a fallen stool and seated myself on it, I made shift to keep up some sort of conversation and to try to bring matters back to a normal footing. I glanced at the shelf, but it was empty. Apparently, the pieces that I had left drying on it had been fired and disposed of. What had happened to my jar, I could not guess and did not very much care. Obviously, the existing circumstances did not lend themselves to any playful interchanges between Gannet and me, nor did they seem to lend themselves to anything else; and I should have made an excuse to steal away, but for my unwillingness to leave the two men together in their present moods.

I did not, however, stay very long; no longer, in fact, than seemed desirable. Presently, Boles, after some restless and apparently aimless rummaging in his cupboard, shut it, locked its door, and, with a sulky farewell to me, took his departure; and, as I had no wish to discuss the quarrel and Gannet seemed to be in a not very sociable mood, I took an early opportunity to bring my visit to an end.

It had been a highly disagreeable episode, and it had a permanent effect on me. Thenceforward, the studio ceased to attract me. Its pleasant, friendly atmosphere seemed to have evaporated. I continued to look in from time to time, but rather to keep an eye on Gannet than to interest myself in the works of the two artists. Like Mrs Gannet, I wondered why these men, hating each other as they obviously did, should perversely continue their association. At any rate, the place was spoiled for me by the atmosphere of hatred and strife that seemed to pervade it, and, even if the abundance of my leisure had continued – which it did not – I should still have been but an occasional visitor.

CHAPTER SEVEN

Mrs Gannet brings Strange Tidings

The wisdom of our ancestors has enriched us with the precept that the locking of the stable door fails in its purpose of security if it is postponed until after the horse has been stolen. Nevertheless (since it is so much easier to be wise after the event than before) this futile form of post-caution continues to be prevalent; of which truth my own proceedings furnished an illustrative instance. For, having allowed my patient to be poisoned with arsenic under my very nose, and that, too, in the crudest and most blatant fashion, I now proceeded to devote my leisure to an intense study of Medical Jurisprudence and Toxicology.

Mine, however, was not a truly representative case. The actual horse had indeed been stolen, but still the stable contained a whole stud of potential horses. I might, and probably should, never encounter another case of poisoning in the practice of a life-time. On the other hand, I might meet with one tomorrow; or if not a poisoning case, perhaps some other form of crime which lay within the province of the medical jurist. There seemed to be plenty of them, judging by the lurid accounts of the authorities whose works I devoured, and I began almost to hope that my labours in their study would not be entirely wasted.

It was natural that my constant preoccupation with the detection and demonstration of crime should react more or less on my habitual state of mind. And it did. Gradually I acquired a definitely Scotland-Yardish outlook and went about my practice – not neglectful, I trust, of the ordinary maladies of my patients – with the idea of criminal possibilities, if not consciously present, yet lurking on the very top surface of the subconscious. Little did my innocent patients or their equally innocent attendants suspect the toxicological balance in which symptoms and ministrations alike were being weighed; and little did the worthy Peter Gannet guess that, even while he was demonstrating the mysteries of stoneware, my perverted mind was canvassing the potentialities of the various glazes that he used for indirect and secret poisoning.

I mention these mental reactions to my late experience and my recent profound study of legal medicine in explanation of subsequent events. And I make no apology. The state of mind may seem odd, but yet it was very natural. I had been caught napping once and I didn't intend to be caught again; and that intention involved these elaborate precautions against possibilities whose probability was almost negligible.

It happened on a certain evening that in the intervals of my evening consultations my thoughts turned to my friend Peter Gannet. It was now some weeks since I had seen him, my practice having of late made a temporary spurt and left me little leisure. I had also been acting as *locum tenens* for the Police Surgeon, who was on leave; and this further diminished my leisure and possibly accentuated the state of mind that I have described. Nevertheless, I was a little disposed to reproach myself, for, solitary man as he was, he had made it clear that he was always pleased to see me. Indeed, it had seemed to me that I was the only friend that he had, for, certainly, Boles could not be regarded in that light; and if the quarrel between them had given me a distaste for the studio, that very occurrence did, in fact, emphasize those obligations of friendship which had led me at first to visit the studio.

I had then felt that it was my duty to keep an eye on him, since some person had certainly tried to poison him. That person had some reason for desiring his death and had no scruple about seeking to compass it; and as the motive, presumably, still existed, there was no denying that, calmly as he had taken the position, Peter Gannet stood definitely in peril of a further and more successful attempt – to say nothing of the chance of his being knocked on the head with a raising hammer in the course of one of his little disagreements with Boles. I ought not to have left him so long without at least a brief visit of inspection.

Thus reflecting, I decided to walk round to the studio as soon as the consultations were finished and satisfy myself that all was well; and, as the time ran on and no further patients appeared, my eye turned impatiently to the clock, the hands of which were creeping towards eight, when I should be free to go. There were now only three minutes to run and the clock had just given the preliminary hiccup by which clocks announce their intention to strike, when I heard the door of the adjoining waiting-room open and close, informing me that a last-minute patient had arrived.

It was very provoking; but, after all, it was what I was there for. So, dismissing Gannet from my mind, I rose, opened the communicating door and looked into the waiting-room.

The visitor was Mrs Gannet; and at the first glance at her my heart sank. For her troubled, almost terrified, expression told me that something was seriously amiss; and my imagination began instantly to frame lurid surmises.

"What is the matter, Mrs Gannet?" I asked, as I ushered her through into the consulting-room. "You look very troubled."

"I am very troubled," she replied. "A most extraordinary and alarming thing has happened. My husband has disappeared."

"Disappeared!" I repeated in astonishment. "Since when?"

"That I can't tell you," she answered. "I have been away from home for about a fortnight, and, when I came back I found the house empty. I didn't think much of it at the time, as I had said, when I wrote to him, that I was not certain as to what time I should get home, and I simply thought that he had gone out. But then I found my letter in the letter box, which seemed very strange, as it must have been lying there two days. So I went up and had another look at his bedroom, but everything was in order there. His bed had not been slept in – it was quite tidily made – and his toilet things and hair brushes were in their usual place. Then I looked over his wardrobe, but none of his clothes seemed to be missing excepting the suit that he usually wears. And then I went down to the hall to see if he had taken his stick or his umbrella, but he hadn't taken either. They were both there; and what was more remarkable, both his hats were on their pegs."

"Do you mean to say," I exclaimed, "that there was no hat missing, at all?"

"No. He has only two hats, and they were both there. So it seems as if he must have gone away without a hat."

"That is very extraordinary," said I. "But surely your maid knows how long he has been absent."

"There isn't any maid," she replied. "Our last girl, Mabel, was under notice and she left a week before I went away; and, as there was no time to get a fresh maid, Peter and I agreed to put it off until I came back. He said that he could look after himself quite well and get his meals out if necessary. There are several good restaurants near.

"Well, I waited in hopes of his return all yesterday, and I sat up until nearly one in the morning, but he never came home, and there has been no sign of him today."

"You looked in at the studio, I suppose?" said I.

"No, I didn't," she replied almost in a whisper. "That is why I have come to you. I couldn't summon up courage to go there."

"Why not?" I asked.

"I was afraid," she answered in the same low, agitated tone, "that there might be something – something there that – well, I don't quite know what I thought, but you know – "

"Yes, I understand," said I, rising – for the clock had struck and I was free. "But that studio ought to be entered at once. Your husband may have had some sudden attack or seizure and be lying there helpless."

I went out into the hall and wrote down on the slate the address where I was to be found if any emergency should arise. Then Mrs Gannet and I set forth together, taking the short cuts through the back streets, with which I was now becoming quite familiar. We walked along at a quick pace, exchanging hardly a word, and, as we went, I cogitated on the strange and disquieting news that she had brought. There was no denying that things had a decidedly sinister aspect. That Gannet should have gone away from home hatless and unprovided with any of his ordinary kit, and leaving no note or message, was inconceivable. Something must have happened to him. But what? My own expectation was that I should find his dead body in the studio, and that was evidently Mrs Gannet's too, as was suggested by her terror at the idea of seeking him there. But that terror seemed to me a little unnatural. Why was she so afraid to go into the studio, even with the expectation of finding her husband dead? Could it be that she had some knowledge or suspicion that she had not disclosed? It seemed not unlikely. Even if she had not been a party to the poisoning, she must have known, or at least strongly suspected, who the poisoner was; and it was most probable that she had been able to guess at the motive of the crime. But she would then realize, as I did, that the motive remained and might induce another crime.

When we reached the house, I tried the wicket in the studio gate, but it was locked, and the key which Gannet had given me was not in my pocket. Meanwhile Mrs Gannet had opened the street door with her latch-key and we entered the house together.

"Are you coming into the studio with me?" I asked as we went through the hall to the side door that opened on the yard.

"No," she replied. "I will come with you to the door and wait outside until you have seen whether he is there or not."

Accordingly we walked together across the yard, and, when we came to the studio door, I tried it. But it was locked; and an inspection by means of my lamp showed that it had been locked from the inside and that the key was in the lock.

"Now," said I, "what are we to do? How are we going to get in?"

"There is a spare key," she replied. "Shall I go and get it?"

"But," I objected, "we couldn't get it into the lock. There is a key there already. And the wicket is locked, too. Have you got a spare key of that?"

She had; so we returned to the house, where she found the key and gave it to me. And as I took it from her trembling hand, I could see – though she made no comment – that the locked door with the key inside had given her a further shock. And, certainly, it was rather ominous. But if the wicket should prove also to be locked from the inside, all hope or doubt would be at an end. It was, therefore, with the most acute anxiety that I hurried out into the street, leaving her standing in the hall, and ran to the wicket. But, to my relief, the key entered freely and turned in the lock and I opened the little gate and stepped through into the studio. Lighting myself with my lamp across the floor, I reached the switch and turned it on, flooding the place with light. A single glance around the studio showed that there was no one in it, alive or dead. Thereupon I unlocked the yard door and threw it open, when I perceived Mrs Gannet standing just outside.

"Well, he isn't here," I reported, whereupon she came, almost on tiptoe, into the lobby and peered round the curtain.

"Oh dear!" she exclaimed, "What a relief! But still, where can he be? I can't help thinking that something must have happened to him."

As I could not pretend to disagree with her, I made no reply to this, but asked: "I suppose you have searched the house thoroughly?"

"I think so," she replied, "and I don't feel as if I could search any more. But if you would be so kind as to take a look round and make sure that I haven't over looked anything – "

"Yes," said I, "I think that would be just as well. But what are you going to do tonight? You oughtn't to be in the house all alone."

"I couldn't be," she replied. "Last night was dreadful, but now my nerves are all on edge. I couldn't endure another night. I shall go to my friend, Miss Hughes – she lives in Mornington Crescent – and see if she will come and keep me company."

"It would be better if she would put you up for the night," said I.

"Yes, it would," she agreed. "Much better. I would rather not stay in this house tonight. As soon as you have made your inspection, I will run round and ask her."

"You needn't wait for me," said I. "Go round to her at once, as it is getting late. Give me the number of her house and I will call on my way home and tell you whether I have discovered any clue to the mystery."

She closed with this offer immediately, being evidently relieved to get away from the silent, desolate house. I walked back with her across the yard, and, when I had escorted her to the street door and seen her start on her mission, I closed the door and went back into the house, not displeased to have the place to myself and the opportunity to pursue my investigations at my leisure and free from observation.

I made a very thorough examination, beginning with the attics at the very top of the house and working my way systematically downwards. On the upper floors there were several unoccupied rooms, some quite empty and others more or less filled with discarded furniture and miscellaneous lumber. All these I searched minutely, opening up every possible – and even impossible – hiding-place, and peering, with the aid of my pocket electric lamp, into the dim and musty recesses of the shapeless closets in the corners of the roof or under the staircases. In the occupied bedrooms I knelt down to look under the beds, I opened the cupboards and wardrobes and prodded the clothes that hung from the pegs to make sure that they concealed no other hanging object. I even examined the chimneys with my lamp and explored their cavities with my walking-stick, gathering a little harvest of soot up my sleeves, but achieving no other result and making no discoveries, excepting that, when I came to examine Gannet's bedroom, I noticed that the pots and pans and the effigy of the monkey had disappeared from the mantelpiece.

It was an eerie business and seemed to become more so (by a sort of auto-suggestion) as I explored one room after another. By the time that I had examined the great stone-paved kitchen and the rather malodorous scullery and searched the cavernous, slug-haunted cellars, even probing the mounds of coal with my stick, I had worked myself up into a state of the most horrid expectancy.

But still there was no sign of Peter Gannet. The natural conclusion seemed to be that he was not there. But this was a conclusion that my state of mind made me unable to accept. His wife's statement set forth that he had disappeared in his ordinary indoor apparel, in which it was hardly imaginable that he could have gone away from the house. But if he had not, then he must be somewhere on the premises. Thus I argued, with more conviction than logic, as I ascended the uncarpeted basement stairs, noting the surprisingly loud sound that my footsteps made as they broke in on the pervading silence.

As I passed into the hall, I paused at the hat-stand to verify Mrs Gannet's statement. There were the two hats, sure enough; a shabby, broad-brimmed, soft felt which I knew well by sight, and a rather trim billy-cock which I had never seen him wear, but which bore his initials in the crown, as I ascertained by taking it down and inspecting it. And there was his stick – a rough, oak crook – and his umbrella with a legible PG on the silver band. There was also another stick which I had never seen before and which struck me as being rather out of character with the bohemian Gannet; a smart, polished cane with a gilt band and a gilt tip to the handle. I took it out of the stand, and, as it seemed to me rather long, I lifted out the oak stick and compared the two, when I found that the cane was the longer by a full inch. There was nothing much in this, and, as the band bore no initials, I was putting it back in the stand when my eye caught a minute monogram on the gilt tip. It was a confused device, as monograms usually are, but eventually I managed to resolve it into the two letters F and B.

Then it was pretty certain that the stick belonged to Frederick Boles. From which it followed that Boles had been to the house recently. But there was nothing abnormal in this, since he worked pretty regularly in the studio and usually approached it through the house. But why had he left his stick? And why had Mrs Gannet made no mention of it, or, indeed, of Boles himself? For if he had been working here, he must have know when Gannet was last seen, since, unless he had a latch-key, he must have been admitted by Gannet himself.

Turning this over in my mind, I decided, before leaving the house, to take another look at the studio. It had certainly been empty when I had looked in previously, and there were no large cupboards or other possible hiding-places. Still, there was the chance that a more thorough examination might throw some light on Gannet's activities and on the question as to the time of his disappearance. Accordingly, I passed out by the side door, and, crossing the yard, opened the studio door, switched on the lights, drew aside the curtain and stepped in.

CHAPTER EIGHT

Dr Oldfield makes some Surprising Discoveries

On entering the studio, I halted close by the curtain and stood awhile surveying the vast, desolate, forbidding interior with no definite idea in my mind. Obviously, there was no one there, dead or alive, nor any closed space large enough to form a hiding-place. And yet as I stood there, the creepy feeling that had been growing on me as I had searched the house seemed to become even more intense. It may have been that the deathly silence and stillness of the place, which I had known only under the cheerful influence of work and companionship, cast a chill over me.

At any rate, there I stood vaguely looking about me with a growing uncomfortable feeling that this great, bare room which had been the scene of Gannet's labours and the centre of his interests, had been in some way connected with his unaccountable disappearance.

Presently my vague, general survey gave place to a more detailed inspection. I began to observe the various objects in the studio and to note what they had to tell of Gannet's recent activities. There was the potter's wheel, carefully cleaned, though never used, according to his invariable orderly practice, and there was a row of "green", unfired jars drying on a shelf until they should be ready for the kiln. But when I looked at the kiln itself, I was struck by something quite unusual, having regard to Gannet's habitual tidiness. The fire-holes which led into the interior of the kiln were all choked with ash; and opposite to each was a large mound of the ash which had been raked out during the firing and left on the hearths. Now, this was singularly unlike Gannet's practice. Usually, as he raked out the ash, he shovelled it up into a bucket and carried it out to the ash-bin in the yard; and as soon as the fires were out, he cleared each of the fireplaces of the remaining ash, leaving them clean and ready for the next firing.

Here, then, was something definitely abnormal. But there was a further discrepancy. The size of the mounds made it clear that there had been a rather prolonged firing and a "high fire". But where were the fired pieces? The shelves on which the pots were usually stored after firing were all empty and there was not a sign of any pottery other than the unfired jars. The unavoidable conclusion was that the "batch" must still be in the kiln. But if this were so, then Gannet's disappearance must have coincided with the end of the firing. But that seemed entirely to exclude the idea of a voluntary disappearance. It was inconceivable that he should have gone away leaving the fires still burning and the kiln unopened.

However, there was no need to speculate. The question could be settled at once by opening the kiln if it was sufficiently cool to handle. Accordingly, I walked over to it and cautiously touched the outside brick casing, which I found to be little more than luke-warm, and then I boldly unlatched and pulled open the big iron, fire-clay lined door, bringing into view the loose fire-bricks which actually closed the opening. As these, too, were only moderately warm, I proceeded to lift them out, one by one, which I was able to do the more easily since they had been only roughly fitted together.

It was not really necessary for me to take them all out, for, as soon as the upper tier was removed, I was able to throw the light of my lamp into the interior. And when I did so, I discovered to my astonishment that the kiln was empty.

The mystery, then, remained. Indeed, it grew more profound. For not only was the problem as to what had become of the fired pottery still unsolved, but there was the remarkable fact that the kiln must have been opened while it was still quite hot – a thing that Gannet would never have done, since a draught of cold air on the hot pottery would probably result in a disaster. And when I took away the rest of the fire-bricks and the interior of the kiln was fully exposed to view, another anomaly presented itself. The floor of the kiln, which during the firing would be covered with burnt flint or bone-ash, was perfectly clean. It had been carefully and thoroughly swept out, and this while the kiln was hot and while the fire-holes remained choked with ash.

As to the missing pottery, there was one possibility, though an unlikely one. It might have been treated with glaze and put into the glost oven. But it had not; for when I opened the oven and looked in, I found it empty and showing no sign of recent use.

It was all very strange; and the strangeness of it did nothing to allay my suspicion that the studio held the secret of Gannet's disappearance. I prowled round with uneasy inquisitiveness, scrutinizing all the various objects in search of some hint or leading fact. I examined the grog-mill and noted that something white had been recently ground in it, and apparently ground dry, to judge by the coating of fine powder on the floor around it. I looked into the big iron mortar and noted that some white material had been pounded in it. I examined the rows of cupels on the shelves by Boles' little muffle, noted that they were badly made and of unusually coarse material, and wondered when Boles had made them. I even looked into the muffle – finding nothing, of course – and observing that the floor of the studio seemed to have been washed recently, speculated on the possible reason for this very unusual proceeding.

But speculation got me no more forward. Obviously, there was something abnormal about the kiln. There had been a prolonged and intense fire, but of the fired ware there was not a trace. What conceivable explanation could there be of such an extraordinary conflict of facts? The possibility occurred to me that the whole batch might have been disposed of by a single transaction or sent to an exhibition. But a moment's reflection showed me that this would not do. There had not been time for the batch to be cooled, finished, glazed and refired, for the kiln was still quite warm inside.

The rough, box-like stool that Gannet had made to sit on at the bench was standing near the kiln. I slipped my hand through the lifting hole and drew the stool up to the open door in order more conveniently to examine the interior. But the examination yielded nothing. I threw the beam of light from my lamp into every corner, but it simply confirmed my original observation. The kiln was empty, and no trace of its late contents remained beyond the few obscure white smears that the brush had left on the fire-clay floor.

I sat there for some minutes facing the open door and reflecting profoundly on this extraordinary problem. But I could make nothing of it, and, at length, I started up to renew my explorations. For it had suddenly occurred to me that I had forgotten to examine the contents of the bins. But as I rose and turned round, I noticed a small white object on the floor which had evidently been covered by the stool before I had moved it. I stooped and picked it up; and at the first glance at it all my vague and formless suspicions seemed to run together into a horrible certainty.

The little object was the ungual phalanx, or terminal joint, of a finger – apparently a fore-finger – burned to the snowy whiteness characteristic of incinerated bone. It was unmistakable. For if I lacked experience in some professional matters, at least my osteology was fresh; and as the instant recognition flashed on me, I stood as if rooted to the ground, staring at the little relic with a shuddering realization of all that it meant.

The mystery of the absent pottery was solved. There had never been any pottery. That long and fierce fire had burned to destroy the evidence of a hideous crime. And the other mysteries, too, were solved. Now I could guess what the white substance was that had been ground in the grog-mill; how it came that the hastily made cupels were of such abnormally coarse material; and why it had been necessary to wash the studio floor. All the anomalies now fell into a horrid agreement and each served to confirm and explain the others.

I laid the little fragile bone tenderly on the stool and proceeded to re-examine the place by the light of this new and dreadful fact. First I went to the shelves by Boles' muffle and looked over the cupels, taking them in my hand the better to examine them. Their nature was now quite obvious. Instead of the finely powdered bone-ash of which they were ordinarily composed, they had been made by cramming fragments of crushed, incinerated bone into the cupel-press; and the cohesion of these was so slight that one of the cupels fell to pieces in my hand.

Laying the loose fragments on the shelf, I turned away to examine the bins, of which there was a row standing against the wall. I began with the clay bins, containing the material for the various "bodies" – stoneware, earthenware and porcelain. But when I lifted the lids, I saw that they contained clay and could contain nothing else. The grog bins were nearly empty and showed nothing abnormal, and the same was true of the plaster bin, though I took the precaution of dipping my hand deeply into the plaster to make sure that there was nothing underneath. When I came to the bone ash bin I naturally surveyed it more critically; for here, with the aid of the mill, the residue of a cremated body could have been concealed beyond the possibility of recognition.

I lifted off the lid and looked in, but at the first glance perceived nothing unusual. The bin was three parts full, and its contents appeared to be the ordinary finely powdered ash. But I was not prepared to accept the surface appearances. Rolling my sleeve up above the elbow, I thrust my hand deep down into the ash, testing its consistency by working it between my fingers and thumb. The result was what the cupels had led me to expect. About eight inches from the surface, the feel of the fine, smooth powder gave place to a sensation as if I were grasping a mixture of gravel and sand with occasional fragments of appreciable size. Some of these I brought up to the surface, dropping them into my other hand and dipping down for further specimens until I had collected a handful, when I carried them over to the cupel shelves and, having deposited them on a vacant space, picked out one or two of the larger fragments and carried them across to the modelling stand to examine them by the light of the big studio lamp.

Of course, there could be no doubt as to their nature. Even to the naked eye, the characteristic structure of bone was obvious, and rendered more so by the burning away of the soft tissues. But I confirmed the diagnosis with the aid of my pocket lens, and then, having replaced the fragments on the shelf, I put the lid back on the bin and began seriously to consider what I should do next. There was no need for further exploration. I had all the essential facts. I now knew what had happened to Peter Gannet, and any further elucidation lay outside my province and within that of those whose business it is to investigate crime.

Before leaving the studio, I looked about for some receptacle in which to pack the little finger-bone; for I knew that it would crumble at a touch, and that, as it was the one piece of undeniable evidence, it must be preserved intact at all costs. Eventually I found a nearly empty match-box, and, having tipped out the remaining matches and torn a strip from my handkerchief, I rolled the little relic in this, packed it tenderly in the match-box and bestowed the latter in my breast pocket. Then I took up my stick and prepared to depart; but, just as I was starting towards the door, it occurred to me that I might as well take a few of the small fragments from the bin to examine more thoroughly at my leisure. Not that I had any doubts as to their nature, but the microscope would put the matter beyond dispute. Accordingly, I collected a handful from the shelf, and, having wrapped them in the remainder of my handkerchief, put the little parcel in my pocket and then made my way to the door, switched off the lights and went out, taking the door-key with me.

Coming out from the glare of the studio into the darkness, I had to light myself across the yard with my pocket lamp, and, as I flashed it about, its beam fell on the big rubbish bin which stood in a corner waiting for the dustman. For a moment, I was disposed to stop and explore it; but then I reflected that it was not my concern to seek further details, and, as it was getting late and I still had to report to Mrs Gannet, I went on into the house, and, passing through the hall, let myself out into the street.

The distance from Jacob Street to Mornington Crescent is quite short; all too short for the amount of thinking that I had to do on the way thither. For it was only when I had shut the door and set forth on my errand that the awkwardness of the coming interview began to dawn on me. What was I to say to Mrs Gannet? As I asked myself the question, I saw that it involved two others. The first was, how much did she know? Had she any suspicion that her husband had been made away with? I did not for a moment believe that she had been privy to the gruesome events that the studio had witnessed, but her agitation, her horror at the idea of spending the night in the house, and, above all, her strange fear of entering the studio, justified the suspicion that, even if she knew nothing of what had happened, she had made some highly pertinent surmises.

Then, how much did I know? I had assumed quite confidently that a body had been cremated in the kiln and that the body was that of Peter Gannet. And I believed that I could name the other party to that grim transaction. But here I recalled Dr Thorndyke's oft-repeated warning to his students never to confuse inference or belief with knowledge and never to go beyond the definitely ascertained facts. But I had done this already; and now, when I revised my convictions by the light of this excellent precept, I realized that the actual facts that I had ascertained (though they justified my inferences) were enough only to call for a thorough investigation.

Then should I tell Mrs Gannet simply what I had observed and leave her to draw her own conclusions? Considered, subject to my strong distrust of the lady, this course did not commend itself. In fact, it was a very difficult question, and I had come to no decision when I found myself standing on Miss Hughes' doorstep, and, in response to my knock, the door was opened by Mrs Gannet herself.

Still temporizing in my own mind, I began by expressing the hope that Miss Hughes was able to accommodate her.

"Yes," she replied as she ushered me into the drawing-room. "I am glad to say that she can give me the spare bedroom. She has been most kind and sympathetic. And how have you got on? You have been a tremendous time. I expected you at least half an hour ago."

"The search took quite a long time," I explained, "for I went through the whole house from the attics to the cellars and examined every nook and corner."

"And I suppose you found nothing, after all?"

"Not a trace in any part of the house."

"It was very good of you to take so much trouble," said she. "I don't know how to thank you, and you such a busy man, too. I suppose you didn't go into the studio again?"

"Yes," I replied. "I thought I would have another look at it, in rather more detail, and I did pick up some information there as to the approximate time when he disappeared, for I opened the big kiln and found it quite warm inside. I don't know how long it takes to cool. Do you?"

"Not very exactly," she answered, "but quite a long time, I believe, if it is kept shut up. At any rate, the fact that it was warm doesn't tell us much more than we know. It is all very mysterious, and I don't know what on earth to do next."

"What about Mr Boles?" I suggested. "He must have been at the studio some time quite lately. Wouldn't it be as well to look him up and see if he can throw any light on the mystery?"

She shook her head disconsolately. "I have," she said. "I went to his flat yesterday and again this morning, but I could get no answer to my knocking and ringing. And the caretaker man in the office says that he hasn't seen him for about a week, though he has been on the look-out for him on account of a parcel that the postman left. He has been up to the flat several times, but could get no answer. And there hasn't been any light in the windows at night. So he must be away from home."

"Did he know when you would be returning?"

"Yes," she replied. "And there is another strange thing. I wrote and told him what day I should be back and asked him to drop in and have tea with me. But he not only never came, but he didn't even answer my letter."

I reflected on this new turn of events, which seemed less mysterious to me than it appeared to her. Then I cautiously approached the inevitable proposal.

"Well, Mrs Gannet," said I, "it is, as you say, all very mysterious. But we can't just leave it at that. We have got to find out what has happened to your husband; and as we haven't the means of doing it ourselves, we must invoke the aid of those who have. We shall have to apply for help to the police."

As I made this proposal, I watched her attentively and was a little relieved to note that it appeared to cause her no alarm. But she was not enthusiastic.

"Do you think it is really necessary?" she asked. "If we call in the police, it will be in all the papers and there will be no end of fuss and scandal; and, after all, he may come back tomorrow."

"I don't think there is any choice," I rejoined, firmly. "The police will have to be informed, sooner or later, and they ought to be notified at once while the events are fresh and the traces more easy to follow. It would never do for us to seem to have tried to hush the affair up."

That last remark settled her. She agreed that perhaps the police had better be informed of the disappearance, and, to my great satisfaction, she asked me to make the communication.

"I don't feel equal to it," said she, "and as you have acted as police surgeon and know the officers, it will be easier for you. Hadn't you better have the latch-key in case they want to look over the house?"

"But won't you want it yourself?" I asked.

"No," she replied. "Miss Hughes has invited me to stay with her for the present. Besides, I have a spare key and I brought it away with me; and, of course, if Peter should come back, he has his own key."

With this she handed me the latch-key and when I had pocketed it I took my leave and set forth at a swinging pace for home, hoping that I should find no messages awaiting me and that a substantial meal would be ready for instant production. I was very well pleased with the way in which the interview had gone off and congratulated myself on having kept my own counsel. For now I need not appear in the investigation at all. The police would, of course, examine the studio, and the discoveries that they would make, on my prompting, could be credited to them.

When I let myself in, I cast an anxious glance at the messages slate and breathed a benediction on the blank surface that it presented. And as a savoury aroma ascending from the basement told me that all was well there, too, I skipped off to the bathroom, there to wash and brush joyfully and reflect on the delight of being really hungry − under suitable conditions.

As I disposed of the excellent dinner − or supper − that my thoughtful housekeeper had provided, it was natural that I should ruminate on the astonishing events of the last few hours. And now that the excitement of the chase had passed off, I began to consider the significance of my discoveries. Those discoveries left me in no doubt (despite Thorndyke's caution) that my friend, Peter Gannet, had been made away with; and I owed it to our friendship, to say nothing of my duty as a good citizen, to do everything in my power to establish the identity of the murderer in order that he − or she − might be brought within the grasp of the law.

Now, who could it be that had made away with my poor friend? I had not the faintest doubt as to, at least, the protagonist in that horrid drama. In the very moment of my realization that a crime had been committed I had confidently identified the criminal. And my conviction remained unshaken. Nevertheless, I turned over the available evidence as it would have to be presented to a stranger and as I should have to present it to the police.

What could we say with certainty as to the personality of the murderer? In the first place, he was a person who had access to the studio. Then he knew how to prepare and fire the kiln. He understood the use and management of the grog-mill and of the cupel-press, and he knew which of the various bins was the bone-ash bin. But, so far as I knew, there was only one person in the world to whom this description would apply – Frederick Boles.

Then, to approach the question from the other direction, were there any reasons for suspecting Boles? And the answer was that there were several reasons. Boles had certainly been at the house when Gannet was there alone, and had thus had the opportunity. He had now unaccountably disappeared, and his disappearance seemed to coincide with the date of the murder. He had already, to my certain knowledge, violently assaulted Gannet, on at least one occasion. But far more to the point was the fact that he was under the deepest suspicion of having made a most determined attempt to kill Gannet by means of poison. Indeed, the word "suspicion" was an under-statement. It was nearly a certainty. Even the cautious Thorndyke had made no secret of his views as to the identity of the poisoner.

It was at this stage of my reflections that I had what, I think, Americans call a "hunch"; a brain wave, or inspiration. Boles had made at least one attempt to poison poor Gannet. We suspected more than one attempt, but of the one I had practically no doubt. Now, one of the odd peculiarities of the criminal mind is its strong tendency to repetition. The coiner, on coming out of prison, promptly returns to the coining industry; the burglar, the forger, the pickpocket, all tend to repeat their successes or even their failures. So, too, the poisoner, foiled at a first attempt, tries again, not only by the same methods, but nearly always makes use of the same poison.

Now, Boles had been alone in the house with Gannet. He had thus had the opportunity, and it might be assumed that he had the means. Was it possible that he might have made yet another attempt, and succeeded? It was true that the appearances rather suggested violence, and that this would be, from the murderer's point of view, preferable to the relatively slow method of poisoning. Nevertheless, a really massive dose of arsenic, if it could be administered, would be fairly rapid in its effects; and, after all, in the assumed circumstances, the time factor would not be so very important.

But there was another consideration. Supposing Boles to have managed to administer a big, lethal dose of arsenic, would any trace of the poison be detectable in the incinerated remains of the body? It seemed doubtful, though I had no experience by which to form an opinion. But it was certainly worth while to try; for if the result of the trial should be negative, no harm would have been done, whereas if the smallest trace of arsenic should be discoverable, demonstrable evidence of the highest importance would have been secured.

I have mentioned that, since the poisoning incident, I had taken various measures to provide against any similar case in the future, and among other precautions, I had furnished myself with a very complete apparatus for the detection of arsenic. It included the appliances for Marsh's test – not the simple and artless affair that is used for demonstration in chemistry classes, but a really up-to-date apparatus, capable of the greatest delicacy and precision. And as a further precaution, I had made several trial analyses with it to make sure that, should the occasion arise, I could rely on my competence to use it.

And now the occasion had arisen. It was not a very promising one, as the probability of a positive result seemed rather remote. But I entered into the investigation with an enthusiasm that accelerated considerably my disposal of the rest of my dinner, and as soon as I had swallowed the last mouthful, I rose and proceeded forthwith to the dispensary which served also as a laboratory. Here I produced from my pocket the match-box containing the finger-bone and the parcel of crushed fragments from the bin. The match-box I opened and tenderly transferred the little bone to a corked glass tube with a plug of cotton wool above and below it, and put the tube away in a locked drawer. Then I opened the parcel of fragments and embarked on the investigation.

I began by examining one or two of the fragments with a low power of the microscope and thereby confirming beyond all doubt my assumption that they were incinerated bone; and, having disposed of this essential preliminary, I fell to work on the chemical part of the investigation. With the details of these operations – which, to tell the truth, I found rather tedious and troublesome – I need not burden the reader. Roughly, and in bare outline, the procedure was as follows. First, I divided the heap of fragments into two parts, reserving one part for further treatment if necessary. The other part I dissolved in strong hydrochloric acid and distilled the mixture into a receiver containing a small quantity of distilled water – a slow and tedious business which tried my patience severely, and which was, after all, only a preliminary to the actual analysis. But at last the fluid in the retort dwindled to a little half dry residue, whereupon I removed the lamp and transferred my attention to the Marsh's apparatus. With this I made the usual preliminary trial to test the purity of the reagents and then set the lamp under the hard glass exit tube, watching it for several minutes after it had reached a bright red heat. As there was no sign of any darkening or deposit in the tube, I was satisfied that my chemicals were free from arsenic – as, indeed, I knew them to be from previous trials.

And now came the actual test. Detaching the receiver from the retort, I emptied its contents – the distilled fluid – into a well-washed measure glass and from this poured it slowly, almost drop by drop, into the thistle funnel of the flask in which the gas was generating. I had no expectation of any result – at least, so I persuaded myself. Nevertheless, as I poured in the "distillate", I watched the exit tube with almost tremulous eagerness. For it was my first real analysis; and after all the trouble that I had taken, a completely negative result would have seemed rather an anticlimax. Hence the yearning and half-expectant eye that turned ever towards the exit tube.

Nevertheless, the result, when it began to appear, fairly astonished me. It was beyond my wildest hopes. For, even before I had finished pouring in the distillate, a dark ring appeared on the inside of the glass exit tube, just beyond the red-hot portion, and grew from moment to moment in intensity and extent until a considerable area of the tube was covered with a typical "arsenic mirror". I sat down before the apparatus and watched it ecstatically, moved not only by the natural triumph of the tyro who has "brought it off" at the first trial, but by satisfaction at the thought that I had forged an instrument to put into the hands of avenging justice.

For now the cause of poor Gannet's death was established beyond cavil. My original surmise was proved to be correct. By some means, the murderer had contrived to administer a dose of arsenic so enormous as to produce an immediately fatal result. It must have been so. The quantity of the poison in the body must have been prodigious; for, even after the considerable loss of arsenic in the kiln, there remained in the ashes a measurable amount, though how much I had not sufficient experience to judge.

I carried the analysis no further. The customary procedure is to cut off the piece of tube containing the "mirror" of metallic arsenic and subject it to a further, confirmatory test. But this I considered unnecessary and, in fact, undesirable. Instead, I carefully detached the tube from the flask and, having wrapped it in several layers of paper, packed it in a cardboard postal tube and put it away with the finger-bone in readiness for my interview with the police on the morrow.

CHAPTER NINE

Inspector Blandy Investigates

On the following morning, as soon as I had disposed of the more urgent visits, I collected the proceeds of my investigations – the finger-bone, the remainder of the bone fragments and the glass tube with the arsenic mirror – and bustled off to the police station, all agog to spring my mine and set the machinery of the law in motion. My entry was acknowledged by the sergeant, who was perched at his desk, with an affable smile and the inquiry as to what he could do for me.

"I wanted, rather particularly, to see the Superintendent, if he could spare me a few minutes," I replied.

"I doubt whether he could," said the sergeant. "He's pretty busy just now. Couldn't I manage your business for you?"

"I think I had better see the Superintendent," I answered. "The matter is one of some urgency and I don't know how far it might be considered confidential. I think I ought to make my communication to him, in the first place."

"Sounds mighty mysterious," said the sergeant, regarding me critically, "however, we'll see what he says. Go in, Dawson, and tell the Superintendent that Dr Oldfield wants to speak to him and that he won't say what his business is."

On this, the constable proceeded to the door of the inner office, on which he knocked, and, having been bidden in a loud, impatient voice to "come in", went in. After a brief delay, occupied, probably, by explanations, he reappeared, followed by the Superintendent, carrying in one hand a large note-book and in the other a pencil. His expression was not genial, but rather irritably interrogative, conveying the question, "Now, then. What about it?"; and, in effect, that was also conveyed by his rather short greeting.

"I should like to have a few words with you, Superintendent," I said, humbly.

"Well," he replied, "they will have to be very few. I am in the middle of a conference will an officer from Scotland Yard. What is the nature of your business?"

"I have come to inform you that I have reason to believe that a murder has been committed," I replied.

He brightened up considerably at this, but still, he accepted the sensational statement with disappointing coolness.

"Do you mean that you think, or suspect, that a murder has been committed?" he asked in an obviously sceptical tone.

"It is more than that," I replied. "I am practically certain. I came to give you the facts that are known to me; and I have brought some things to show you which I think you will find pretty convincing."

He reflected for a moment; then, still a little irritably, he said:

"Very well. You had better come in and let us hear what you have to tell us."

With this, he indicated the open door, and when I had passed through, he followed me and closed it after us.

As I entered the office I was confronted by a gentleman who was seated at the table with a number of papers before him. A rather remarkable-looking gentleman, slightly bald, with a long, placid face and a still longer, and acutely-pointed nose, and an expression in which concentrated benevolence beamed on an undeserving world. I don't know what his appearance suggested, but it certainly did *not* suggest a detective-inspector of the Criminal Investigation Department. Yet that was his actual status, as appeared when the Superintendent introduced him to me – by the name of Blandy – adding:

"This is Dr Oldfield, who has come to give us some information about a case of suspected murder."

"How good of him!" exclaimed Inspector Blandy, rising to execute a deferential bow and beaming a benediction on me as he pressed my hand with affectionate warmth. "I am proud, sir, to make your acquaintance. I am always proud to make the acquaintance of members of your learned and invaluable profession."

The Superintendent smiled sourly and offered me a chair.

"I suppose, Inspector," said he, "we had better adjourn our other business and take the Doctor's information?"

"Surely, surely," replied Blandy. "A capital crime must needs take precedence. And as the Doctor's time is even more valuable than ours, we can rely on him to economize both."

Accordingly, the Superintendent, with a distinct return to the "what about it?" expression, directed me shortly to proceed, which I did; and, bearing in mind the Inspector's polite hint, I plunged into the matter without preamble.

I need not record my statement in detail since it was but a repetition, suitably condensed, of the story that I have already told. I began with the disappearance of Peter Gannet, went on to my search of the house (to which the Superintendent listened with undissembled impatience) and then to my examination of the studio and my discoveries therein, producing the finger-bone and the packet of fragments in corroboration. To the latter part of my statement both officers listened with evidently aroused interest, asking only such questions as were necessary to elucidate the narrative; as, for instance, how I came to know so much about the kiln and Gannet's methods of work.

At the conclusion of this part of my statement, I paused while the two officers pored over the little bone in its glass container and the open package of white, coral-like fragments. Then I prepared to play my trump card. Taking off the paper wrapping from the cardboard case, I drew out from the latter the glass tube and laid it on the table.

The Superintendent glared at it suspiciously while the Inspector picked it up and regarded it with deep and benevolent interest.

"To my untutored eye," said he, "this dark ring seems to resemble an arsenic mirror."

"It is an arsenic mirror," said I.

"And what is its connection with these burnt remains?" the Superintendent demanded.

"That arsenic," I replied impressively, "was extracted from a quantity of bone fragments similar to those that I have handed to you," and with this, I proceeded to give them an account of my investigations with the Marsh's apparatus, to which the Superintendent listened with open incredulity.

"But," he demanded, when I had finished, "what on earth led you to test these ashes for arsenic? What suggested to you that there might be arsenic in them?"

Of course, I had expected this question, but yet, curiously enough, I was hardly ready for it. The secret of the poisoning had been communicated to Gannet, but otherwise I had, on Thorndyke's advice, kept my own counsel. But now this was impossible. There was nothing for it but to give the officers a full account of the poisoning affair, including the fact that the discovery had been made and confirmed by Dr Thorndyke.

At the mention of my teacher's name, both men pricked up their ears, and the Superintendent commented:

"Then Dr Thorndyke would be available as a witness."

"Yes," I replied, "I don't suppose he would have any objection to giving evidence on the matter."

"Objection be blowed!" snorted the Superintendent. "He wouldn't be asked. He could be subpoenaed as a common witness to the fact that this man, Gannet, was suffering from arsenic poisoning. However, before we begin to talk of evidence, we have got to be sure that there is something like a *prima facie* case. What do you think, Inspector?"

"I agree with you, Superintendent, as I always do," the Inspector replied. "We had better begin by checking the Doctor's observations on the state of affairs in Gannet's studio. If we find the conditions to be as he has described them – which I have no doubt that we shall – and if we reach the same conclusions that he has reached, there will certainly be a case for investigation."

"Yes," the Superintendent agreed. "But our conclusions on the primary facts would have to be checked by suitable experts; and I suppose an independent analysis would be desirable. The Doctor's evidence is good enough, but counsel like to produce a specialist with a name and a reputation."

"Very true," said the Inspector. "But the analysis can wait. It is quite possible that the arsenic issue may never be raised. If we find clear evidence that a human body has been burned to ashes in that kiln, we shall have the very strongest presumptive evidence that a murder has been committed. The method used doesn't really concern us, and an attempt to prove that deceased was killed in some particular manner might only confuse and complicate the case."

"I was thinking," said the superintendent, "of what the Doctor has told us about the attempt to poison Gannet. The presence of arsenic in the bones might point to certain possible suspects, considered in connection with that previous attempt."

"Undoubtedly," agreed the Inspector, "if we could prove who administered that arsenic. But we can't. And, if Gannet is dead, I don't see how we are going to, he being the only really competent witness. No, Superintendent. My feeling is that we shall be wise to ignore the arsenic, or, at any rate, keep it up our sleeve for the present. But to come back to the immediate business; we want to see that studio, Doctor. How can it be managed without making a fuss?"

"Quite easily," I replied. "I have the keys, and I have Mrs Gannet's permission to enter the house and to admit you, if you want to inspect the premises. I could hand you the keys if necessary, but I would much rather admit you myself."

"And very proper, too," said the Inspector. "Besides, we should want you to accompany us, as you know all about the studio and we don't. Now, when could you manage the personally conducted exploration? The sooner the better, you know, as the matter is rather urgent."

"Well," I replied, "I have got several visits to make, and it is about time that I started to make them. It won't do for me to neglect my practice."

"Of course it won't," the Inspector agreed. "If duty calls you must away; and, after all, a live patient is better than a dead potter. What time shall we say?"

"I think I shall be clear by four o'clock. Will that do?"

"It will do for me," replied the Inspector, glancing inquiringly at his brother officer; and as the latter agreed, it was arranged that they should call at my house at four o'clock and that we should proceed together to the studio.

As I rose to depart, my precious mirror tube – despised by Blandy but dear to me – caught my eye, and I proceeded unostentatiously to resume possession of it, remarking that I would take care of it in case it should ever be wanted. As neither officer made any objection, I returned it to its case; and the packet of bone ash having served its purpose, I closed it and slipped it into my pocket with the tube.

On leaving the police station, I glanced rapidly through the entries in my visiting-list, and, having planned out a convenient route, started on my round, endeavouring – none too successfully – to banish from my mind all thoughts of the Gannet mystery that I might better concentrate my attention on the clinical problems that my patients presented. But if I suffered some distraction from my proper business, there was compensation in the matter of speed, for I dispatched my round of visits in record time, and, even after a leisurely lunch, found myself with half an hour to spare before my visitors were due to arrive; which half-hour I spent, with my hat on, pacing my consulting-room in an agony of apprehension lest an inopportune professional call should hinder me from keeping my appointment. But, fortunately, no message came, and, punctually at four o'clock, Inspector Blandy was announced and conducted me to a large, roomy car which was drawn up outside the house.

"The Superintendent couldn't come," Blandy explained as he ushered me into the car. "But it doesn't matter. This is not a case for the local police. If there is anything in it, the CID will have to carry out the investigation."

"And what are you proposing to do now?" I asked.

"Just to check your report," he replied. "Personally, having seen you and noted your careful and exact methods, I accept it without any hesitation. But our people take nothing on hearsay if they can get observed facts, so I must be in a position to state those facts on my own knowledge and the evidence of my own eyesight; though, as you and I know, my eyesight would have been of no use without yours."

I was beginning a modest disclaimer, suggesting that I was but an amateur investigator, but he would have none of it, exclaiming:

"My dear Doctor, you under-value yourself. The whole discovery is your own. Consider, now, what would have happened if I had looked into the studio as you did. What should I have seen? Nothing, my dear sir, nothing. My mere bodily senses would have perceived the visible objects but their significance would never have dawned on me. Whereas you, bringing an expert eye to bear on them, instantly detected the signs of some abnormal happenings. By the way, I am assuming that I am going to have the benefit of your co-operation and advice on this occasion."

I replied that I should be very pleased to stay for a time and help him, (being, in fact, on the very tip-toe of curiosity as to his proceedings) on which he thanked me warmly, and was still thanking me when the car drew up opposite the Gannets' front door. We both alighted, Blandy lifting out a large, canvas-covered suit-case, which he set down on the pavement while he stood taking a general view of the premises.

"Does that gate belong to Gannet's house?" he asked, indicating the wide, double-leaved studio door.

"Yes," I replied. "It opens directly into the studio. Would you like to go in that way? I have the key of the wicket."

"Not this time," said he. "We had better go in through the house so that I may see the lie of the premises."

Accordingly, I let him in by the front door and conducted him through the hall, where he looked about him inquisitively, giving special attention to the hat-rack and stand. Then I opened the side door and escorted him out into the yard, where, again, he inspected the premises and especially the walls and houses which enclosed the space. Presently he espied the rubbish bin, and, walking over to it, lifted its lid and looked thoughtfully into its interior.

"Is this domestic refuse?" he inquired, "or does it belong to the studio?"

"I think it is a general dump," I replied, "but I know that Gannet used it for ashes and anything that the dustmen would take away."

"Then," said he, "we had better take it in with us and look over the contents before the dustman has his innings."

As I had by this time got the studio door unlocked, we took the bin by its two handles and carried it in. Then, at the Inspector's suggestion, I shut the door and locked it on the inside.

"Now, I suppose," said I, "you would like me to show you round the studio and explain the various appliances."

"Thank you, Doctor," he replied, "but I think we will postpone that, if it should be necessary after your singularly lucid description, and get on at once with the essential part of the inquiry."

"What is that?" I asked.

"Our present purpose," he replied, beaming on me benevolently, "is to establish what the lawyers call the *corpus delicti* – to ascertain whether a crime has been committed, and, if so, what sort of crime it is. We begin by finding out what those bone fragments really amount to. I have brought a small sieve with me, but probably there is a better one here, preferably a fairly fine one."

"There is a set of sieves for sifting grog and other powders," said I. "The coarser ones are of wire gauze and the finer of bolting cloth, so you can take your choice. The number of meshes to the linear inch is marked on the rims."

I took him across to the place where the sieves were stacked, and, when he had looked through the collection, he selected the finest of the wire sieves, which had twenty meshes to the inch. Then I found him a scoop, and, when he had tipped the contents of one grog bin into another and placed the empty bin by the side of that containing the bone-ash, he spread out on the bench a sheet of white paper from his case, laid the sieve on the empty bin and fell to work.

For a time the proceedings were quite uneventful, as the upper part of the bin was occupied by the finely ground ash, and when a scoopful of this was thrown on to the sieve, it sank through at once. But presently, as the deeper layers were reached, larger fragments, recognizable as pieces of burnt bone, began to appear on the wire-gauze surface, and these, when he had tapped the sieve and shaken all the fine dust through, the Inspector carefully tipped out on to the sheet of paper. Soon he had worked his way down completely past the deposit of fine powder, and now each scoopful consisted almost entirely of bone-fragments; and, as these lay on the gauze surface, Blandy bent over them, scrutinizing them with amiable intentness and shaking the sieve gently to spread them out more evenly.

"There can be no doubt," said he, as he ran his eye over a fresh scoopful thus spread out, "that these are fragments of bone; but it may be difficult to prove that they are human bones. I wish our unknown friend hadn't broken them up quite so small."

"You have the finger bone," I reminded him. "There's no doubt that that is human."

"Well," he agreed, "if you are prepared to swear positively that it is a human bone, that will establish a strong probability that the rest of the fragments are human. But we want proof if we can get it. In a capital case, the court isn't taking anything for granted."

Here he stooped closer over the sieve with his eyes riveted on one spot. Then, very delicately with finger and thumb, he picked out a small object, and, laying it on the palm of his other hand, held it out to me with a smile of concentrated benevolence. I took it from his palm, and, placing it on my own, examined it closely, first with the naked eye and then with my pocket lens.

"And what is the diagnosis?" he asked as I returned it to him.

"It is a portion of a porcelain tooth," I replied. "A front tooth, I should say, but it is such a small piece that it is impossible to be sure. But it is certainly part of a porcelain tooth."

"Ha!" said he, "there is the advantage of expert advice and co-operation. It is pronounced authoritatively to be certainly a porcelain tooth. But as the lower animals do not, to the best of my knowledge and belief, ever wear porcelain teeth, we have corroborative evidence that these remains are human. That is a great step forward. But how far does it carry us? Can you suggest any particular application of the fact?"

"I can," said I. "It is known to me that Peter Gannet had a nearly complete upper dental plate. I saw it in a bowl when he was ill."

"Excellent!" the Inspector exclaimed. "Peter Gannet wore porcelain teeth, and here is part of a porcelain tooth. The evidence grows. But if he wore a dental plate, he must have had a dentist. I suppose you cannot give that dentist a name?"

"It happens that I can. He is a Mr Hawley of Wigmore Street!"

"Really, now," exclaimed the Inspector, "you are positively spoiling me. You leave me nothing to do. I have only to ask for information and it is instantly supplied."

He laid the fragment of tooth tenderly on the corner of the sheet of paper and made a note in his pocket-book of the dentist's address. Then, having tipped the contents of the sieve on to the paper, he brought up another scoopful of bone fragments and shook it out on the gauze surface.

I need not follow the proceedings in detail. Gradually, we worked our way through the entire contents of the bone-ash bin, finishing up by holding the bin itself upside down over the sieve and shaking out the last grains. The net result was a considerable heap of bone fragments on the sheet of paper and no less than four other pieces of porcelain. As to the former, they were, for the most part, mere crumbs of incinerated bone with just a sprinkling of lumps large enough to have some recognizable character. But the fragments of porcelain were more informative, for close examination and a few tentative trials at fitting them together left little doubt that they were all parts of the same tooth.

"But we won't leave it at that," said Blandy as he dropped them, one by one, into a glass tube that he produced from his case. "We've got a man at Headquarters who is an expert at mending up broken articles. He'll be able to cement these pieces together so that the joins will hardly be visible. Then I'll take the tooth along to Mr Hawley and see what he has to say about it."

He slipped the tube into his pocket and then, having produced from his case a large linen bag, shovelled the bone fragments into it, tied up its mouth and stowed it away in the case.

"This stuff," he remarked, "will have to be produced at the inquest, if we can identify it definitely enough to make an inquest possible. But I shall go over it again, tea-spoonful at a time, to make sure that we haven't missed anything; and then it will be passed to the Home Office experts. If they decide that the remains are certainly human remains we shall notify the coroner."

While he was speaking, his eyes turned from one object to another, taking in all the various fittings of the studio, and finally his glance lighted on Boles' cupboard and there remained fixed.

"Do you happen to know what is in that cupboard?" he asked.

"I know that it belongs to Mr Boles," I replied, "and I think he uses it to keep his materials in."

"What are his materials?" the Inspector asked.

"Principally gold and silver, especially gold. But he keeps some of his enamel material there and the copper plates for his plaques."

The Inspector walked over to the cupboard and examined the keyhole narrowly.

"It isn't much of a lock," he remarked, "for a repository of precious metals. Looks like a common ward lock that almost any key would open. I think you said that Mr Boles is not available at the moment?"

"I understand from Mrs Gannet that he has disappeared from his flat and that no one knows where he is."

"Pity," said Blandy. "I hate the idea of opening that cupboard in his absence, but we ought to know what is in it. And, as I have a search warrant, it is my duty to search. H'm! I happen to have one or two keys in my case. Perhaps one of them might fit this very simple lock."

He opened his case and produced from it a bunch of keys, and very odd-looking keys they were; so much so that I ventured to inquire:

"Are those what are known as skeleton keys?"

He beamed on me with a slightly deprecating expression.

"The word 'skeleton'," said he, "as applied to keys, has disagreeable associations. I would rather call these simplified keys; just ordinary ward keys without wards. You will see how they act."

He illustrated their function by trying them one after another on the keyhole. At the third trial the key entered the hole, whereupon he gave it a turn and the door came open.

"There, you see," said he. "We break nothing, and when we go away we leave the cupboard locked as we found it."

The opened door revealed one or two shelves on which were glass pots of the powdered enamels, an agate mortar and a few small tools. Below the shelves were several small but deep drawers. The Inspector pulled out one of these and looked inquisitively into it as he weighed it critically in his hand.

"Queer-looking stuff, this, Doctor," said he, "and just feel the weight of it. All these lumps of gold in a practically unlocked cupboard. Are these the things that Mr Boles makes?"

As he spoke he turned the drawer upside down on the paper that still covered the bench and pointed contemptuously to the heap of pendants, rings and brooches that dropped out of it.

"Did you ever see such stuff?" he exclaimed. "Jewellery, indeed! Why, it might have been made by a plumber's apprentice. And look at the quantity of metal in it. Look at that ring. There's enough gold in it to make a bracelet. This stuff reminds me of the jewellery that the savages produce, only it isn't nearly so well made. I wonder who buys it. Do you happen to know?"

"I have heard," I replied, "that Mr Boles exhibits it at some of the private galleries, and I suppose some of it gets sold. It must, you know, or he wouldn't go on making it."

Inspector Blandy regarded me with a rather curious, cryptic smile, but he made no rejoinder. He simply shot "the stuff" back into the drawer, replaced the latter, and drew out the next.

The contents of this seemed to interest him profoundly, for he looked into the drawer with an expression of amiable satisfaction and seemed to meditate on what he saw as if it conveyed some new idea to him. At length he tipped the contents out on to the paper and smilingly invited me to make any observations that occurred to me. I looked at the miscellaneous heap of rings, brooches, lockets and other trinkets and noted that they seemed to resemble the ordinary jewellery that one sees in shop windows excepting that the stones were missing.

"I don't think Mr Boles made any of these," said I.

"I am quite sure he didn't," said Blandy, "but I think he took the stones out. But what do you make of this collection?"

"I should guess," I replied, "that it is old jewellery that he bought cheap to melt down for his own work."

"Yes," agreed Blandy, "he bought it to melt down and work up again. But he didn't buy it cheap if he bought from the trade. You can't buy gold cheap in the open market. Gold is gold, whether old or new. It has its standard price per ounce and you can't get it any cheaper; and you can always sell it at that price. I am speaking of the open market."

Once more he regarded me with that curious inscrutable smile, and then, sweeping the jewellery back into its drawer, he passed on to the next.

This drawer contained raw material proper; little ingots of gold, buttons from cupels or crucibles, and a few pieces of thin gold plate. It did not appear to me to present any features of interest, but evidently Blandy thought otherwise, for he peered into the drawer with a queer, benevolent smile for quite a considerable time. And he did not tip out its contents on to the bench. Instead, he took a pair of narrow-nosed pliers from one of the shelves and with these he delicately picked out the pieces of gold plate, and, having examined them on both sides, laid them carefully on the paper.

"You seem to be greatly interested in those bits of plate," I remarked.

"I am," he replied. "There are two points of interest in them. First, there is the fact that they are pieces of gold plate such as are supplied to the trade by bullion-dealers. That goes to show that he bought some of his gold from the dealers in the regular way. He didn't get it all second-hand. The other point is this."

He picked up one of the pieces of plate with the pliers and exhibited it to me, and I then observed that its polished surface was marked with the impression of a slightly greasy finger.

"You mean that fingerprint?" I suggested.

"Thumbprint," he corrected, "apparently a left thumb; and on the other side, the print of a fore-finger. Both beautifully clear and distinct, as they usually are on polished metal."

"Yes," said I, "they are clear enough. But what about it? They are Mr Boles' fingerprints. But this is Mr Boles' cupboard. We knew that he had used it and that he had frequented this studio. I don't see that the fingerprints tell you anything that you didn't know."

The Inspector smiled at me, indulgently. "It is remarkable," said he, "how the scientific mind instantly seizes the essentials. But there is a little point that I think you have missed. We find that Mr Boles is a purchaser of second-hand jewellery. Now, in the Fingerprint Department we have records of quite a number of gentlemen who are purchasers of second-hand jewellery. Of course, it is quite incredible that Mr Boles' fingerprints should be among them. But the scientific mind will realize that proof is better than belief. The fingerprint experts will be able to supply the proof."

The hint thus delicately expressed conveyed a new idea to me and caused me to look with rather different eyes on the contents of the next, and last, drawer. These consisted of three small cardboard boxes, which, being opened, were found to contain unmounted stones. One was nearly half-filled with the less-precious kinds; moonstones, turquoises, garnets, agates, carnelians and the like. The second held a smaller number of definitely precious stones such as rubies, sapphires and emeralds, while the third contained only diamonds, mostly quite small. The Inspector's comments expressed only the thought which had instantly occurred to me.

"These stones," said he, "must have been picked out of the second-hand stuff. I shouldn't think he ever buys any stones from the dealers, for only two of his pieces are set with gems, and those only with moonstone and carnelian. He doesn't seem to use stones often; too much trouble; easier to stick on a blob of enamel. So he must sell them. I wonder who buys them from him."

I could offer no suggestion on this point, and the Inspector did not pursue the subject. Apparently, the examination was finished, for he began to pack up the various objects that we had found in the drawers, bestowing especial care on the pieces of gold plate.

"As Mr Boles seems to have disappeared," said he, "I shall take these goods into my custody. They are too valuable to leave in an unoccupied studio. And I must take temporary possession of these premises, as we may have to make some further investigations. We haven't examined the dust-bin yet, and it is too late to do it now. In fact, it is time to go. And what about the key, Doctor? I shall seal these doors before I leave – the wicket on the inside and the yard door on the outside – and the place will have to be watched. I should take it as a favour if you would let me have the key so that I need not trouble Mrs Gannet. You won't be using it yourself?"

As I saw that he meant to have it, and, as it was of no further use to me, I handed it to him, together with the spare key of the wicket; on which he thanked me profusely and made ready to depart.

"Before we go," said he, "I will just make a note of Mrs Gannet's present address in case we have to communicate with her, and you may as well give me Mr Boles', too. We shall have to get into touch with him, if possible."

I gave him both addresses, rather reluctantly as to the former, for I suspected that Mrs Gannet was going to suffer some shocks. But there was no help for it. The police would have to communicate with her if only to acquaint her with the fact of her husband's death. But I was sorry for her, little as I liked her and little as I approved of her relations with Boles.

When the Inspector had locked, bolted and sealed the wicket, he took up his case and we went into the yard, where he locked the door with the key that I had left in it, pocketed the latter and sealed the door. Then we went out to the car, and, when the driver had put away his book and his cigarette, we started homeward and arrived at my premises just in time for my evening consultations.

Chapter Ten

Inspector Blandy is Inquisitive

My forebodings concerning Mrs Gannet were speedily and abundantly justified. On the morning of the third day after the search of the studio, an urgent note, delivered by hand, from Miss Hughes informed me that her guest had sustained a severe shock and was in a state of complete nervous prostration. She had expressed a wish to see me, and Miss Hughes hoped that I would call as soon as possible.

As the interview promised to be a somewhat lengthy one, I decided to dispose of the other patients on my modest visiting-list and leave myself ample time for a leisurely talk, apart from the professional consultation. As a result, it was well past noon when I rang the bell at the house in Mornington Crescent. The door was opened by Miss Hughes herself, from whom I received forthwith the first instalment of the news.

"She is in an awful state, poor thing," said Miss Hughes. "Naturally, she was a good deal upset by her husband's extraordinary disappearance. But yesterday a gentleman called to see her – a police officer he turned out to be, though you'd never have suspected it to look at him. I don't know what he told her – it seems that she was sworn to secrecy – but he stayed a long time, and when he had gone and I went into the sitting-room, I found her lying on the sofa in a state of collapse. But I mustn't keep you here talking. I made her stay in bed until you'd seen her, so I will take you up to her room."

Miss Hughes had not overstated the case. I should hardly have recognized the haggard, white-faced woman in the bed as the sprightly lady whom I had known. As I looked at her pallid, frightened face, turned so appealingly to me, all my distaste of her – it was hardly dislike – melted away in natural compassion for her obvious misery.

"Have you heard of the awful thing that has happened, Doctor?" she whispered when Miss Hughes had gone, discreetly shutting the door after her. "I mean what the police found in the studio."

"Yes, I know about that," I replied, not a little relieved to find that my name had not been mentioned in connection with the discovery. "I suppose that the officer who called on you was Inspector Blandy?"

"Yes, that was the name, and I must say that he was most polite and sympathetic. He broke the horrible news as gently as he could and told me how sorry he was to be the bearer of such bad tidings; and he did seem to be genuinely sorry for me. I only wished he would have left it at that. But he didn't. He stayed ever so long, telling me over and over again how sincerely he sympathized with me, and then asking questions; dozens of questions he asked until I got quite hysterical. I think he might have given me a day or two to recover a little before putting me through such a catechism."

"It does seem rather inconsiderate," said I, "but you must make allowances. The police have to act promptly and they naturally want to get at the facts as quickly as possible."

"Yes. That is the excuse he made for asking so many questions. But it was an awful ordeal. And although he was so polite and sympathetic, I couldn't help feeling that he suspected me of knowing more about the affair than I admitted. Of course, he didn't say anything to that effect."

"I think that must have been your imagination," said I. "He couldn't have suspected you of any knowledge of the – er – the tragedy, seeing that you were away from home when it happened."

"Perhaps not," said she. "Still, he questioned me particularly about my movements while I was away and wanted all the dates, which, of course, I couldn't remember off-hand. And then he asked a lot of questions about Mr Boles, particularly as to where he was on certain dates; and somehow he gave me the impression that he knew a good deal about him."

"What sort of questions did he put about Mr Boles?" I asked with some curiosity, recalling Blandy's cryptic reference to the fingerprint files at Scotland Yard.

"It began with his asking me whether the two men, Peter and Fred, were usually on good terms. Well, as you know, Doctor, they were not. Then he asked me if they had always been on bad terms; and when I told him that they used to be quite good friends, he wanted to know exactly when the change in their relations occurred and whether I could account for it in any way. I told him quite truthfully that I could not; and as to the time when they first fell out, I could only say that it was some time in the latter part of last year. Then he began to question me about Mr Boles' movements; where he was on this and that date, and, of course, I couldn't remember, if I had ever known. But his last question about dates I was able to answer. He asked me to try to remember where Mr Boles was on the 19th of last September. I thought about it a little and then I remembered, because Peter had gone down to spend a long week-end with him and I had taken the opportunity to make a visit to Eastbourne. As I was at Eastbourne on the 19th of September I knew that Peter and Mr Boles must have been at Newingstead on that date."

"Newingstead!" I exclaimed, and then stopped short.

"Yes," said she, looking at me in surprise. "Do you know the place?"

"I know it slightly," I replied, drawing in my horns rather suddenly as the fingerprint files came once more into my mind. "I happen to know a doctor who is in practice there."

"Well, Mr Blandy seemed to be very much interested in Mr Boles' visit to Newingstead and particularly with the fact that Peter was there with him on that day; and he pressed me to try to remember whether that date seemed to coincide with the change in their feelings to each other. It was an extraordinary question. I can't imagine what could have put the idea into his head. But when I came to think about it, I found that he was right, for I remember quite clearly that when I came back from Eastbourne I saw at once that there was something wrong. They weren't a bit the same. All the old friendliness seemed to have vanished and they were ready to quarrel on the slightest provocation. And they did quarrel dreadfully. I was terrified; for they were both strong men and both inclined to be violent."

"Did you ever get any inkling as to what it was that had set them against each other?"

"No. I suspected that something had happened when they were away together, but I could never find out what it was. I spoke to them both and asked them what was the matter, but I couldn't get anything out of either of them. They simply said that there was nothing the matter; that it was all my imagination. But I knew that it wasn't, and I was in a constant state of terror as to what might happen."

"So I suppose," said I, "that the – er – the murder has not come as a complete surprise?"

"Oh, don't call it a murder!" she protested. "It couldn't have been that. It must have been some sort of accident. When two strong and violent men start fighting, you never know how it will end. I am sure it must have been an accident – that is, supposing that it was Mr Boles who killed Peter. We don't know that it was. It's only a guess."

I thought that it was a pretty safe guess, but I did not say so. My immediate concern was with the future. For Mrs Gannet was my patient and I chose to regard her as my friend. She had been subjected to an intolerable strain, and I suspected that there was worse to come. The question was, what was to be done about it?

"Did the Inspector suggest that he would require any further information from you?" I asked.

"Yes. He said that he would want me to come to his office at Scotland Yard one day pretty soon to make a statement and sign it. That will be an awful ordeal. It makes me sick with terror to think of it."

"I don't see why you need be," said I. "You are not in any way responsible for what has happened."

"You know that I am not," said she, "but the police don't; and I am absolutely terrified of Mr Blandy. He is a most extraordinary man. He is so polite and sympathetic and yet so keen and searching, and he asks such unexpected questions and seems to have such uncanny knowledge of our affairs. And, as I told you, I am sure that he suspects that I had something to do with what has happened."

"I suppose he didn't seem to know anything about that mysterious affair of the arsenic poisoning?" I suggested.

"No," she replied, "but I am certain that he will worm it out of me when he has me in his office; and then he will think that it was I who put the poison into poor Peter's food."

At this point she broke down and burst into tears, sobbing hysterically and mingling incoherent apologies with her sobs. I tried to comfort her as well as I could, assuring her – with perfect sincerity – of my deep sympathy. For I realized that her fears were by no means unfounded. She probably had more secrets than I knew; and once within the dreaded office in the presence of a committee of detective officers, taking down in writing every word that she uttered, she might easily commit herself to some highly incriminating statements.

"It is a great comfort to me, Doctor," said she, struggling to control her emotion, "to be able to tell you all my troubles. You are the only friend that I have; the only friend, I mean, that I can look to for advice and help."

It wrung my heart to think of this poor, lonely woman in her trouble and bereavement, encompassed by perils at which I could only guess, facing those perils, friendless, alone, and unprotected save by me – and what was I that I could give her any effective support? As I met the look of appeal that she cast on me, so pathetic and so confiding, it was borne in on me that she needed some more efficient adviser and that the need was urgent and ought to be met without delay.

"I am very willing," said I, "to help you, but I am not very competent. The advice that you want is legal, not medical. You ought to have a lawyer to protect your interests and to advise you."

"I suppose I ought," she agreed, "but I don't know any lawyers; and I trust in you because you know all about my affairs and because you have been such a kind friend. But I will do whatever you advise. Perhaps you know a lawyer whom you could recommend."

"The only lawyer whom I know is Dr Thorndyke," I replied.

"Is he a lawyer?" she exclaimed in surprise. "I thought he was a doctor."

"He is both," I explained, "and what is more to the point, he is a criminal lawyer who knows all the ropes. He will understand your difficulties and also those of the police. Would you like me to see him and ask him to advise us?"

"I should be most grateful if you would," she replied, earnestly. "And you may take it that I agree to any arrangements that you may make with him. But," she added, "you will remember that my means are rather small."

I brushed this proviso aside in view of Thorndyke's known indifference to merely financial considerations, and the fact that my own means admitted of my giving material assistance if necessary. So it was agreed that I should seek Thorndyke's advice forthwith and that whatever he might advise should be done.

"That will be a great relief," said she. "I shall have somebody to think for me, and that will leave me free to think about all that has to be done. There will be quite a lot of things to attend to. I can't stay here for ever, though dear Miss Hughes protests that she loves having me. And then there are the things at the gallery. They will have to be removed when the exhibition closes. And there are some pieces on loan at another place – but there is no hurry about them."

"What exhibition are you referring to?" I asked.

"The show at the Lyntondale Gallery in Bond Street. It is a mixed exhibition and some of Peter's work is being shown and a few pieces of Mr Boles'. Whatever is left unsold will have to be fetched away at once to make room for the next show."

"And the other exhibition?" I asked, partly from curiosity and partly to keep her attention diverted from her troubles.

"That is a sort of small museum and art gallery at Hoxton. They show loan collections there for the purpose of educating the taste of the people, and Peter has lent them some of his pottery on two or three occasions. This time he sent only a small collection – half a dozen bowls and jars and the stoneware figure that used to be on his bedroom mantelpiece. I dare say you remember it."

"I remember it very well," said I. "It was a figure of a monkey."

"Yes, that was what he called it, though it didn't look to me very much like a monkey. But then I don't understand much about art. At any rate, he sent it, and, as he set a good deal of value on it, I took it myself and delivered it to the director of the museum."

As we talked, principally on topics not directly connected with the tragedy, her agitation subsided by degrees until, by the time when my visit had to end, she had become quite calm and composed.

"Now don't forget," said I, as I shook her hand at parting, "that you have nothing further to fear from Inspector Blandy. You are going to have a legal adviser, and he won't let anybody put undue pressure on you."

Her gratitude was quite embarrassing; and as she showed signs of a slight recrudescence of emotion, I withdrew my hand (which she was pressing fervently) at the first opportunity and bustled out of the room.

On my way home I considered my next move. Obviously, no time ought to be lost in making the necessary arrangements. But, although I had the afternoon free, Thorndyke probably had not. He was a busy man and it would be futile for me to make a casual call on the chance of finding him at home and disengaged. Accordingly, as soon as I had let myself in and ascertained that there were no further engagements, I rang him up on the telephone to inquire when I could have a few words with him. In reply, a voice, apparently appertaining to a person named Polton, informed me that the Doctor was out; that he would be in at three-thirty and that he had an engagement elsewhere at four-fifteen. Thereupon I made an appointment to call at three-thirty, and, having given my name, rang off, and proceeded without delay to dispatch my immediate business, including the dispensing of medicine, the writing up of the Day Book and the wash and brush-up preliminary to lunch.

As I had no clear idea of the geography of the Temple, I took the precaution of arriving at the main gate well in advance of the appointed time; with the result that, having easily located King's Bench Walk, I found myself opposite the handsome brick portico of Number 5A at the very moment when a particularly soft-toned bell ventured most politely to suggest that it was a quarter past three.

There was, therefore, no need to hurry. I whiled away a few minutes inspecting the portico and surveying the pleasant surroundings of the dignified old houses – doubtless still more pleasant before the fine, spacious square had become converted into a car-park; then I entered and took my leisurely way up the stairs to the first-floor landing, where I found myself confronted by a grim-looking, iron-bound door, above which was painted the name, "Dr Thorndyke". I was about to press the electric bell-push at the side of the door when I perceived, descending the stairs from an upper floor, a gentleman who appeared to belong to the premises, a small gentleman of a sedate and even clerical aspect, but very lively and alert.

"Have I the honour, sir, of addressing Dr Oldfield?" he inquired suavely.

I replied that I was, in fact, Dr Oldfield. "But," I added, "I think I am a little before my time."

Thereupon, like Touchstone, "he drew a dial from his poke', and, regarding it thoughtfully (but by no means "with lack-lustre eye") announced that it was now twenty-four minutes and fifteen seconds past three. While he was making his inspection I looked at the watch, which was a rather large silver timepiece with an audible and very deliberate tick, and, as he was putting it away, I ventured to remark that it did not appear to be quite an ordinary watch.

"It is not, sir," he replied, hauling it out again and gazing at it fondly. "It is an eight-day pocket chronometer; a most admirable timepiece, sir, with the full chronometer movement and even a helical balance-spring."

Here he opened the case and then, in some miraculous way, turned the whole thing inside out, exhibiting the large, heavy balance and an unusual-looking balance-spring which I accepted as helical.

"You can't easily see the spring detent," said he, "but you can hear it; and you will notice that it beats half-seconds."

He held the watch up towards my ear, and I was able to distinguish the peculiar sound of the escapement. But at this moment he, also, assumed a listening attitude; but he was not listening to the watch, for, after a few moments of concentrated attention, he remarked, as he closed and put away the chronometer:

"You are not much too early, sir. I think I hear the Doctor coming along Crown Office Row and Dr Jervis with him."

I listened attentively and was just able to make out the faint sound of quick footsteps which seemed to be approaching; but I had not my small friend's diagnostic powers, which, however, were demonstrated when the footsteps passed in at the entry, ascended the stairs and materialized into the bodily forms of Thorndyke and Jervis. Both men looked at me a little curiously, but any questions were forestalled by my new acquaintance.

"Dr Oldfield, sir, made an appointment by telephone to see you at half-past three. I told him of your engagement at four-fifteen."

"Thank you, Polton," said Thorndyke. "So now, Oldfield, as you know the position, let us go in and make the best use of the available half-hour; that is, if this is anything more than a friendly call."

"It is considerably more," said I, as Mr Polton opened the two doors and ushered us into a large room. "I have come on quite urgent business, but I think we can dispatch it easily in half an hour."

Here Mr Polton, after an interrogative glance at Thorndyke, took himself off, closing after him both the inner and outer doors.

"Now, Oldfield," said Jervis, setting out three chairs in a triangle, "sit down and let the bulgine run."

Thereupon we all took our seats facing one another and I proceeded, without preamble, to give a highly condensed account of the events connected with Gannet's disappearance with a less-condensed statement of Mrs Gannet's position in relation to them. To this account Thorndyke listened with close attention, but quite impassively and without question or comment. Not so Jervis. He did, indeed, abstain from interruptions; but he followed my recital with devouring interest, and I had hardly finished when he burst out:

"But, my good Oldfield, this is a first-class murder mystery. It is a sin to boil it down into a mere abstract. I want details, and more details, and, in short – or rather in long – the whole story."

"I am with you, Jervis," said Thorndyke. "We must get Oldfield to tell us the story *in extenso*. But not now. We have an immediate and rather urgent problem to solve; how to protect Mrs Gannet."

"Does she need protecting?" demanded Jervis. "The English police are not in the habit of employing 'third degree' methods."

"True," Thorndyke agreed. "The English police have usually the desire and the intention to deal fairly with persons who have to be interrogated. But an over-zealous officer may easily be tempted to press his examination – in the interests of justice, as he thinks – beyond the limits of what is strictly admissible. We must remember that, under our system of police procedure in the matter of interrogation, the various restrictions tend to weight the dice rather against the police and in favour of the accused person."

"But Mrs Gannet is not an accused person," I protested.

"No," Thorndyke agreed. "But she may become one, particularly if she should make any indiscreet admissions. That is what we have to guard against. We don't know what the views of the police are, but one notes that our rather foxy friend, Blandy, was not disposed to be over-scrupulous. To announce to a woman that her husband has been murdered and his body burned to ashes, and then, while she is still dazed by the shock, to subject her to a searching interrogation, does not impress one as a highly considerate proceeding. I think her fear of Blandy is justified. No further interrogation ought to take place excepting in the presence of her legal adviser."

"She isn't legally bound to submit to any interrogation until she is summoned as a witness," Jervis suggested.

"In practice she is," said Thorndyke. "It would be highly improper for her to withhold from the police any assistance that she could give them. And it would be extremely impolitic, as it would suggest that she had something serious to conceal. But it would be perfectly proper for her to insist that her legal adviser should accompany her and be present at the interrogation. And that is what will have to be done. She will have to be legally represented. But by whom? Can you make any suggestion, Jervis? It is a solicitor's job."

"What about the costs?" asked Jervis. "Is the lady pretty well off?"

"We can waive that question," said I. "The costs will be met. I will make myself responsible for that."

"I see," said Jervis. "Your sympathy takes a practical form. Well, if you are going to back the bill, we must see that it doesn't get too obese. A swagger solicitor wouldn't do; besides, he would be too busy to attend in person. But we should want a good man. Preferably a young man with a rather small practice. Yes, I think I know the very man. What do you say, Thorndyke, to young Linnell? He was Marchmont's managing clerk, but he has gone into practice on his own account and he has distinct leanings towards criminal work."

"I remember him," said Thorndyke. "A very promising young man. Could you get into touch with him?"

"I will see him today before he leaves his office and I think there is no doubt that he will undertake the case gladly. At any rate, Oldfield, you can take it that the matter is in our hands and that the lady will be fully protected, even if I have to accompany her to Scotland Yard myself. But you must play your hand, too. You are her doctor, and it is for you to see that she is not subjected to any strain that she is not fit to bear. A suitable medical certificate will put the stopper even on Blandy."

As Jervis ceased speaking, the soft-voiced bell of the unseen clock, having gently chimed the quarters, now struck (if one may use so violent an expression) the hour of four. I rose from my chair, and, having thanked both my friends profusely for their ready help, held out my hand.

"One moment, Oldfield," said Thorndyke. "You have tantalized us with a bare précis of the astonishing story that you have to tell. But we want the unabridged edition. When are we to have it? We realize that you are rather tied to your practice. But perhaps we could look in on you when you have some time to spare, say one evening after dinner. How would that do?"

"Why after dinner?" I demanded. "Why not come and dine with me and do the pow-wow after?"

"That would be very pleasant," said Thorndyke. "Don't you agree, Jervis?"

Jervis agreed emphatically; and, as it appeared that both my friends were free that very evening, it was settled that we should meet again at Osnaburgh Street and discuss the Gannet case at length.

"And remember," said I, pausing in the doorway, "that consultation hours are usually more or less blank, so you can come as early as you like."

With this parting admonition, I shut the door after me and went on my way.

CHAPTER ELEVEN

Mr Bunderby Expounds

As I emerged from the Temple gateway into Fleet Street I was confronted by a stationary omnibus, held up temporarily by a block in the traffic; and, glancing at it casually, my eye caught, among the names on its rear-board, those of Piccadilly and Bond Street. The latter instantly associated itself with the gallery of which Mrs Gannet had spoken that morning, and the effect of the association was to cause me to jump on to the omnibus just as it started to move. I had nearly two hours to spare, and in that time could easily inspect the exhibition of Gannet's work.

I was really quite curious about this show, for Gannet's productions had always been somewhat of a mystery to me. They were so amazingly crude and so deficient, as I thought, in any kind of ceramic quality. And yet, I felt, there must be something more in them than I had been able to discover. There must be some deficiency in my own powers of perception and appreciation; for it was a fact that they had not only been publicly exhibited but actually sold, and sold at quite impressive prices; and one felt that the people who paid those prices must surely know what they were about. At any rate, I should now see the pottery in its appropriate setting and perhaps hear some comments from those who were better able than I to form a judgment.

I had no difficulty in finding the Lyntondale Gallery, for a flag bearing its name hung out boldly from a first-floor window; and when I had paid my shilling entrance fee and a further shilling for a catalogue, I passed in through the turnstile and was straightway spirited aloft in an electric lift.

On entering the principal room of the gallery I was aware of a knot of people – about a dozen – gathered before a large glass case and appearing to surround a stout, truculent-looking gentleman with a fine, rich complexion and a mop of white hair which stood up like the crest of a cockatoo. But my attention was more particularly attracted by another gentleman, who stood apart from the knot of visitors and appeared to be either the proprietor of the gallery or an attendant. What drew my attention to him was an indefinite something in his appearance that seemed familiar. I felt that I had seen him somewhere before. But I could not place him; and while I was trying to remember where I might have seen him, he caught my eye and approached with a deferential smile.

"You have arrived quite opportunely, sir," said he. "Mr Bunderby, the eminent art critic, is just about to give us a little talk on the subject of Peter Gannet's very remarkable pottery. It will be worth your while to hear it. Mr Bunderby's talks are always most illuminating."

I thanked him warmly for the information, for an illuminating talk on this subject by a recognized authority was precisely what I wanted to hear; and as the cockatoo gentleman – whom I diagnosed as Mr Bunderby – had just opened a show-case and transferred one of the pieces to a small revolving stand, like a modeller's turn-table, I joined the group that surrounded him and prepared to "lend him my ears".

The piece that he had placed on the stand was one of Gannet's roughest; and uncouth vessel, in appearance something between a bird's nest and a flower-pot. I noticed that the visitors stared at it in obvious bewilderment, and Mr Bunderby watched their expressions with a satisfied smile.

"Before speaking to you," said he, "of these remarkable works, I must say just a few words about their creator. Peter Gannet is a unique artist. Whereas the potters of the past have striven after more and yet more sophistication, Gannet has perceived the great truth that pottery should be simple and elemental, and, with wonderful courage and insight, he has set himself to retrace the path along which mankind has strayed, back to that fountain-head of culture, the New Stone Age. He has cast aside the potter's wheel and all other mechanical aids, and relies solely on that incomparable instrument, the skilled hand of the artist.

"So in these works, you must not look for mechanical accuracy or surface finish. Gannet is, first and foremost, a great stylist, who subordinates everything to the passionate pursuit of essential form. So much for the man. And now we will turn to the pottery."

He paused a few moments and stood with half-closed eyes and his head on one side, contemplating the bowl on the stand. Then he resumed his discourse.

"I begin," said he, "by showing you this noble and impressive work because it is typical of the great artist by whose genius it was created. It presents in a nut-shell," (he might have said a coco-nut shell) "the aims, the ambitions and the inmost thoughts and emotions of its maker. Looking at it, we realize with respectful admiration the wonderful power of analysis, the sensibility – at once subtle and intense – that made its conception possible; and we can trace the deep thought, the profound research – the untiring search for the essentials of abstract form."

Here a lady, who spoke with a slight American intonation, ventured to remark that she didn't quite understand this piece. Mr Bunderby fixed her with his truculent blue eye and replied, impressively:

"You don't understand it! But of course you don't. And you shouldn't try to. A great work of art is not to be understood. It is to be felt. Art is not concerned with intellectual expositions. Those it leaves to science. It is the medium of emotional transfer whereby the soul of the artist conveys to kindred spirits the reactions of his own sensibility to problems of abstract form".

Here another Philistine intervened with the objection that he was not quite clear as to what was meant by "abstract form".

"No," said Mr Bunderby, "I appreciate your difficulty. Mere verbal language is a clumsy medium for the expression of those elusive qualities that are to be felt rather than described. How shall I explain myself? Perhaps it is impossible. But I will try.

"The words, 'abstract form', then, evoke in me the conception of that essential, pervading, geometric substructure which persists when all the trivial and superficial accidents of mere visual appearances have been eliminated. In short, it is the fundamental rhythm which is the basic aesthetic factor underlying all our abstract conceptions of spatial limitation. Do I make myself clear?"

"Oh, perfectly, thank you," the Philistine replied, hastily, and forthwith retired deep into his shell and was heard no more.

I need not follow Mr Bunderby's discourse in detail. The portion that I have quoted is a representative sample of the whole. As I listened to the sounding phrases with their constantly recurring references to "rhythm" and "essential abstract form", I was conscious of growing disappointment. All this nebulous verbiage conveyed nothing to me. I seemed merely to be listening to Peter Gannet at second-hand (though probably it was the other way about; that I had, in the studio talks, been listening to Bunderby at second hand). At any rate, it told me nothing about the pottery; and, so far from resolving my doubts and misgivings, left me only still more puzzled and bewildered.

But enlightenment was to come. It came, in fact, when the whole collection seemed to have been reviewed. There was an impressive pause while Mr Bunderby passed his fingers through his crest, making it stand up another two inches, and glared at the empty stand.

"And now," said he, "as a final *bonne bouche,* I am going to show you another facet of Peter Gannet's genius. May we have the decorated jar, Mr Kempster?"

As the name was uttered, my obscure recognition of the proprietor was instantly clarified. But close as his resemblance was to the diamond merchant of Newingstead, he was obviously not the same man. Indeed he could not have been. Nevertheless, I observed him with interest as he advanced with slow steps, treading delicately and holding the precious jar in both hands as if it had been the Holy Grail or a live bomb. At length he placed it, with infinite care and tenderness, on the stand, slowly withdrew his hands and stepped back a couple of paces, still gazing at it reverentially.

"There," said Bunderby, "look at *that!*"

They looked at it; and so did I – with bulging eyes and mouth agape. It was amazing – incredible. And yet it was impossible that I could be mistaken. Every detail of it was familiar, including the marks of my own latch-key and the little dents made by the clinical thermometer. Eagerly, I awaited Bunderby's exposition; and when it came it surpassed even my expectations.

"I have reserved this, the gem of the collection, to the last, because, though, at the first glance, it is different from the others, it is typical. It affords the perfect and unmistakable expression of Peter Gannet's artistic personality. Even more than the others, it testifies to the rigorous, single-minded search for essential form and abstract rhythm. It is the fine flower of hand-built pottery. And mark you, not only does its hand-built character leap to the eye (the expert eye, of course); it is obvious that by no method but that of direct modelling by hand could it have been created.

"Then consider the ornament. Note this charming *guilloche*, executed with the most masterly freedom with the thumb-nail – just the simple thumb-nail; a crude instrument, you may say; but no other could produce exactly this effect, as the ancient potters knew."

He ran his finger lovingly over the mustard-spoon impressions and continued:

"Then look at these lovely rosettes. They tell us that when the artist created them he had in his mind the idea of 'what o'clocks' – the dandelion head. Profoundly stylized as the form is, generalized from the representational plane to that of ultimate abstraction, we can still trace the thought."

As he paused, one of the spectators remarked that the rosettes seemed to have been executed with the end of a key.

"They do," Bunderby agreed, "and it is quite possible that they were. And why not? The genius asks for no special apparatus. He uses the simple means that lie to his hand. But that hand is the hand of a master which transmutes to gold the very clay that feels its touch.

"So it has done in this little masterpiece. It has produced what we feel to be a complete epitome of abstract three-dimensional form. And then, the rhythm! the rhythm!"

He paused, having apparently exhausted his vocabulary (if such a thing were possible). Then, suddenly, he looked at his watch and started.

"Dear me!" he exclaimed. "How the time flies! I must be running away. I have four more galleries to inspect. Let me thank you for the courteous interest with which you have listened to my simple comments and express the hope that some of you may be able to secure an example of the work of a great and illustrious artist. I had intended to say a few words about Mr Boles' exquisite neo-primitive jewellery, but my glass has run out. I wish you all 'good afternoon'."

He bowed to the assembly and to Mr Kempster and bustled away; and I noticed that with his retirement all interest in the alleged masterpieces seemed to lapse. The visitors strayed away to other parts of the gallery, and the majority soon strayed towards the door.

Meanwhile Mr Kempster took possession of the jar and carried it reverently back to its case. I followed him with my eyes and then with the rest of my person. For, like Mr Tite Barnacle (or, rather, his visitor) I "wanted to know, you know". I had noticed a red wafer stuck to the jar, and this served as an introduction.

"So the masterpiece is sold," said I. "Fifteen guineas, according to the catalogue. It seems a long price for a small jar."

"It does," he admitted. "But it is a museum piece; hand-built and by an acknowledged master."

"It looks rather different from most of Gannet's work. I suppose there is no doubt that it is really from his hand?"

Mr Kempster was shocked. "Good gracious, no!" he replied. "He drew up the catalogue, himself. Besides – "

He picked up the jar quickly (no Holy Grail touch this time) and turned it up to exhibit the bottom.

"You see," said he, "the piece is signed and numbered. There is no question as to its being Gannet's work."

If the inference was erroneous, the fact was correct. On the bottom of the jar was Gannet's distinctive mark; a sketchy gannet, the letters "PG" with the number, Op. 961. That disposed of the possibility which had occurred to me that the jar might have been put among Gannet's own works by mistake, possibly by Mrs Gannet. The fraud had evidently been deliberate.

As he replaced the jar on its shelf, I ventured to indulge my curiosity on another point.

"I heard Mr Bunderby mention your name. Do you happen to be related to Mr Kempster of Newingstead?"

"My brother," he replied. "You noticed the likeness, I suppose. Do you know him?"

"Very slightly. But I was down there at the time of the robbery; in fact, I had to give evidence at the inquest on the unfortunate policeman. It was I who found him by the wood."

"Ah, then you will be Dr Oldfield. I read the report of the inquest, and, of course, heard all about it from my brother. It was a disastrous affair. It appears that the diamonds were not covered by insurance, and I am afraid that it looks like a total loss. The diamonds are hardly likely to be recovered now. They are probably dispersed, and it would be difficult to identify them singly."

"I was sorry," said I, "to miss Mr Bunderby's observations on Mr Boles' jewellery. It seems to me to need some explaining."

"Yes," he admitted, "it isn't to everybody's taste. My brother, for instance, won't have it at any price, though he knows Mr Boles and rather likes him. And speaking of Newingstead, it happens that Mr Boles is a native of that place."

"Indeed. Then that, I suppose, is how your brother came to know him?"

"I can't say, but I rather think not. Probably he made the acquaintance through business channels. I know that he has had some dealings – quite small transactions – with Mr Boles."

"But surely," I exclaimed, "Mr Boles doesn't ever use diamonds in his neolithic jewellery?"

"Neo-primitive," he corrected with a smile. "No, I should think he was a vendor rather than a buyer, or he may have made exchanges. Like most jewellers, Mr Boles picks up oddments of old or damaged jewellery, when he can get it cheap, to use as scrap. Any diamonds or faceted stones will be useless to him as he uses only simple stones, cabochon cut, and not many of those. But that is only a surmise based on remarks that Mr Boles has let fall; I don't really know much about his affairs."

At this moment I happened to glance at a clock at the end of the gallery, and, to my dismay, saw that it stood at ten minutes to six. With a few words of apology and farewell, I rushed out of the gallery, clattered down the stairs, and darted out into the street. Fortunately, an unoccupied taxi was drifting towards me and slowed down as I hailed it. In a moment I had given my address, scrambled in and slammed the door and was moving on at a pace that bid fair to get me home within a minute or two of six.

The short journey gave me little time for reflection. Yet, in those few minutes, I was able to consider the significance of my recent experiences sufficiently to be conscious of deep regret and disillusionment. Of the dead, one would wish not only to speak but to think nothing but good; and though Peter Gannet had been rather an acquaintance than a friend, and one for whom I had entertained no special regard, I was troubled that I could no longer even pretend to think of him with respect. For the doubts that I had felt and tried to banish were doubts no longer. The bubble was pricked. Now I knew that his high pretensions were mere clap-trap, his "works of art" a rank imposture.

But even worse than this was the affair of "the decorated jar". To pass off as his own work a piece that had been made by another – though that other were but an incompetent beginner – was unspeakably shabby; to offer it for sale was sheer dishonesty. Not that I grudged the fifteen guineas, since they would benefit poor Mrs Gannet, nor did I commiserate the "mug" who had paid that preposterous price. Probably, he deserved all he got – or lost. But it irked me to think that Gannet, whom I had assumed to be a gentleman, was no more than a common rogue.

As to Bunderby, obviously, he was an arrant quack. An ignoramus, too, if he really believed my jar to have been handbuilt, for a glance at its interior would have shown the most blatant traces of the wheel. But at this point my meditations were interrupted by the stopping of the taxi opposite my house. I hopped out, paid the driver, and fished out my latch-key, and had it in the keyhole at the very moment when the first – and, as it turned out, also the last – of the evening's patients arrived on the doorstep.

CHAPTER TWELVE

A Symposium

To the ordinary housewife, the casual invitation to dinner of two large, able-bodied men would seem an incredible proceeding. But such is the way of bachelors; and perhaps it is not, after all, a bad way. Still, as I immured the newly arrived patient in the waiting-room, it did dawn on me that my housekeeper, Mrs Gilbert, ought to be notified of the expected guests. Not that I had any anxiety. For Mrs Gilbert appeared to credit me with the appetite of a Gargantua (and, in fact, I had a pretty good "twist") and seemed to live in a state of chronic anxiety lest I should develop symptoms of impending starvation.

Having discharged my bombshell down the kitchen stairs, I proceeded to deal with the patient – fortunately, a "chronic" who required little more than a "repeat" – and, having safely launched him, bottle in hand, from the door-step, repaired to the little glory-hole, known as "the study", to make provision for my visitors. Of their habits I knew nothing; but it seemed to me that a decanter of whisky, another of sherry, a syphon, and a box of cigars would meet all probable exigencies; and I had just finished these preparations when my guests arrived.

As they entered the study, Jervis looked at the table on which the decanters were displayed and grinned.

"It's all right, Thorndyke," said he. "Oldfield has got the restoratives ready. You won't want your smelling-salts. But he is evidently going to make our flesh creep properly."

"Don't take any notice of him, Oldfield," said Thorndyke. "Jervis is a perennial juvenile. But he takes quite an intelligent interest in this case, and we are both all agog to hear your story. Where shall I put my writing block? I want to take rather full notes."

As he spoke, he produced a rather large block of ruled paper and fixed a wistful eye on the table; whereupon, having, after a brief discussion, agreed to take the restoratives as read, we transferred the whole collection – decanters, syphon, and cigar-box – to the top of a cupboard and Thorndyke laid his block on the vacant table and drew up a chair.

"Now, Oldfield," said Jervis, when we had all taken our seats and filled our pipes, "fire away. Art is long but life is short. Thorndyke is beginning to show signs of senile decay already, and I'm not as young as I was."

"The question is," said I, "where shall I begin?"

"The optimum place to begin," replied Jervis, "is at the beginning."

"Yes, I know. But the beginning of the case was the incident of the arsenic poisoning, and you know all about that."

"Jervis doesn't," said Thorndyke, "and I only came in at the end. Tell us the whole story. Don't be afraid of repetition and don't try to condense."

Thus directed, I began with my first introduction to the Gannet household and traced the history of my attendance up to the point at which Thorndyke came into the case, breaking off at the cessation of my visits to the hospital.

"I take it," said Jervis, "that full notes and particulars of the material facts are available if they should be wanted."

"Yes," Thorndyke replied. "I have my own notes and a copy of Woodfield's; and I think Oldfield has kept a record."

"I have," said I, "and I had intended to send you a copy. I must write one out and send it to you."

"Don't do that," said Jervis. "Lend it to me, and I will have a typewritten copy made. But get on with the story. What was the next phase?"

"The next phase was the return home of Peter Gannet. He called on me to report, and informed me that, substantially, he was quite fit."

"Was he, by Jove?" exclaimed Jervis. "He had made a pretty rapid recovery, considering the symptoms. And how did he seem to like the idea of coming home? Seem at all nervous?"

"Not at all. His view was that, as the attempt had been spotted and we should be on our guard, they wouldn't risk another. And apparently he was right – up to a certain point. I don't know what precautions he took – if he took any. But nothing further happened until – but we shall come to that presently. I will carry the narrative straight on."

This I did, making a brief and sketchy reference to my visits to the studio and the activities of Gannet and Boles. But at this point Jervis pulled me up.

"A little vague and general, this, Oldfield. Better follow the events more closely and in fuller detail."

"But," I protested, "all this has really nothing to do with the case."

"Don't you let Thorndyke hear you say that, my child. He doesn't admit that there is such a thing as an irrelevant fact, ascertainable in advance as such. Detail, my friend, detail; and again I say detail."

I did not take him quite literally, but I acted as if I did. Going back to the beginning of the studio episode, I recounted it with the minutest and most tedious circumstantiality, straining my memory in sheer malice to recall any trivial and unmeaning incident that I could recover, and winding up with a prolix and exact description of my prentice efforts with the potter's wheel and the creation of the immortal jar. I thought I had exhausted their powers of attention, but, to my surprise, Thorndyke asked:

"And what did your masterpiece look like when you had finished it?"

"It was very thick and clumsy, but it was quite a pleasant shape. The wheel tends to produce pleasant shapes if you let it."

"Do you know what became of it?"

"Yes. Gannet fired it and passed it off as his own work. But I will tell you about that later. I only discovered the fraud this afternoon."

He nodded and made a note on a separate slip of paper and I then resumed my narrative; and as this was concerned with the discovery of the crime, I was genuinely careful not to omit any detail, no matter how unimportant it might appear to me. They both listened with concentrated attention, and Thorndyke, apparently, took my statement down verbatim in shorthand.

When I had finished with the gruesome discoveries in the studio, I paused and prepared to play my trump card, confident that, unlike Inspector Blandy, they would appreciate the brilliancy of my inspiration and its important bearing on the identity of the criminal. And I was not disappointed, at least as to the impression produced, for, as I described how the "brain wave" had come to me, Thorndyke looked up from his note-block with an appearance of surprise and Jervis stared at me, open-mouthed.

"But my dear Oldfield!" he exclaimed, "what in the name of Fortune gave you the idea of testing the ashes for arsenic?"

"Well, there had been one attempt," I replied, "and it was quite possible that there might have been another. That was what occurred to me."

"Yes, I understand," said he. "But surely you did not expect to get an arsenic reaction from incinerated bone?"

"I didn't, very much. It was just a chance shot; and I must admit that the result came quite as a surprise."

"The result!" he exclaimed. "What result?"

"I will show you," said I; and forthwith I produced from a locked drawer the precious glass tube with its unmistakable arsenic mirror.

Jervis took it from me and stared at it with a ludicrous expression of amazement, while Thorndyke regarded him with a quiet twinkle.

"But," the former exclaimed, when he had partially recovered from his astonishment, "the thing is impossible. I don't believe it." Whereupon Thorndyke chuckled aloud.

"My learned friend," said he, "reminds me of that German professor who, meeting a man wheeling a tall bicycle – a thing that he had never seen the like of – demonstrated conclusively to the cyclist that it was impossible to ride the machine for the excellent reason that, if you didn't fall off to the right, you must inevitably fall off to the left."

"That's all very well," Jervis retorted, "but you don't mean to tell me that you accept this mirror at its face value?"

"It is certainly a little unexpected," Thorndyke replied, "but you will remember that Soderman and O'Connell state definitely that it has been possible to show the presence of arsenic in the ashes of cremated bodies."

"Yes. I remember noting their statement and finding myself unable to accept it. They cited no instances and they gave no particulars. A mere *ipse dixit* has no evidential weight. I am convinced that there is some fallacy in this case. What about your reagents, Oldfield? Is there a possibility that any of them might have been contaminated with arsenic?"

"No," I replied, "it is quite impossible. I tested them exhaustively. There was no sign of arsenic until I introduced the bone ash."

"By the way," Thorndyke asked, "did you use up all your material, or have you any left?"

"I used only half of it, so, if you think it worth while to check the analysis, I can let you have the remainder."

"Excellent!" said Thorndyke. "A control experiment will settle the question whether the ashes do, or do not, contain arsenic. Meanwhile, since the mirror is an undeniable fact, we must provisionally adopt the affirmative view. I suppose you told the police about this?"

"Yes, I showed them the tube. Inspector Blandy spotted the arsenic mirror at a glance, but he took up a most extraordinary attitude. He seemed to regard the arsenic as of no importance whatever; quite irrelevant, in fact. He would, apparently, like to suppress it altogether; which appears to me a monstrous absurdity."

"I think you are doing Blandy an injustice," said Thorndyke. "From a legal point of view he is quite right. What the prosecution has to prove is, first, the fact that a murder has been committed, second, the identity of the person who has been murdered, and, third, the identity of the person who committed the murder. Now, the fact of the murder is established by the condition of the remains and the circumstances in which they were found. The exact cause of death is, therefore, irrelevant. The arsenic has no bearing as proof of murder, because the murder is already proved. And it has no bearing on the other two questions."

"Surely," said I, "it indicates the identity of the murderer, in view of the previous attempt to poison Gannet."

"Not at all," he rejoined. "There was never any inquiry as to who administered that poison and there is no evidence. The court would not listen to mere surmises or suspicions. The poisoner is an unknown person, and, at present, the murderer is an unknown person. But you cannot establish the identity of an unknown quantity by proving that it is identical with another unknown quantity. No, Oldfield, Blandy is perfectly right. The arsenic would be only a nuisance and a complication to the prosecution. But it would be an absolute godsend to the defence."

"Why?" I demanded.

"Well," he replied, "you saw what Jervis' attitude was. That would be the attitude of the defence. The defending counsel would pass lightly over all the facts that had been proved and that he could not contest, and fasten on the one thing that could not be proved, and that he could make a fair show of disproving. The element of doubt introduced by the arsenic might wreck the case for the prosecution and be the salvation of the accused. But we are wandering away from your story. Tell us what happened next."

I resumed my narrative, describing my visit to the police station and Blandy's investigations at the studio, dwelling especially on the interest shown by the Inspector in Boles' works and materials. They appeared to arouse a similar interest on the part of my listeners, for Jervis commented:

"The plot seems to thicken. There is a distinct suggestion that the studio was the scene of activities other than pottery and the making of modernist jewellery. I wonder if those fingerprints will throw any light on the subject."

"I rather suspect that they have," said I, "judging by the questions that Blandy put to Mrs Gannet. He had got some information from somewhere."

"I don't want to interrupt the narrative," said Thorndyke, "but when we have finished with the studio, we might have Blandy's questions. They probably represent his views on the case, and, as you say, they may enable us to judge whether he knows more about it than we do."

"There is only one more point about the studio," said I, "but it is a rather important one, as it seems to bear on the motive for the murder"; and with this, I gave a detailed account of the quarrel between Gannet and Boles, an incident that, in effect, brought my connection with the place and the men to an end.

"Yes," Thorndyke agreed, "that is important, for all the circumstances suggest that it was not a mere casual falling-out but a manifestation of a deep-seated enmity."

"That was what I thought," said I, "and so, evidently, did Mrs Gannet; and it was on this point that Blandy's questions were so particularly searching. First, he elicited the fact that the two men were formerly quite good friends and that the change had occurred quite recently. He inquired as to the cause of the change, but she was quite unable to account for it. Then he wanted to know when the change occurred, but she was able only to say that it occurred some time in the latter part of last year. The next questions related to Boles' movements about that time, and, naturally, she couldn't tell him very much. And then he asked a most remarkable question, which was, could she remember where Boles was on the 19th of last September? And it happened that she could. For at that time Gannet had gone to spend a week-end with Boles and she had taken the opportunity to spend a week-end at Eastbourne. And as she remembered clearly that she was at Eastbourne on the 19th of September, it followed that, on that date, Boles and Gannet were staying together at a place called Newingstead."

At the mention of Newingstead Thorndyke looked up quickly, but he made no remark, and I continued:

"This information seemed greatly to interest Inspector Blandy, especially the fact that the two men were at Newingstead together on that date; and he pressed Mrs Gannet to try to remember whether the sudden change from friendship to enmity seemed to coincide with that date. The question, naturally, astonished her; but, on reflection, she was able to recall that she first noticed the change when she returned from Eastbourne."

"There is evidently something significant," said Jervis, "about that date and that place, but I can't imagine what it can be."

"I think," said I, "that I can enlighten you to some extent, for it happens that I, also, was at Newingstead on the 19th of last September."

"The deuce you were!" exclaimed Jervis. "Then it seems that you did not begin your story at the beginning, after all."

"I take it," said Thorndyke, "that you are the Dr Oldfield who gave evidence at the inquest on Constable Murray?"

"That is so. But how do you come to know about that inquest? I suppose you read about it in the papers? But it is odd that you should happen to remember it."

"It isn't, really," said Thorndyke. "The fact is that Mr Kempster – the man who was robbed, you remember – consulted me about the case. He wanted me to trace the thief, and, if possible, to trace the diamonds, too. Of course, I told him that I had no means of doing anything of the kind. It was purely a police case. But he insisted on leaving the matter in my hands and he provided me with a verbatim report of the inquest from the local paper. Don't you remember the case, Jervis? I know you read the report."

"Yes," replied Jervis. "I begin to have a hazy recollection of the case. I remember now that a constable was murdered in a wood; killed with his own truncheon, wasn't he?"

"Yes," I replied; "and some very distinct fingerprints were found on the truncheon – fingerprints from a left hand, with a particularly clear thumbprint."

"Ha!" said Jervis. "Yes, of course, I remember; and I think I begin to 'rumble' Mr Blandy, as Miller would say. Did you see those fingerprints on the gold plate?"

"I just had a look at them, though I was not particularly interested. But they were extremely clear – they would be, on polished gold plate. There was a thumb on one side and a forefinger on the reverse."

"Do you know whether they were left or right?"

"I couldn't tell; but Blandy said they were from a left hand."

"I expect he was right," said Jervis. "I am not fond of Blandy, but he certainly does know his job. It looks as if there are going to be some startling developments in this case. What do you think, Thorndyke?"

"It depends," replied Thorndyke, "on what Blandy found at the studio. If the fingerprints on the gold plate were the same as those found on the truncheon, they can be assumed to be those of the man who murdered the constable; and as Blandy will have assumed – quite properly – that they were the fingerprints of Boles, we can understand his desire to ascertain where Boles was on the day of the murder, and his intense interest in learning from Mrs Gannet that Boles was actually at Newingstead on that very day. Further, I think we can understand his disinclination to have any dealings with the arsenic."

"I don't quite see why," said I.

"It is partly a matter of legal procedure," he explained. "Boles cannot be charged with any crime until he is caught. But, if he is arrested, and his fingerprints are found to be the same as those on the truncheon, he will be charged with the murder of the constable. He may also be charged with the murder of Gannet. Thus when it comes to the trial, there will be two indictments. But whereas – in the circumstances that we are assuming – the evidence against him in the matter of the murder at Newingstead appears to be conclusive and unanswerable, that relating to the murder of Gannet is much less convincing; in fact, there is hardly enough, at present, to support the charge.

"Hence it is practically certain that the first indictment would be the one to be proceeded with; and, as this would almost certainly result in a conviction, the other would be of no interest. The police would not be willing to waste time and effort on preparing a difficult and inconclusive case which would never be brought to trial. That is how the matter presents itself to me."

"Yes," Jervis agreed, "that seems to be the position. But yet we can't dismiss the Gannet murder altogether. Boles is the principal suspect, but he hasn't the monopoly. He might have had an accomplice – an accessory, either before or after the fact. As I see the case, it seems to leave Mr Boles fairly in the soup and Mrs Gannet, so to speak, sitting on the edge of the tureen. But I may be wrong."

"I think you are," said I, with some warmth. "I don't believe that Mrs Gannet has any guilty knowledge of the crime at all."

"I am inclined to agree with you, Oldfield," said Thorndyke. "But I think Jervis was referring to the views of the police, which may be different from ours."

At this moment the clock in the adjacent consulting-room struck eight, and, before its reverberations had died away, the welcome sound of the gong was heard summoning us to dinner. I conducted my guests to the dining-room, and a quick glance at the table as I entered assured me that Mrs Gilbert had been equal to the occasion. And that conviction deepened as the meal proceeded and evidently communicated itself to my guests, for Jervis remarked, after an appreciative sniff at his claret glass:

"Oldfield seems to do himself pretty well for a struggling GP."

"Yes," Thorndyke agreed. "I think we may congratulate him on his housekeeper."

"And his wine merchant," added Jervis. "I propose a vote of thanks to them both."

I bowed my acknowledgments and promised to convey the sentiments of the company to the proper quarters (which I did, subsequently, to our mutual satisfaction), and we then reverted to the activities proper to the occasion, Presently, Jervis looked up at me as if a sudden thought had struck him.

"When you were describing Gannet's method of work, Oldfield, you didn't give us a very definite idea of the result. I gather that he posed as a special kind of artist potter. Did you consider that his productions justified that claim?"

"To tell the truth," I replied, "I didn't know what to think. To my eye, his pottery looked like the sort of rough, crude stuff that is made by primitive peoples – but not so good – or the pottery that children turn out at the kindergartens. But, you see, I am not an expert. It seemed possible that it might have some subtle qualities that I was too ignorant to detect."

"A very natural state of mind for a modest man," said Thorndyke, "and a perfectly proper one; but a dangerous one, nevertheless. For it is just that self-distrust, that modest assumption that 'there must be something in it, after all', that lets in the charlatan and the impostor. I saw some of Gannet's pottery in his bedroom, including that outrageous effigy, and I am afraid that I was less modest than you were, for I decided, definitely, that the man who made it was no potter."

"And you were absolutely right," said I. "The question has been settled conclusively, so far as I am concerned, this very day. I have just visited an exhibition of Gannet's works, and the bubble of his reputation was burst before my eyes. I will give you the particulars. It was quite a quaint experience."

With this, I produced the catalogue from my pocket, and, having read to them Bunderby's introduction, I gave them a full description of the proceedings, including as much of Bunderby's discourse as I could remember, and finishing up with the amazing incident of the "decorated jar". They both listened with deep interest and with appreciative chuckles, and, when I had concluded, Jervis remarked:

"Well, the jar incident fairly puts the lid on it. Obviously the whole of the pottery business was what the financiers call a ramp. And I should say that Bunderby was in it up to the neck."

"That is not so certain," said Thorndyke. "He is either an ignoramus or a sheer impostor, and possibly both. It doesn't matter much, as he is, apparently, not our pigeon. But the affair of the jar – a mere beginner's experiment – is more interesting, for it concerns Gannet, who is our pigeon. As Jervis says, it explodes Gannet's pretensions as a skilled artist, and thus convicts him of deliberate imposture, but it also proves him guilty of an act, not only mean but quite definitely dishonest. For the jar might conceivably be sold."

"It is sold," said I; "for fifteen guineas."

"Which," Jervis pronounced, oracularly, "illustrates the proverbial lack of cohesion between a fool and his money. I wonder who the mug is."

"I didn't discover that; in fact, I didn't ask. But I picked up some other items of information. I had quite a long chat with Mr Kempster, the proprietor of the gallery."

"Mr Kempster," Thorndyke repeated with a note of interrogation.

"Yes, but not your Mr Kempster. This man is the brother of your client and a good deal like him. That is how I came to speak to him."

"And what did you learn from Mr Kempster?" Thorndyke asked.

"I learned, in the first place, the Boles is a Newingstead man; that he is acquainted with your Mr Kempster, and that they have had certain business transactions."

"Of what kind?" asked Thorndyke.

"Either the sale or exchange of stones. It seems that Boles buys up oddments of old or damaged jewellery to melt down for his own work. If they contain any diamonds, he picks them out and passes them on to Kempster, either in exchange for the kind of stones that he uses, or else, I suppose, for cash. Apparently, the transactions are on quite a small scale."

"Small or large," said Jervis, "it sounds a bit fishy. Wouldn't Blandy be interested?"

"I don't quite see why," said I. "Blandy is all out on the murder charge. It wouldn't help him if he could prove Boles to be a receiver, or even a thief."

"I think you are wrong there," said Thorndyke. "If you recall the circumstances of the diamond robbery, which led to the murder of the constable, you will see that what you have told us has a distinct bearing. It was assumed that the thief was a chance stranger who had strayed into the premises. But a man who was suspected of being either a receiver or a thief, who had had dealings with Kempster – possibly in that very house – and knew something of his habits, and who happened to be in Newingstead at the time of the robbery, would fit into the picture much better than a chance stranger. However, that case really turns on the fingerprint. If the print on the truncheon is Boles' print, Boles will hang if he is caught; and if it is not, he is innocent both of the murder and of the robbery."

I did not pursue the topic any farther, and the conversation drifted into other channels. But suddenly it occurred to me that nothing had been said on the very subject that had occasioned the present meeting.

"By the way," said I, "you haven't told me what has been done about poor Mrs Gannet. I hope you have been able to make some arrangements."

"We have," said Jervis. "You need have no further anxiety about her. I called on Linnell this afternoon and put the proposal to him, and he agreed, not only quite willingly but with enthusiasm, to undertake the case. He is keen on criminal practice, and he has, for a solicitor, an unusual knowledge of criminal law and procedure. So we can depend on him in both respects. He will see that Mrs Gannet's rights and interests are properly safeguarded, and, on the other hand, he won't obstruct and antagonize the police."

"I am relieved to hear that," said I, "for I was most distressed to think of the terrible position that this poor lady finds herself in. I feel the deepest sympathy for her."

"Very properly," said Thorndyke, "as her medical adviser, and I think I am disposed to agree with your view of the case. But we must be cautious. We must not take sides. In the words of a certain ecclesiastic, 'we must keep a warm heart and a cool head.' You will remember that, when the arsenic poisoning occurred, both you and I, having regard to Mrs Gannet's relations with Boles, felt that she was a possible suspect, either as an accessory or a principal. And that view was perfectly correct; and I must remind you that nothing has changed since then. The general probabilities remain. I do not believe that she had any hand in this crime, but you and I may both be wrong. At any rate, the police will consider all the possibilities, and our business is to see that Mrs Gannet gets absolutely fair treatment; and that we shall do."

"Thank you, sir," said I. "It is most kind of you to take so much interest and so much trouble in this case, seeing that you have no personal concern in it. Indeed, I don't quite know why you have interested yourselves in it the way that you have done."

"That is easily explained," replied Thorndyke. "Jervis and I are medico-legal practitioners, and here is a most unusual crime of the greatest medico-legal interest. Such cases are naturally studied for the sake of the knowledge and experience that may be gleaned from them. But there is another reason. It has repeatedly happened that when we have studied some unusual case from the outside for its mere professional interest, we have suddenly acquired a personal interest in it by being called on to act for one of the parties. Then we have had the great advantage of being able to take it up with full and considered knowledge of most of the facts."

"Then," I asked somewhat eagerly, "if you were asked to take up this case on behalf of Mrs Gannet, would you be willing – assuming, of course, that the costs would be met?"

"The costs would not be an essential factor," he replied. "I think that if a charge should be brought against Mrs Gannet, I should be willing to investigate the case – with an open mind and at her risk as to what I might discover – and, if I were satisfied of her innocence, to undertake her defence."

"Only if you were satisfied of her innocence?"

"Yes. Reasonably satisfied when I had all the facts. Remember, Oldfield, that I am an investigator. I am not an advocate."

I found this slightly disappointing, but, as no charge was probable, and as Thorndyke's view of the case was substantially similar to my own, I pursued the subject no farther. Shortly afterwards, we all adjourned to the study and spent the remainder of the evening discussing Gannet's pottery and the various aspects of modernist art.

CHAPTER THIRTEEN

The Inquiry

The results of Mr Linnell's activities on Mrs Gannet's behalf were slightly disappointing, though she undoubtedly derived great encouragement from the feeling that his advice and support were always available. But Inspector Blandy was quietly but doggedly persistent in his search for information. Characteristically, he welcomed Linnell with almost affectionate warmth. It was such a relief to him to know that this poor lady now had a really competent and experienced legal adviser to watch over her interests. He had formerly been so distressed at her friendless and solitary condition. Now he was quite happy about her, though he deplored the necessity of troubling her occasionally with tiresome questions.

Nevertheless he returned to the charge again and again in spite of Linnell's protests that all available information had been given. There were two points on which he yearned for more exact knowledge. The first related to the movements of Mr Boles; the second to her own movements during the time that she had been absent from home. As to the first, the last time she had seen Boles was about a week before she went away, and she then understood that he was proposing to take a short holiday at Burnham-on-Crouch. Whether, in fact, he did go to Burnham she could not say. She had never seen or heard from him since that day. As to his usual places of resort, he had an aunt at Newingstead with whom he used to stay from time to time as a paying guest. She knew of no other place which he was in the habit of visiting, and she had no idea whatever as to where he might be now.

As to her own movements, she had been staying at Westcliff-on-Sea with an old servant who had a house there and let lodgings to visitors. While there, she had usually walked along the sea front to Southend in the mornings and returned to tea or dinner. Sometimes she spent the whole day at Southend and went to a theatre or other entertainment, coming back at night by train. Naturally she could not give exact dates or say positively where she was at a certain time on a given day, though she tried to remember. And when the questions were repeated on subsequent occasions, the answers that she gave inevitably tended to vary.

From these repeated questionings, it was evident to Linnell (from whom, as well as from Mrs Gannet, I had these particulars) that, in the intervals, Blandy had checked all these statements by exhaustive inquiries on the spot; and further, that he had been carefully studying the fast train service between Southend and London. Apparently he had discovered no discrepancy, but yet it seemed that he was not satisfied; that he still harboured a suspicion that Mrs Gannet knew more about the affair than she had admitted and that she could, if she chose, give a useful hint as to where Boles was in hiding.

Such was the state of affairs when I received a summons to attend and give evidence at an inquest "on certain remains, believed to be human, found on the premises of No. 12 Jacob Street". The summons came rather as a surprise, and, on receiving it, I gave very careful consideration to the questions that I might be asked and the evidence that I should give. Should I, for instance, volunteer any statements as to the arsenic poisoning and my analysis of the bone-ash? As to the latter, I knew that Blandy would have liked me to suppress it, and my own enthusiasm on the subject had largely evaporated after witnessing Jervis' open incredulity. But I should be sworn to tell the whole truth, and as the analysis was a fact, it would have to be mentioned. However, as will be seen, the choice was not left to me; the far-sighted Blandy had anticipated my difficulty and provided the necessary counterblast.

On the morning of the inquest, I made a point of calling on Mrs Gannet to satisfy myself that she was in a fit state to attend and to ascertain whether Linnell would be there to represent her. On both points I was reassured; for, though naturally a little nervous, she was quite composed and prepared to face courageously what must necessarily be a rather painful ordeal.

"I can never be grateful enough to you and Dr Thorndyke," said she, "for sending Mr Linnell to me. He is so kind and sympathetic and so wise. I should have been terrified of this inquest if I had had to go to it alone; but now that I know Mr Linnell will be there to support me, I feel quite confident. For, you know, I really haven't anything that I need conceal."

"Of course you haven't," I replied cheerfully, though with not very profound conviction, "and there is nothing at all for you to worry about. You can trust Mr Linnell to keep Inspector Blandy in order."

With this I took my departure, greatly relieved to find her in so satisfactory a state, and proceeded to dispatch my visits so as to leave the afternoon clear. For my evidence would probably occupy a considerable time and I wanted, if possible, to hear the whole of the inquiry; and I managed this so successfully that I was able to present myself only a few minutes late and before the business had actually commenced.

Looking round the room as I entered, I was surprised to find but a mere handful of spectators; not more than a dozen, and these occupied two benches at the back, while the witnesses were accommodated on a row of chairs in front of them. Before seating myself on the vacant chair at the end, I glanced along the row, which included Blandy, Thorndyke, Jervis, Mrs Gannet, Linnell and one or two other persons who were unknown to me.

I had hardly taken my seat when the coroner opened the proceedings with a brief address to the jury.

"The general nature of this inquiry," said he, "has been made known to you in the course of your visit to the studio in Jacob Street. There are three questions to which we have to find answers. First, are these fragments of burnt bones the remains of a human being? Second, if they are, can we give a name and an identity to that person? And third, how did that person come by his death? To these questions the obvious appearances and the known circumstances suggest certain answers; but we must disregard all preconceived opinions and consider the facts with an open mind. To do that, I think that the best plan will be to trace in the order of their occurrence the events which seem to be connected with the subject of our inquiry. We will begin by taking the evidence of Dr Oldfield."

Here I may say that I shall not follow the proceedings in detail since they dealt with matters with which the reader is already acquainted; and for such repetition as is unavoidable, I hereby offer a comprehensive apology.

When the preliminaries had been disposed of, the coroner opened his examination with the question:

"When, and in what circumstances, did you first meet Peter Gannet?"

"On the 16th of December, 1930," I replied. "I was summoned to attend him professionally. He was then an entire stranger to me."

"What was the nature of his illness?"

"He was suffering from arsenic poisoning."

"Did you recognize the condition immediately?"

"No. The real nature of his illness was discovered by Dr Thorndyke, whom I consulted."

Here, in answer to a number of questions, I described the circumstances of the illness up to the time when Peter Gannet called on me to report his recovery.

"Were you able to form any opinion as to who administered the poison to Gannet?"

"No. I had no facts to go upon other than those that I have mentioned."

"You have referred to a Mr Frederick Boles as being in attendance on Gannet. What was his position in the household?"

"He was a friend of the family and he worked with Gannet in the studio."

"What were his relations with Gannet? Were they genuinely friendly?"

"I thought so at the time, but afterwards I changed my opinion."

"What were the relations of Boles and Mrs Gannet?"

"They were quite good friends."

"Should you say that their relations were merely friendly? Nothing more?"

"I never had any reason to suppose that they were anything more than friends. They seemed to be on the best of terms, but their mutual liking was known to Gannet and he used to refer to it without any sign of disapproval. He seemed to accept their friendship as quite natural and proper."

The questions now concerned themselves with what I may call the second stage: my relations with Gannet up to the time of the disappearance, including the quarrel in the studio which I had overheard. This evidently produced a deep impression, and evoked a number of searching questions from the coroner and one or two of the jury. Then came the disappearance itself, and as I told the story of my search of the house and my discoveries in the studio, the profound silence in the court and the intent looks of the jury testified to the eager interest of the listeners. When I had finished the account of my doings in the studio, the coroner (who I suspected had been primed by Blandy), asked:

"What about the sample of bone-ash that you took away with you? Did you make any further examination of it?"

"Yes. I examined it under the microscope and confirmed my belief that it was incinerated bone; and I also made a chemical test to ascertain whether it contained any arsenic."

"Had you any expectation that it would contain arsenic?"

"I thought it just possible that it might contain traces of arsenic. It was the previous poisoning incident that suggested the examination."

"Did you, in fact, find any arsenic?"

"Yes. To my surprise I discovered a considerable quantity. I don't know how much as I did not attempt to estimate it, but I could see that there was a comparatively large amount."

"And what conclusion did you reach from this fact?"

"I concluded that deceased, whoever he was, had died from the effects of a very large dose of arsenic."

"Is that still your opinion?"

"I am rather doubtful. There may have been some source of error which is not known to me, but the arsenic was certainly there. Really, its significance is a matter for an expert, which I am not."

This, substantially, brought my evidence to an end. I was followed by Sir Joseph Armadale, the eminent medico-legal authority, acting for the Home Office. As he took his place near the coroner, he produced and laid on the table a shallow, glass-topped box. In reply to the coroner's question, he deposed:

"I have examined a quantity of fragments of incinerated bone submitted to me by the Commissioner of Police. Most of them were too small to have any recognizable character, but some were large enough to identify as parts of particular bones. These I found, in every case, to be human bones."

"Would you say that all these fragments are the remains of a human being?"

"That, of course, is an inference, but it is a reasonable inference. All I can say is that every fragment that I was able to recognize as part of a particular bone was part of a human bone. It is reasonable to infer that the unrecognizable fragments were also human. I have picked out all the fragments that were identifiable and put them in this box, which I submit for your inspection."

Here the box was passed round and examined by the jury, and while the inspection was proceeding, the coroner addressed the witness.

"You have heard Dr Oldfield's evidence as to the arsenic that he found in the ashes. Have you any comments to make on his discovery?"

"Yes. The matter was mentioned to me by Inspector Blandy and I accordingly made an analysis to check Dr Oldfield's findings. He is perfectly correct. The ashes contain a considerable quantity of arsenic. From two ounces of the ash I recovered nearly a tenth of a grain."

"And do you agree that the presence of that arsenic is evidence that deceased died from arsenic poisoning?"

"No. I do not associate the arsenic with the body of deceased at all. The quantity is impossibly large. As a matter of fact, I do not believe that, if deceased had been poisoned even by a very large dose of arsenic any trace of the poison would have been discoverable in the ashes. Arsenic is a volatile substance which changes into a vapour at a comparatively low temperature – about 300 degrees Fahrenheit. But these bones had been exposed for hours to a very high temperature – over 2,000 Fahrenheit. I should say that the whole of the arsenic would have been driven off in vapour. At any rate, the quantity which was found in the ashes was quite impossible as a residue. The arsenic must have got into the ashes in some way after they had become ashes."

"Can you suggest any way in which it could have got into the ashes?"

"I can only make a guess. Inspector Blandy has informed me that he found a jar of arsenic in the studio among the materials for making glazes or enamels. So it appears that arsenic was one of the materials used, in which case it would have been possible for it to have got mixed with the ashes either in the grinding apparatus or in the bin. But that is only a speculative suggestion. There may be other possibilities."

"Yes," the coroner agreed. "But it doesn't matter much. The important point is that the arsenic was not derived from the body of deceased, and you are clear on that?"

"Perfectly clear," replied Sir Joseph; and that completed his evidence.

The next witness was Mr Albert Hawley, who described himself as a dental surgeon and deposed that he had attended Mr Peter Gannet professionally, and had made for him a partial upper denture which included the four incisors. The coroner then handed to him a small stoppered tube which I could see contained a tooth, remarking:

"I think you have seen that before, but you had better examine it."

"Yes," the witness replied as he withdrew the stopper and shook the tooth out into the palm of his hand. "It was shown to me by Inspector Blandy. It is a porcelain tooth – a right upper lateral incisor – which has been broken into several fragments and very skilfully mended. It is of the type known as Du Trey's."

"Does it resemble any of the teeth in the denture which you made for Peter Gannet?"

"Yes. I used Du Trey's teeth in that denture, so this is exactly like the right upper lateral incisor in that denture."

"You can't say, I suppose, whether this tooth actually came from that denture?"

"No. The teeth are all alike when they come from the makers, and if I have to make any small alterations in adjusting the bite, no record is kept. But nothing seems to have been done to this tooth."

"If it were suggested to you that this tooth came from Gannet's denture, would you have any reason to doubt the correctness of that suggestion?"

"None whatever. It is exactly like a tooth in his denture and it may actually be that tooth. Only I cannot say positively that it is."

"Thank you," said the coroner. "That is all that we could expect of you, and I think we need not trouble you any further."

Mr Hawley was succeeded by Inspector Blandy, who gave his evidence with the ease and conciseness of the professional witness. His description of the researches in the studio and the discovery of the fragments of the tooth were listened to by the jury with the closest interest, though, in the matter of sensation I had rather "stolen his thunder". But the turning out of Boles' cupboard was a new feature and several points of interest arose from it. The discovery, for instance, of a two-pound jar of arsenic, three-quarters full, was one of them.

"You had already learned of Dr Oldfield's analysis?"

"Yes. He showed me the tube with the arsenic deposit in it, but I saw at once that there must be some mistake. It was too good to be true. There was too much arsenic for a cremated body."

"Did you gather what the arsenic was used for?"

"No. The cupboard contained a number of chemicals, apparently used for preparing enamels and fluxes, and I presumed that the arsenic was used for the same purposes."

The discovery of the fingerprints raised some other interesting questions, particularly as to their identity, concerning which the coroner asked:

"Can you say whose fingerprints those were?"

"Not positively. But there were quite a lot of them on various objects, on bottles and jars, and some on tool handles, and they were all from the same person; and as the cupboard was Boles' cupboard and the tools and bottles were his, it is fair to assume that the fingerprints were his."

"Yes," the coroner agreed, "that seems a reasonable assumption. But I don't see the importance of it, unless the fingerprints are known to the police. Is it expedient to ask whether they are?"

"I don't want to go into particulars," said Blandy, "but I may say that these fingerprints are known to the police and that their owner is wanted for a very serious crime against the person, a crime involving extreme violence. That is their only bearing on this case. If they are Boles' fingerprints, then Boles is known to be a violent criminal; and there seems to be evidence in this case that a violent crime has been committed."

"Have you had an opportunity of interviewing Mr Boles?" the coroner asked.

The Inspector smiled grimly. "No," he replied. "Mr Boles disappeared just about the time when the body was burned, and, so far, he has managed to keep out of sight. Apparently he doesn't desire an interview."

That was the substance of the Inspector's evidence, and, as he was disposed to be evasive and reticent, the coroner discreetly refrained from pressing him. Accordingly, when the depositions had been read and signed, he was allowed to retire to his seat and the name of Letitia Gannet was called. As she advanced to the table, where a chair was placed for her, I watched her with some uneasiness; for though I felt sure that she knew nothing that she had not already disclosed, the atmosphere of the court was not favourable. It was easy to see that the jury regarded her with some suspicion, and that Blandy's habitually benevolent expression but thinly disguised a watchful attention which was not entirely friendly.

As I had expected, the coroner began with an attempt to get more light on the incident of the arsenic poisoning, and Mrs Gannet recounted the history of the affair in so far as it was known to her.

"Of what persons did your household consist at that time?" the coroner asked.

"Of my husband, myself, and one maid. Perhaps I should include Mr Boles, as he worked in the studio with my husband and usually took his meals with us and was at the house a good deal."

"Who prepared your husband's food?"

"I did, while he was ill. The maid did most of the other cooking."

"And the barley-water. Who prepared that?"

"Usually I did; but sometimes Mr Boles made it."

"And who took the food and drink to your husband's room?"

"I usually took it up to him myself, but sometimes I sent the maid up with it and occasionally Mr Boles took it up."

"Is the maid still with you?"

"No. As soon as I heard from my husband that there had been arsenic in his food, I sent the girl away with a month's wages in lieu of notice."

"Why did you do that? Did you suspect her of having put the arsenic in the food?"

"No, not in the least, but I thought it best to be on the safe side."

"Did you form any opinion as to who might have put it in?"

"No, there was nobody whom I could suspect. At first I thought that there must have been some mistake, but when Dr Oldfield explained to me that no mistake was possible, I supposed that the arsenic must have got in by accident; and I think so still."

The next questions were concerned with the relations existing between Gannet and Boles and the time and circumstances of the break-up of their friendship.

"As to the cause of this sudden change from friendship to enmity, did you ever learn from either of the men what the trouble was?"

"Neither of them would admit that there was any trouble, though I saw that there must be. But I could never guess what it was."

"Did it ever occur to you that your husband might be jealous on account of your intimacy with Mr Boles?"

"Never; and I am sure he was not. Mr Boles and I were relatives – second cousins – and had known each other since we were children. We were always the best of friends, but there was never anything between us that could have occasioned jealousy on my husband's part, and he knew it. He never made the least objection to our friendship."

"You spoke of Mr Boles as working with your husband in the studio. What, precisely, does that mean? Was Mr Boles a potter?"

"No. He sometimes helped my husband, particularly in firing the kiln; but his own work, for the last year or two, was the making of certain kinds of jewellery and enamels."

"You say, 'for the last year or two'. What was his previous occupation?"

"He was originally a dental mechanic; but when my husband took the studio, as it contained a jeweller's and enameller's plant, Mr Boles came there and began to make jewellery."

Here I caught the eye of Inspector Blandy, and a certain fluttering of the eyelid recalled his observations on Mr Boles' "neo-primitive" jewellery. But a dental mechanic is not quite the same as a plumber's apprentice.

The inquiry now proceeded to the circumstances of Peter Gannet's disappearance and the dates of the various events.

"Can you remember exactly when you last saw Mr Boles?"

"I think it was on Tuesday, the 21st of April; about a week before I went away. He came to the studio and had lunch with us, and he then told us that he was going to spend a week or ten days at Burnham in Essex. I never saw or heard from him after that."

"You say that you went away. Can we have particulars as to when and where you went?"

"I left home on the 29th of April to stay for a fortnight at Westcliff-on-Sea with an old servant, Mrs Hardy, who has a house there and lets rooms to visitors in the season. I returned home on Thursday, the 14th of May."

"Between those two dates, were you continuously at Westcliff, or did you go to any other places?"

To this she replied in the same terms that she had used in her answers to Blandy, which I have already recorded. Here again I suspected that the coroner had received some help from the Inspector, for he inquired minutely into the witness' doings from day to day while she was staying at Westcliff.

"In effect," said he, "you slept at Westcliff, but you frequently spent whole days elsewhere. During that fortnight, did you ever come to London?"

"No."

"If you had wished to spend a day in London, could you have done so without your landlady being aware of it?"

"I suppose so. There is a very good train service. But I never did."

"And what about Burnham? That is not so very far from Westcliff. Did you ever go there during your stay?"

"No. I never went farther than Southend."

"During that fortnight, did you ever write to your husband?"

"Yes, twice. The first letter was sent a day or two after my arrival at Westcliff and he replied to it a couple of days later. The second letter I wrote before my return, telling him when he might expect me home. I received no answer to that, and when I got home I found it in the letter box."

"Can you give us the exact dates of those letters? You see that they are important as they give, approximately, the time of the disappearance. Can you remember the date of your husband's reply to your first letter? Or, perhaps you have the letter itself."

"I have not. It was only a short note, and, when I had read it I tore it up. My first letter was written and posted, I am nearly sure, on Monday, the 4th of May. I think his reply reached me by the first post on Friday, the 8th, so it will have been sent off on Thursday, the 7th. My second letter, I remember quite clearly, was written and posted on Sunday, the 10th of May, so it will have been delivered at our house early on Monday, the 11th."

"That is the one that you found in the letter box. Is it still in existence?"

"No. Unfortunately, I destroyed it. I took it from the letter box and opened it to make sure that it was my letter, and then, when I had glanced at it, I threw it on the fire that I had just lit. But I am quite sure about the date."

"It is a pity you destroyed the letter," said the coroner, "but no doubt your memory as to the date is reliable. Now we come to the incidents connected with the disappearance. Just give us an account of all that happened from the time when you arrived home."

In reply to this, Mrs Gannet told the story of her alarming discovery in much the same words as she had used in telling it to me, but in greater detail and including her visit to me and our joint examination of the premises. Her statement was amplified by various questions from the coroner, but her answers to them conveyed nothing new to me with one or two exceptions. For instance, the coroner asked:

"You looked at the hall stand and noticed that your husband's hats and stick were there. Did you notice another walking-stick?"

"I saw that there was another stick in the stand."

"Did you recognize it as belonging to any particular person?"

"No, I had never seen it before."

"Did you form any opinion as to whose stick it was?"

"I felt sure that it did not belong to my husband. It was not the kind of stick that he would have used; and as there was only one other person who was likely to be the owner – Mr Boles – I assumed that it was his."

"Did you take it out and examine it?"

"No, I was not interested in it. I was trying to find out what had become of my husband."

"But you assumed that it was Mr Boles' stick. Did it not occur to you as rather strange that he should have left his stick in your stand?"

"No. I supposed that he had gone out of the studio by the wicket and forgotten about his stick. He was sometimes inclined to be forgetful. But I really did not think much about it."

"Was that stick in the stand when you went away from home?"

"No. I am sure it was not."

"You have mentioned that you called at Mr Boles' flat. Why did you do that?"

"For two reasons. I had written to him telling him when I should be home and asking him to come and have tea with us. As he had not answered my letter and did not come to the house, I thought that something unusual must have happened. But, especially, I wanted to find out whether he knew anything about my husband."

"When you found that he was not at his flat, did you suppose that he was still at Burnham?"

"No, because I learned that he had returned about a week previously at night and had slept at the flat and had the next day gone away again."

"Did you know, or could you guess, where he had gone to?"

"No, I had not the least idea."

"Have you any idea as to where he may be at this moment?"

"Not the slightest."

"Do you know of any places to which he is in the habit of going?"

"The only place I know of is his aunt's house at Newingstead. But I understand from Inspector Blandy that inquiries have been made there and that his aunt has not seen or heard of him for some months. I know of no other place where he might be."

"When you were describing your search of the premises, you said that you did not look in the studio. Why did you not? Was it not the most likely place in which he might be?"

"Yes, it was. But I was afraid to go in. Since my husband and Mr Boles had been on bad terms, they had quarrelled dreadfully. And they were both rather violent men. On one occasion – which Dr Oldfield has mentioned – I heard them actually fighting in the studio, and I think it had happened on other occasions. So, when I could find no trace of my husband in the house, I began to fear that something might have happened in the studio. That was why I was afraid to go there."

"In short, you were afraid that you might find your husband's dead body in the studio. Isn't that what you mean?"

"Yes, I think that was in my mind. I suspected that something awful had happened."

"Was it only a suspicion? Or did you know that there had been some trouble?"

"I knew nothing whatever about any trouble. I did not even know whether the two men had met since I went away. And it was hardly a suspicion; only, remembering what had happened in the past, the possibility occurred to me."

When the coroner had written down this answer, he sat for a few moments looking reflectively at the witness. Apparently he could think of nothing further to ask her, for presently, turning to the jury, he said:

"I think the witness has told us all that she knows about this affair, but possibly some members of the jury might wish to ask a further question."

There was a short pause, during which the members of the jury gazed solemnly at the witness. At length one enterprising juryman essayed a question.

"Could we ask Mrs Gannet if she knows, or has any idea, who murdered her husband?"

"I don't think," the coroner replied with a faint smile, "that we could ask that question, even if it were a proper one to put to a witness, because we have not yet decided that anyone murdered Peter Gannet, or even that he is dead. Those are precisely the questions that you will have to answer when you come to consider your verdict."

He paused and still regarded the jury inquiringly, but none of them made any sign; then, after waiting for yet a few more moments, he read the depositions, took the signature, released the witness, and pronounced the name of her successor, Dr Thorndyke, who came forward and took the place which she had vacated. Having been sworn, he deposed, in answer to the coroner's question:

"I attended Peter Gannet in consultation with Dr Oldfield last January. I formed the opinion that he was suffering from arsenic poisoning."

"Had you any doubt on the subject?"

"No. His symptoms were the ordinary symptoms of poisoning by arsenic, and, when I had him in the hospital under observation, it was demonstrated chemically that there was arsenic in his body. The chemical tests were made by Professor Woodfield and by me."

He then went on to confirm the account which I had given, including the analysis of the arrowroot and the barley-water. When he had finished his statement, the coroner asked, tentatively:

"I suppose you were not able to form an opinion as to how, or by whom, the poison was administered, or whether the poisoning might have been accidental?"

"No. I had no first-hand knowledge of the persons or the circumstances. As to accidental poisoning, I would not say that it was impossible, but I should consider it too improbable to be seriously entertained. The poisoning affected only one person in the house, and, when the patient returned home after the discovery it did not recur. Those facts are entirely opposed to the idea of accidental poisoning."

"What do you say about the arsenic that Dr Oldfield found in the ashes?"

"I agree with Sir Joseph Armadale that there must have been some contamination of the ashes. I do not associate the arsenic with the body of the person who was burned – assuming the ashes to be those of a burned human body."

"On that matter," said the coroner, "perhaps you will give us your opinion on the fragments which Sir Joseph Armadale has shown us."

He handed the box to Thorndyke, who took it and examined the contents with an appearance of the deepest interest, assisting his eyesight with his pocket lens. When he had – apparently – inspected each separate fragment, he handed the box back to the coroner, who asked, as he replaced it on the table:

"Well, what do you say about those fragments?"

"I have no doubt," replied Thorndyke, "that they are all fragments of human bones."

"Would it be possible to identify deceased from these fragments?"

"I should say that it would be quite impossible."

"Do you agree that the ashes as a whole may be assumed to be the remains of a burned human body?"

"That is an obviously reasonable assumption, though it is not susceptible of proof. It is the assumption that I should make in the absence of any reasons to the contrary."

That concluded Thorndyke's evidence, and, when he retired, his place was taken by Professor Woodfield. But I need not record the Professor's evidence, since it merely repeated and confirmed that of Thorndyke and Sir Joseph. With the reading and signing of his depositions the body of evidence was completed and, when he had returned to his seat, the coroner proceeded to his summing up.

"In opening this inquiry," he began, "I said that there were three questions to which we had to find answers. First, are these ashes the remains of a human being? Second, if they are, can we identify that human being as any known person? And, third, if we can so identify him, can we decide how he came by his death?

"Let us take these questions in their order. As to the first, it is definitely answered for us by the medical evidence. Sir Joseph Armadale and Dr Thorndyke, both authorities of the highest eminence, have told us that all the fragments which are large enough to have any recognizable characters are undoubtedly portions of human bones; and they agree – as, indeed, common sense suggests – that the unrecognizable remainder of the ashes must also be presumed to be fragments of human bones. Thus our first question is answered in the affirmative. The bone ashes found in the studio are the remains of a human being.

"The next question presents much more difficulty. As you have heard from Dr Thorndyke, the fragments are too small to furnish any clue to the identity of deceased. Our efforts to discover who this person was must be guided by evidence of another kind. We have to consider the person, the places and the special circumstances known to us.

"As to the place: these remains were found in the studio occupied by Peter Gannet; and we learn that Peter Gannet has disappeared in most mysterious circumstances. I need not repeat the evidence in detail, but the fact that, when he disappeared, he was wearing his indoor clothing only, seems to preclude the possibility of his having gone away from his home in any ordinary manner. Now, the connection between a man who has mysteriously disappeared, and unrecognizable human remains found on his premises after his disappearance, appears strongly suggestive and invites the inquiry, What is the nature of the connection? To answer this, we must ask two further questions: When did the man disappear? and – When did the remains make their appearance?

"Let us take the first question. We learn from Mrs Gannet's evidence that she received a letter from her husband on the 8th of May. That letter, we may presume, was written on the 7th. Then, she wrote and posted a letter to him on the 10th of May, and we may assume that it was delivered on the 11th. Most unfortunately, she destroyed that letter, so we cannot be absolutely certain about the date on which it was delivered, but we can feel little doubt that it was delivered in the ordinary way on the 11th of May. If that is so, we can say with reasonable confidence that Peter Gannet was undoubtedly alive on the 7th of May; but, inasmuch as Mrs Gannet found her letter in the letter box, we must conclude that at the date of its delivery, Peter Gannet had already disappeared. That is to say that his disappearance occurred at some time between the 7th and the 11th of May.

"Now let us approach the problem from another direction. You have seen the kiln. It is a massive structure of brick and fire-clay with enormously thick walls. During the burning of the body, we know from the condition of the bones that its interior must have been kept for several hours at a temperature which has been stated in evidence as well over 2,000 degrees Fahrenheit; that is to say, at a bright-red heat. When Dr Oldfield examined it, the interior was just perceptibly warm. Now, I don't know how long a great mass of brick and fire-clay such as this would take to cool down to that extent. Allowing for the fact that it had been opened to extract the ashes, as it had then been reclosed, its condition was undoubtedly favourable to slow cooling. We can confidently put down the time taken by the cooling which had occurred at several days; probably somewhere about a week. Now, Dr Oldfield's inspection was made on the evening of the 15th. A week before that was the 8th. But we have seen that the disappearance occurred between the 7th and the 11th of May; and the temperature of the kiln shows that the burning of the body must have occurred at some time before the 11th, and almost certainly, after the 7th. It thus appears that the disappearance of Peter Gannet and the destruction of the body both occurred between those two dates. The obvious suggestion is that the body which was burned was the body of Peter Gannet.

"Is there any evidence to support that conclusion? There is not very much. The most striking is the discovery among the ashes of a porcelain tooth. You have heard Mr Hawley's evidence. He identifies that tooth as one of a very distinctive kind, and he tells us that it is identically and indistinguishably similar to a tooth on the denture which he supplied to Peter Gannet. He will not swear that it is the same tooth; only that it is the exact facsimile of that tooth. So you have to consider what are the probabilities that the body of some unknown person should have been burned in Peter Gannet's kiln and that that person should have worn a denture containing a right upper lateral incisor of the type known as Du Trey's, in all respects identical with that in Peter Gannet's denture; and how such probabilities compare with the alternative probability that the tooth came from Peter Gannet's own denture.

"There is one other item of evidence. It is circumstantial evidence and you must consider it for what it seems to be worth. You have heard from Dr Oldfield and Dr Thorndyke that, some months ago, Peter Gannet suffered from arsenic poisoning. Both witnesses agree that the suggestion of accidental poisoning cannot be entertained. It is therefore practically certain that some person or persons administered this poison to Gannet with the intention of causing his death. That intention was frustrated by the alertness of the doctors. The victim survived and recovered.

"But let us see how those facts bear on this inquiry. Some unknown person or persons desired the death of Peter Gannet and sought, by means of poison, to compass it. The attempted murder failed; but we have no reason to suppose that the motive ceased to exist. If it did not, then Peter Gannet went about in constant peril. There was some person who desired his death and who was prepared, given the opportunity, to take appropriate means to kill him.

"Apply these facts to the present case. We see that there was some person who wished Gannet to die and who was prepared to realize that wish by murdering him. We find in Gannet's studio the remains of a person who may be assumed to have been murdered. Gannet has unaccountably disappeared, and the date of his disappearance coincides with that of the appearance of these remains in his studio. Finally, among these remains, we find a tooth of a rather unusual kind which is in every respect identical with one known to have been worn by Peter Gannet. Those are the facts known to us; and I think you will agree with me that they yield only one conclusion; that the remains found in Peter Gannet's studio were the remains of Peter Gannet himself.

"If you agree with that conclusion, we have answered two of the three questions to which we had to find answers. We now turn to the third: How, and by what means, did deceased come by his death? It appears almost an idle question, for the body of deceased was burned to ashes in a kiln. By no conceivable accident could this have happened, and deceased could not have got into the kiln by himself. The body must have been put in by some other person and deliberately destroyed by fire. But such destruction of a body furnishes the strongest presumptive evidence that the person who destroyed the body had murdered the dead person. We can have no reasonable doubt that deceased was murdered.

"That it as far as we are bound to go. It is not our function to fix the guilt of this crime on any particular person. Nevertheless, we are bound to take notice of any evidence that is before us which seems to point to a particular person as the probable perpetrator of the crime. And there is, in fact, a good deal of such evidence. I am not referring to the arsenic poisoning. We must ignore that, since we have no certain knowledge as to who the poisoner was. But there are several important points of evidence bearing on the probable identity of the person who murdered Peter Gannet. Let us consider them.

"In the first place, there is the personality of the murderer. What do we know about him? Well, we know that he must have been a person who had access to the studio, and he must have had some acquaintance with its arrangements; where the various appliances were to be found, which of the bins was the bone-ash bin, and so on. Then he must have known how to prepare and fire the kiln and where the fuel was kept; and he must have understood the use and management of the appliances that he employed – the grinding mills and the cupel-press, for instance.

"Do we know of any person to whom this description applies? Yes, we know of one such person, and only one – Frederick Boles. He had free access to the studio, for it was his own workshop and he had the key. He was familiar with all its arrangements, and some of the appliances, such as the cupel-press, were his own. He knew all about the kiln, for we have it in evidence that he was accustomed to helping Gannet to light and stoke it when pottery was being fired. He agrees completely with the description, in these respects, which we know must have applied to the murderer; and, I repeat, we know of no other person to whom it would apply.

"Thus there is a *prima facie* probability that the murderer was Frederick Boles. But that probability is conditioned by possibility. Could Boles have been present in the studio when the murder was committed? Our information is that he had been staying at Burnham. But he came home one night and passed that night at his flat and then went away again. What night was it that he spent at the flat? Now, Mrs Gannet came home on the 14th of May, and she called at Boles' flat on the following day, the 15th. There she learned that he had come to the flat about a week previously, spent the night there and gone away the next day. Apparently, then, it would have been the night of the 8th that he spent at the flat; or it might have been the 7th or the 9th. But Gannet's death occurred between the 7th and the 11th. Consequently, Boles would appear to have been in London at the time when the murder was committed.

"But is there any evidence that he was actually on these premises at this time? There is. A walking-stick was found by Dr Oldfield in the hall-stand on the night of the 15th. You have seen that stick and I pass it round again. On the gilt mount on the handle you can see the initials, 'FB' – Boles' initials. Mrs Gannet had no doubt that it belonged to Boles, and, indeed, there is no one else to whom it could belong. But she has told us that it was not in the hall-stand when she went away. Then it must have been deposited there since. But there is only one day on which it could have been deposited; the day after Boles' arrival at the flat. We have thus clear evidence that Boles was actually on the premises on the 8th, the 9th, or the 10th, that is to say, that his presence on these premises seems to coincide in time with the murder of Peter Gannet; and we further note the significant fact that, at the time when Boles came to the house, Gannet – if still alive – was there all alone.

"Thus the circumstantial evidence all points to Boles as the probable murderer and we know of no other person against whom any suspicion could rest. Add to this the further fact that the two men – Boles and deceased – are known to have been on terms of bitter enmity and actually, on at least one occasion, to have engaged in violent conflict; and that evidence receives substantial confirmation.

"I think I need say no more than this. You have heard the evidence and I have offered you these suggestions as to its bearing. They are only suggestions. It is you who have to decide on your verdict; and I think you will have little difficulty in answering the three questions that I mentioned in opening this inquiry."

The coroner was right up to a certain point. The jury had apparently agreed on their verdict before he had finished speaking, but found some difficulty in putting it into words. Eventually, however, after one or two trials on paper, the foreman announced that he and his fellow jurors had reached a conclusion; which was that the ashes found in the studio were the remains of the body of Peter Gannet, and that the said Peter Gannet had been murdered by Frederick Boles at some time between the 7th and 11th of May.

"Yes," said the coroner, "that is the only verdict possible on the evidence before us. I shall record a verdict of wilful murder against Frederick Boles." He paused, and, glancing at Inspector Blandy, asked the latter: "Is there any object in my issuing a warrant?"

"No, sir," Blandy replied. "A warrant has already been issued for the arrest of Boles on another charge."

"Then," said the coroner, "that brings these proceedings to an end, and I can only hope that the perpetrator of this crime may shortly be arrested and brought to trial."

On this the court rose. The reporters hurried away intent on gorgeous publicity; the spectators drifted out into the street; and the four experts (including myself for this occasion only) after a brief chat with the coroner and the Inspector, departed also and went their respective ways. And here it is proper for me to make my bow to the reader and retire from the post of narrator. Not that the story is ended, but that the pen now passes into another, and, I hope, more capable, hand. My function has been to trace the antecedents and describe the intimate circumstances of this extraordinary crime, and this I have done to the best of my humble ability. The rest of the story is concerned with the elucidation; and the centre of interest is now transferred from the rather drab neighbourhood of Cumberland Market to the historic precincts of the Inner Temple.

BOOK II

Narrated by Christopher Jervis, MD

CHAPTER FOURTEEN

Dr Jervis is Puzzled

The stage which the train of events herein recorded had reached when the office of narrator passed to me from the hands of my friend Oldfield, found me in a state of some mental confusion. It seemed that Thorndyke was contemplating some kind of investigation. But why? The Gannet case was no concern of ours. No client had engaged us to examine it; and a mere academic interest in it would not justify a great expenditure of valuable time and effort.

But, further, what was there to investigate? In a medico-legal sense there appeared to be nothing. All the facts were know; and though they were lurid enough, they were of little scientific interest. Gannet's death presented no problem, since it was a bald and obvious case of murder; and if his mode of life seemed to be shrouded in mystery, that was not our affair, nor, indeed, that of anybody else now that he was dead.

But it was precisely this apparently irrelevant matter that seemed to engage Thorndyke's attention. The ostensible business of the studio had, almost certainly, covered some other activities, doubtful if not actually unlawful, and Thorndyke seemed to be set on ascertaining what they were; whereas, to me, that question appeared to be exclusively the concern of the police in their efforts to locate the elusive Boles.

I had the first inkling of Thorndyke's odd methods of approach to this problem on the day after our memorable dinner at Osnaburgh Street. On our way home, he had proposed that we should look in at the gallery where Gannet's pottery was on view, and I had agreed readily, being quite curious as to what these remarkable works were really like. So it happened naturally enough that when, on the following day, we entered the temple of the Fine Arts, my attention was at first entirely occupied with the exhibits.

I will not attempt to describe those astonishing works, for I feel that my limited vocabulary would be unequal to the task. There are some things that must be seen to be believed, and Gannet's pottery was one of them. Outspoken as Oldfield had been in his description of them, I found myself totally unprepared for the outrageous reality. But I need not dwell on them. Merely remarking that they looked to me like the throw-outs from some very juvenile handwork class, I will dismiss them – as I did, in fact – and proceed to the apparent purpose of our visit.

Perhaps the word "apparent" is inappropriate, for, in truth, the purpose of our visit was not apparent to me at all. I can only record this incomprehensible course of events, leaving their inner meaning to emerge at a later stage of this history. By the time that I had recovered from the initial shock and convinced myself that I was not the subject of an optical illusion, Thorndyke had already introduced himself to the gallery proprietor, Mr Kempster, and seemed to be discussing the exhibits in terms of the most extraordinary irrelevance.

"Having regard," he was saying as I joined them, "to the density of the material and the thickness of the sides, I should think that these pieces must be rather inconveniently ponderous."

"They are heavy," Mr Kempster admitted, "but you see they are collector's pieces. They are not intended for use. You wouldn't want, for instance, to hand this one across the dinner table."

He picked up a large and massive bowl and offered it to Thorndyke, who took it and weighed it in his two hands with an expression of ridiculous earnestness.

"Yes," he said, as he returned it to Mr Kempster, "it is extremely ponderous for its size. What should you say it weighs? I should guess it at nearly eight pounds."

He looked solemnly at the obviously puzzled Kempster, who tried it again and agreed to Thorndyke's estimate. "But," he added, "there's no need to guess. If you are interested in the matter, we can try it. There is a pair of parcel scales in my office. Would you like to see what it really does weigh?"

"If you would be so kind," Thorndyke replied; whereupon Kempster picked up the bowl and we followed him in procession to the office, as if we were about to perform some sacrificial rite, where the uncouth pot was placed on the scale and found to be half an ounce short of eight pounds.

"Yes," said Thorndyke, "it is abnormally heavy even for its size. That weight suggests an unusually dense material."

He gazed reflectively at the bowl, and then, producing a spring tape from his pocket, proceeded carefully to measure the principal dimensions of the piece while Mr Kempster looked on like a man in a dream. But not only did he take the measurements. He made a note of them in his pocket book together with one of the weight.

"You appear," said Mr Kempster, as Thorndyke pocketed his note book, "to be greatly interested in poor Mr Gannet's work."

"I am," Thorndyke replied, "but not from the connoisseur's point of view. As I mentioned to you, I am trying, on Mrs Gannet's behalf, to elucidate the very obscure circumstances of her husband's death."

"I shouldn't have supposed," said Kempster, "that the weight of his pottery would have had much bearing on that. But, of course, you know more about evidence than I do; and you know – which I don't – what obscurities you want to clear up."

"Thank you," said Thorndyke. "If you will adopt that principle, it will be extremely helpful."

Mr Kempster bowed. "You may take it, Doctor," said he, "that, as a friend of poor Gannet's, though not a very intimate one, I shall be glad to be of assistance to you. Is there anything more that you want to know about his work?"

"There are several matters," Thorndyke replied; "in fact, I want to know all that I can about his pottery, including its disposal and its economic aspects. To begin with the latter, was there much of it sold? Enough, I mean, to yield a living to the artist?"

"There was more sold than you might have expected, and the pieces realized good prices – ten to twenty guineas each. But I never supposed that Gannet made a living by his work. I assumed that he had some independent means."

"The next question," said Thorndyke, "is what became of the pieces that were sold? Did they go to museums or to private collectors?"

"Of the pieces sold from this gallery – and I think that this was his principal market – one or two were bought by provincial museums, but all the rest were taken by private collectors."

"And what sort of people were those collectors?"

"That," said Kempster, with a deprecating smile, "is a rather delicate question. The things were offered for sale in my gallery and the purchasers were, in a sense, my clients."

"Quite so," said Thorndyke. "It was not really a fair question; and not very necessary as I have seen the pottery. I suppose you don't keep any records of the sales or the buyers?"

"Certainly I do," replied Kempster. "I keep a day-book and a ledger. The ledger contains a complete record of the sales of each of the exhibitors. Would you like to see Mr Gannet's account?"

"I am ashamed to give you so much trouble," Thorndyke replied, "but if you would be so very kind – "

"It's no trouble at all," said Kempster, stepping across to a tall cupboard and throwing open the doors. From the row of books therein revealed, he took out a portly volume and laid it on the desk, turning over the leaves until he found the page that he was seeking.

"Here," he said, "is a record of all of Mr Gannet's works that have been sold from this gallery. Perhaps you may get some information from it."

I glanced down the page while Thorndyke was examining it and was a little surprised at the completeness of the record. Under the general heading "Peter Gannet, Esq." was a list of the articles sold with a brief description of each, and, in separate columns, the date, the price, and the name and address of the purchaser.

"I notice," said Thorndyke, "that Mr Francis Broomhill of Stafford Square has made purchases on three occasions. Probably he is a collector of modernist work?"

"He is," replied Kempster, "and a special admirer of Mr Gannet. You will observe that he bought one of the two copies of the figurine in stoneware of a monkey. The other copy, as you see, went to America."

"Did Mr Gannet ever execute any other figurines?" Thorndyke asked.

"No," Kempster replied. "To my surprise, he never pursued that form of art, though it was a striking success. Mr Bunderby, the eminent art critic, was enthusiastic about it, and, as you see, the only copies offered realized fifty guineas each. But perhaps if he had lived he might have given his admirers some further examples."

"You speak of copies," said Thorndyke "so I presume that they were admittedly replicas, probably squeezed in a mould or possibly slip-casts? It was not pretended that they were original modellings?"

"No, they couldn't have been. A small pottery figure must be made in a mould, either squeezed or cast, to get it hollow. Of course, it would be modelled in the solid in the first place and the mould made from the solid model."

"There was a third specimen of this figurine," said Thorndyke. "I saw it in Gannet's bedroom. Would that also be a squeeze, or do you suppose it might be the original? It was certainly stoneware."

"Then it must have been squeezed from a mould," replied Kempster. "It couldn't have been fired solid; it would have cracked all to pieces. The only alternative would have been to excavate the solid original; which would have been extremely difficult and quite unnecessary, as he certainly had a mould."

"From your recollection of the figurines, should you say that they were as thick and ponderous as the bowls and jars?"

"I can't say, positively," replied Kempster, "but they could hardly have been. A figure is more likely to crack in the fire than an open bowl or jar, but the thinner it is, in reason, the safer it is from fire-cracks. And it is just as easy to make a squeeze thin as thick."

This virtually brought our business with Mr Kempster to an end. We walked out into the gallery with him, when Thorndyke had copied out a few particulars from the ledger, but our conversation, apart from a brief discussion of Boles' jewellery exhibits, obviously had no connection with the purpose of our visit – whatever that might be. Eventually, having shaken his hand warmly and thanked him for his very courteous and helpful treatment of us, we took our departure, leaving him, I suspect, as much puzzled by our proceedings as I was myself.

"I suppose, Thorndyke," said I, as we walked away down Bond Street, "you realize that you have enveloped me in a fog of quite phenomenal density?"

"I can understand," he replied, "that you find my approach to the problem somewhat indirect."

"The problem!" I exclaimed. "What problem? I don't see that there is any problem. We know that Gannet was murdered, and we can fairly assume that he was murdered by Boles. But whether he was or not is no concern of ours. That is Blandy's problem; and, in any case, I can't imagine that the weight and density of Gannet's pottery has any bearing on it, unless you are suggesting that Boles biffed deceased on the head with one of his own pots."

Thorndyke smiled indulgently as he replied:

"No, Jervis. I am not considering Gannet's pots as possible lethal weapons, but the potter's art has its bearing on our problem, and even the question of weight may be not entirely irrelevant."

"But what problem are you alluding to?" I persisted.

"The problem that is in my mind," he replied, "is suggested by the very remarkable story that Oldfield related to us last night. You listened to that story very attentively and, no doubt, you remember the substance of it. Now, recalling that story as a whole and considering it as an account of a series of related events, doesn't it seem to you to suggest some very curious and interesting questions?"

"The only question that it suggested to me was how the devil that arsenic got into the bone ash. I could make nothing of that."

"Very well," he rejoined, "then try to make something of it. The arsenic was certainly there. We agree that it could not have come from the body. Then it must have got into the ash after the firing. But how? There is one problem. Take it as a starting-point and consider what explanations are possible; and, further, consider what would be the implications of each of your explanations."

"But," I exclaimed, "I can't think of any explanation. The thing is incomprehensible. Besides, what business is it of ours? We are not engaged in the case."

"Don't lose sight of Blandy," said he. "He hasn't shot his bolt yet. If he can lay hands on Boles, he will give us no trouble, but if he fails in that, he may think it worth while to give some attention to Mrs Gannet. I don't know whether he suspects her of actual complicity in the murder, but it is obvious that he does suspect her of knowing and concealing the whereabouts of Boles. Consequently, if he can get no information from her by persuasion, he might consider the possibility of charging her as an accessory either before or after the fact."

"But," I objected, "the choice wouldn't lie with him. You are surely not suggesting that either the police or the Public Prosecutor would entertain the idea of bringing a charge for the purpose of extorting information – virtually as a measure of intimidation?"

"Certainly not," he replied, "unless Blandy could make out a *prima facie* case. But it is possible that he knows more than we do about the relations of Boles and Mrs Gannet. At any rate, the position is that I have made a conditional promise to Oldfield that, if any proceedings should be taken against her, I will undertake the defence. It is not likely that any proceedings will be taken, but still it is necessary for me to know as much as I can learn about the circumstances connected with the murder. Hence these inquiries."

"Which seem to me to lead nowhere. However, as Kempster remarked, you know – which I do not – what obscurities you are trying to elucidate. Do you know whether there is going to be an inquest?"

"I understand," he replied, "that an inquest is to be held in the course of a few days and I expect to be summoned to give evidence concerning the arsenic poisoning. But I should attend in any case, and I recommend you to come with me. When we have heard what the various witnesses, including Blandy, have to tell, we shall have a fairly complete knowledge of the facts, and we may be able to judge whether the Inspector is keeping anything up his sleeve."

As the reader will have learned from Oldfield's narrative – which this account overlaps by a few days – I adopted Thorndyke's advice and attended the inquest. But though I gained thereby a knowledge of all the facts of the case, I was no nearer to any understanding of the purpose that Thorndyke had in view in his study of Gannet's pottery; nor did I find myself entirely in sympathy with his interest in Mrs Gannet. I realized that she was in a difficult and trying position, but I was less convinced than he appeared to be of her complete innocence of any complicity in the murder or the very suspicious poisoning affair that had preceded it.

But his interest in her was quite remarkable. It went so far as actually to induce him to attend the funeral of her husband and even to persuade me to accept the invitation and accompany him. Not that I needed much persuasion, for the unique opportunity of witnessing a funeral at which there was no coffin and no corpse – where "our dear departed brother" might almost have been produced in a paper bag – was not to be missed.

But it hardly came up to my expectations, for it appeared that the ashes had been deposited in the urn before the proceedings began, and the funeral service took its normal course, with the terra-cotta casket in place of the coffin. But I found a certain grim humour in the circumstance that the remains of Peter Gannet should be enshrined in a pottery vessel of obviously commercial origin which in all its properties – in its exact symmetry and mechanical regularity – was the perfect antithesis of his own masterpieces.

CHAPTER FIFTEEN

A Modernist Collector

My experiences at Mr Kempster's gallery were only a foretaste of what Thorndyke could do in the way of mystification. For I need not say that the most profound cogitation on Oldfield's story and on the facts which had transpired at the inquest had failed completely to enlighten me. I was still unable to perceive that there was any real problem to solve, or that, if there were, the physical properties of Gannet's pottery could possibly be a factor in its solution.

But obviously I was wrong. For Thorndyke was no wild goose hunter or discoverer of mare's nests. If he believed that there was a problem to investigate, I could safely assume that there was such a problem; and if he believed that Gannet's pottery held a clue to it, I could assume – and did assume – that he was right. Accordingly I waited, patiently and hopefully, for some further developments which might dissipate the fog in which my mind was enshrouded.

The further developments were not long in appearing. On the third day after the funeral, Thorndyke announced to me that he had made, by letter, an appointment, which included me, with Mr Francis Broomhill of Stafford Square, for a visit of inspection of his famous collection of works of modernist art. I gathered, subsequently, by the way in which we were received, that Thorndyke's letter must have been somewhat misleading, in tone if not in matter. But any little mental reservations as to our views

184

on contemporary art were, I suppose, admissible in the circumstances.

Of course, I accepted, gleefully. For I was on the tiptoe of curiosity as to Thorndyke's object in making the appointment. Moreover, the collection included Gannet's one essay in the art of sculpture; which, if it matched his pottery, ought certainly to be worth seeing. Accordingly, we set forth together in the early afternoon and made our way to the exclusive and aristocratic region in which Mr Broomhill had his abode.

The whole visit was a series of surprises. In the first place the door was opened by a footman, a type of organism that I had supposed to be virtually extinct. Then, no sooner had we entered the grand old Georgian house than we seemed to become enveloped in an atmosphere of unreality suggestive of *Alice in Wonderland* or of a nightmare visit to a lunatic asylum. The effect began in the entrance hall, which was hung with strange, polychromatic picture frames enclosing objects which obviously were not pictures but appeared to be panels or canvases on which some very extravagant painter had cleaned his palette. Standing about the spacious floor were pedestals supporting lumps of stone or metal, some – to my eye – completely shapeless, while others had faint hints of obscure anthropoidal character such as one might associate with the discarded failures from the workshop of some Easter Island sculptor. I glanced at them in bewilderment as the footman, having taken possession of our hats and sticks, solemnly conducted us along the great hall to a fine pedimented doorway, and, opening a noble, many-panelled mahogany door, ushered us into the presence.

Mr Francis Broomhill impressed me favourably at the first glance: a tall, frail-looking man of about forty with a slight stoop and the forward poise of the head that one associates with near sight. He wore a pair of deep concave spectacles mounted in massive tortoiseshell frames; and, looking at those spectacles with a professional eye, I decided that without them his eyesight would have been negligible. But though the pale blue eyes, seen through those powerful lenses, appeared ridiculously small, they were kindly eyes that conveyed a friendly greeting; and the quiet, pleasant voice confirmed the impression.

"It is exceedingly kind of you," said Thorndyke, when we had shaken hands, "to give us this opportunity of seeing your treasures."

"But not at all," was the reply. "It is I who am the beneficiary. The things are here to be looked at and it is a delight to me to show them to appreciative connoisseurs. I don't often get the chance; for, even in this golden age of artistic progress, there still lingers a hankering for the merely representational and anecdotal aspects of art."

As he was speaking, I glanced round the room and especially at the pictures which covered the walls, and as I looked at them they seemed faintly to recall an experience of my early professional life, when for a few weeks, I had acted as *locum tenens* for the superintendent of a small lunatic asylum (or "mental hospital" as we say nowadays). The figures in them – when recognizable as such – all seemed to have a certain queer psychopathic quality as if they were looking out at me from a padded cell.

After a short conversation, during which I maintained a cautious reticence and Thorndyke was skilfully elusive, we proceeded on a tour of inspection round the room under the guidance of Mr Broomhill, who enlightened us with comment and exposition, somewhat in the Bunderby manner. There was a quite considerable collection of pictures, all by modern artists – mostly foreign, I was glad to note – and all singularly alike. The same curious psychopathic quality pervaded them all, and the same odd absence of the traditional characteristics of pictures. The drawing – when there was any – was childish, the painting was barbarously crude, and there was a total lack of any sort of mental content or subject matter.

"Now," said our host, halting before one of these masterpieces, "here is a work that I am rather fond of though it is a departure from the artist's usual manner. He is not often as realistic as this."

I glanced at the gold label beneath it and read: "Nude. Israel Popoff"; and nude it certainly was – apparently representing a naked human being with limbs like very badly made sausages. I did not find it painfully realistic. But the next picture – by the same artist – fairly "got me guessing", for it appeared to consist of nothing more than a disorderly mass of streaks of paint of various rather violent colours. I waited for explanatory comments as Mr Broomhill stood before it, regarding it fondly.

"This," said he, "I regard as a truly representative example of the Master; a perfect piece of abstract painting. Don't you agree with me?" he added, turning to me, beaming with enthusiasm.

The suddenness of the question disconcerted me. What the deuce did he mean by "abstract painting"? I hadn't the foggiest idea. You might as well – it seemed to me – talk about "abstract amputation at the hip-joint". But I had got to say something, and I did.

"Yes," I burbled incoherently, gazing at him in consternation. "Certainly – in fact, undoubtedly – a most remarkable and – er – " (I was going to say "cheerful" but mercifully saw the red light in time) "most interesting demonstration of colour contrast. But I am afraid I am not perfectly clear as to what the picture represents."

"Represents!" he repeated in a tone of pained surprise. "It doesn't represent anything. Why should it? It is a picture. But a picture is an independent entity. It doesn't need to imitate something else."

"No, of course not," I spluttered mendaciously. "But still, one has been accustomed to find in pictures representations of natural objects – "

"But why?" he interrupted. "If you want the natural objects, you can go and look at them; and if you want them represented, you can have them photographed. So why allow them to intrude into pictures?"

I looked despairingly at Thorndyke but got no help from that quarter. He was listening impassively; but, from long experience of him, I knew that, behind the stony calm of his exterior, his inside was shaking with laughter. So I murmured a vague assent, adding that it was difficult to escape from the conventional ideas that one had held from early youth; and so we moved on to the next "abstraction". But, warned by this terrific experience, I maintained thereafter a discreet silence tempered by carefully prepared ambiguities, and thus managed to complete our tour of the room without further disaster.

"And now," said our host as we turned away from the last of the pictures, "you would like to see the sculptures and pottery. You mentioned in your letter that you were especially interested in poor Mr Gannet's work. Well, you shall see it in appropriate surroundings, as he would have liked to see it."

He conducted us across the hall to another fine door which he threw open to admit us to the sculpture gallery. Looking around me as we entered, I was glad that I had seen the pictures first; for now I was prepared for the worst and could keep my emotions under control.

I shall not attempt to describe that chamber of horrors. My first impression was that of a sort of infernal Mrs Jarley's; and the place was pervaded by the same mad-house atmosphere as I had noticed in the other room. But it was more unpleasant. For debased sculpture can be much more horrible than debased painting; and in the entire collection there was not a single work that could be called normal. The exhibits ranged from almost formless objects, having only that faint suggestion of a human head or figure that one sometimes notices in queer-shaped potatoes or flint nodules, to recognizable busts or torsos; but in these the faces were hideous and bestial and the limbs and trunks mis-shapen and characterized by a horrible obesity suggestive of dropsy or myxoedema. There was a little pottery, all crude and coarse, but Gannet's pieces were easily the worst.

"This, I think," said our host, "is what you specially wanted to see."

He indicated a grotesque statuette labelled, "Figurine of a Monkey: Peter Gannet", and I looked at it curiously. If I had met it anywhere else it would have given me quite a severe shock; but here, in this collection of monstrosities, it looked almost like the work of a sane barbarian.

"There was some question," Mr Broomhill continued, "that you wanted to settle, was there not?"

"Yes," Thorndyke replied, "in fact, there are two. The first is that of priority. Gannet executed three versions of this figurine. One has gone to America, one is on loan at a London museum, and this is the third. The question is, which was made first?"

"There ought not to be any difficulty about that," said our host. "Gannet used to sign and number all his pieces and the serial number should give the order of priority at a glance."

He lifted the image carefully, and, having inverted it and looked at its base, handed it to Thorndyke.

"You see," said he, "that the number is 571.B. Then there must have been a 571.A. and a 571.C. But, clearly, this must have been the second one made, and if you can examine the one at the museum, you can settle the order of the series. If that is 571.A., then the American copy must be 571.C. or vice versa. What is the other question?"

"That relates to the nature of the first one made. Is it the original model or is it a pressing from a mould? This one appears to be a squeeze. If you look inside, you can see traces of the thumb impressions, so it can't be a cast."

He returned it to Mr Broomhill, who peered into the opening of the base and then, having verified Thorndyke's observation, passed it to me. I was not deeply interested, but I examined the base carefully and looked into the dark interior as well as I could. The flat surface of the base was smooth but unglazed, and in it was inscribed in blue around the central opening, "Op.571.B., PG." with a rudely drawn figure of a bird, which might have been a goose but which I knew was meant for a gannet, interposed between the number and the initials. Inside, on the uneven surface I could make out a number of impressions of a thumb – apparently a right thumb. Having made these observations, I handed the effigy back to Mr Broomhill who replaced it on its stand, and resumed the conversation.

"I should imagine that all of the three versions were pressings, but that is only an opinion. What is your view?"

"There are three possibilities, and, bearing in mind Gannet's personality, I don't know which of them is the most probable. The original figure was certainly modelled in the solid. Then Opus 571.A. may either be that model, fired in the solid, or that model excavated and fired, or a squeeze from the mould."

"It would hardly have been possible to fire it in the solid," said Mr Broomhill.

"That was Mr Kempster's view, but I am not so sure. After all, some pottery articles are fired solid. Bricks, for instance."

"Yes, but a few fire-cracks in a brick don't matter. I think he would have had to excavate it, at least. But why should he have taken that trouble when he had actually made a mould?"

"I can imagine no reason at all," replied Thorndyke, "unless he wished to keep the original. The one now at the museum was his own property and I don't think it had ever been offered for sale."

"If the question is of any importance," said our host – who was obviously of opinion that it was not – "it could perhaps be settled by inspection of the piece at the museum, which was probably the first one made. Don't you think so?"

"It might," Thorndyke replied, "or it might not. The most satisfactory way would be to compare the respective weights of the two pieces. An excavated figurine would be heavier than a pressing, and, of course, a solid one would be much heavier."

"Yes," Mr Broomhill agreed with a slightly puzzled air, "that is true. So I take it that you would like to know the exact weight of this piece. Well, there is no difficulty about that."

He walked over to the fireplace and pressed the bell-push at its side. In a few moments the door opened and the footman entered the room.

"Can you tell me, Hooper," Mr Broomhill asked, "if there is a pair of scales that we could have to weigh this statuette?"

"Certainly, sir," was the reply. "There is a pair in Mr Law's pantry. Shall I bring them up, sir?"

"If you would, Hooper – with the weights, of course. And you might see that the pan is quite clean."

Apparently the pan was quite clean, for, in a couple of minutes Hooper reappeared carrying a very spick and span pair of scales with a complete set of weights. When the scales had been placed on the table with the weights beside them, Mr Broomhill took up the effigy with infinite care and lowered it gently on to the scale-pan. Then, with the same care to avoid jars or shocks, he put on the weights, building up a little pile until the pan rose, when he made the final adjustment with a half-ounce weight.

"Three pounds, three and a half ounces," said he. "Rather a lot for a small figure."

"Yes," Thorndyke agreed, "but Gannet used a dense material and was pretty liberal with it. I weighed some of his pottery at Kempster's gallery and found it surprisingly heavy."

He entered the weight of the effigy in his notebook, and, when the masterpiece had been replaced on its stand and the scales borne away to their abiding-place, we resumed our tour of the room. Presently Hooper entered, bearing a large silver tray loaded with the materials for afternoon tea, which he placed on a small circular table.

"You needn't wait, Hooper," said our host. "We will help ourselves when we are ready"; and, as the footman retired, he turned to the last of the exhibits – a life-sized figure of a woman, naked, contorted, and obese, whose brutal face and bloated limbs seemed to shout for thyroid extract – and, having expatiated on its noble rendering of abstract form and its freedom from the sickly prettiness of "mere imitative sculpture", dismissed the masterpieces and placed chairs for us by the table.

"Which museum is it," he asked, as we sipped the excellent China tea, "that is showing Mr Gannet's work?"

"It is a small museum at Hoxton," Thorndyke replied, "known as 'The People's Museum of Modern Art'."

"Ah!" said Broomhill, "I know it; in fact, I occasionally lend some of my treasures for exhibition there. It is an excellent institution. It gives the poor people of that uncultured region an opportunity of becoming acquainted with the glories of modern art – the only chance they have."

"There is the Geffrye Museum close by," I reminded him.

"Yes," he agreed, "but that is concerned with the obsolete furniture and art of the bad old times. It contains nothing of this sort," he added, indicating his collection with a wave of the hand. Which was certainly true. Mercifully, it does not.

"And I hope," he continued, "that you will be able to settle your question when you examine the figurine there. It doesn't seem to me to matter very much, but you are a better judge of that than I am."

When we had taken leave of our kind and courteous host and set forth on our homeward way, we walked for a time in silence, each occupied with his own thoughts. As to Thorndyke's ultimate purpose in this queer transaction, I could not make the vaguest guess and I gave it no consideration. But the experience itself had been an odd one with a peculiar interest of its own. Presently I opened the subject with a question.

"Could you make anything of this stuff of Broomhill's or of his attitude to it?"

Thorndyke shook his head. "No," he replied. "It is a mystery to me. Evidently Broomhill gets a positive pleasure from these things, and that pleasure seems to be directly proportionate to their badness; to the absence in them of all the ordinary qualities – fine workmanship, truth to nature, intellectual interest, and beauty – which have hitherto been considered to be the essentials of works of art. It seems to be a cult, a fashion, associated with a certain state of mind; but what that state of mind is, I cannot imagine. Obviously it has no connection with what has always been known as art, unless it is a negative connection. You noticed that Broomhill was utterly contemptuous of the great work of the past, and that,

I think, is the usual modernist attitude. But what can be the state of mind of a man who is completely insensitive to the works of the accomplished masters of the older schools, and full of enthusiasm for clumsy imitations of the works of savages or ungifted children, I cannot begin to understand."

"No," said I, "that is precisely my position," and with this, the subject dropped.

CHAPTER SIXTEEN

At the Museum

"It is curious to reflect," Thorndyke remarked, as we took our way eastward along Old Street, "that this, which is commonly accounted one of the meanest and most squalid regions of the town, should be, in a sense, the last outpost of a disappearing culture."

"To what culture are you referring?" I asked.

"To that of the industrial arts," he replied, "of which we may say that it is substantially the foundation of all artistic culture. Nearly everywhere else, those arts are dead or dying, killed by machinery and mass-production, but here we find little groups of surviving craftsman who still keep the lamp burning. To our right in Curtain Road and various small streets adjoining, are skilled cabinet-makers, making chairs and other furniture in the obsolete tradition of what Broomhill would call the bad old times of Chippendale and his contemporaries; near by in Bunhill Row the last of the makers of fine picture frames have their workshops, and farther ahead in Bethnal Green and Spital-fields a remnant of the ancient colony of silk weavers are working with the hand-loom as they did in the eighteenth century."

"Yes," I agreed, "it seems rather an anomaly; and our present mission seems to rub in the discrepancy. I wonder what inspired the founders of The People's Museum of Modern Art to dump it down in this neighbourhood and almost in sight the Geffrye Museum."

Thorndyke chuckled softly. "The two museums," said he, "are queer neighbours; the one treasuring the best work of the past and the other advertising the worst work of the present. But perhaps we shan't find it as bad as we expect."

I don't know what Thorndyke expected, but it was bad enough for me. We located it without difficulty by means of a painted board inscribed with its name and description set over what looked like a reconstructed shop front, to which had been added a pair of massive folding doors. But those doors were closed and presumably locked, for a large card affixed to the panel with drawing-pins bore the announcement, "Closed temporarily. Re-open 11.15."

Thorndyke looked at his watch. "We have a quarter of an hour to wait," said he, "but we need not wait here. We may as well take a stroll and inspect the neighbourhood. It is not beautiful, but it has a character of its own which is worth examining."

Accordingly, we set forth on a tour of exploration through the narrow streets where Thorndyke expounded the various objects of interest in illustration of his previous observations. In one street we found a row of cabinet-makers' shops, through the windows of which we could see the half-finished carcases of wardrobes and sideboards and "period" chairs, seatless and unpolished; and I noticed that the names above the shops were mostly Jewish and many of them foreign. Then, towards Shoreditch, we observed a timber yard with a noble plank of Spanish mahogany at the entrance, and noted that the stock inside seemed to consist mainly of hard-woods suitable for making furniture. But there was no time to make a detailed examination, for the clock of a neighbouring church now struck the quarter and sent us hurrying back to the temple of modernism, where we found that the card had vanished and the doors stood wide open, revealing a lobby and an inner door.

As we opened the latter and entered the gallery we were met by an elderly tired-looking man, who regarded us expectantly.

"Are you Mr Sancroft?" Throndyke asked.

"Ah!" said our friend, "then I was right. You will be Dr Thorndyke. I hope I haven't kept you waiting."

"Only a matter of minutes," Thorndyke replied in his suavest manner, "and we spent those quite agreeably."

"I am so very sorry," said Sancroft, with evidently genuine concern, "but it was unavoidable. I had to go out, and, as I am all alone here, I had to lock up the place while I was away. It is very awkward having no one to leave in charge."

"It must be," Thorndyke agreed, sympathetically. "Do you mean that you have no assistant of any kind; not even a doorkeeper?"

"No one at all," replied Sancroft. "You see, the society who run this museum have no funds but their own contributions. There's only just enough to keep the place going, without paying any salaries. I am a voluntary worker, but I have my living to earn. Mostly, I can do my work in the curator's room – I am a law writer – but there are times when I have to go out on business, and then – well, you saw what happened this morning."

Thorndyke listened to this tale of woe not only with patience but with a concern that rather surprised me.

"But," said he, "can't you get some of your friends to give you at least a little help? Even a few hours a day would solve your difficulties."

Mr Sancroft shook his head wearily. "No," he replied, "it is a dull job, minding a small gallery, especially as so few visitors come to it, and I have found nobody who is willing to take it on. I suppose," he added, with a sad smile, "you don't happen to know of any enthusiast in modern art who would make the sacrifice in the interests of popular enlightenment and culture?"

"At the moment," said Thorndyke, "I can think of nobody but Mr Broomhill, and I don't suppose that he could spare the time. Still, I will bear your difficulties in mind, and if I should think of any person who might be willing to help, I will try my powers of persuasion on him."

I must confess that this reply rather astonished me. Thorndyke was a kindly man, but he was a busy man and hardly in a position to enter into Mr Sancroft's difficulties. And, with him, a promise was a promise, not a mere pleasant form of words; a fact which I think Sancroft hardly realized, for his expression of thanks seemed to imply gratitude for a benevolent intention rather than any expectation of actual performance.

"It is very kind of you to wish to help me," said he. "And now, as to your own business. I understand that you want to make some sort of inspection of the works of Mr Gannet. Does that involve taking them out of the case?"

"If that is permissible," Thorndyke replied. "I wanted, among other matters, to feel the weight of them."

"There is no objection to your taking them out," said Sancroft, "for a definite purpose. I will unlock the case and put the things in your custody for the time being. And then I will ask you to excuse me. I have a lease to engross, and I want to get on with it as quickly as I can."

With this, he led us to the glass case in which Gannet's atrocities were exposed to view, and, having unlocked it, made us a little bow and retired into his lair.

"That lease," Thorndyke remarked, "is a stroke of luck for us. Now we can discuss the matter freely."

He reached into the case and, lifting out the effigy, began to examine it in the closest detail, especially as to the upturned base.

"The questions, as I understand them," said I, "are, first, priority, and second, method of work; whether it was fired solid, or excavated, or squeezed in a mould. The priority seems to be settled by the signature. This is 571.A. Then it must have been the first piece made."

"Yes," Thorndyke agreed, "I think we may accept that. What do you say as to the method?"

"That, also, seems to be settled by the character of the base. It is a solid base without any opening, which appears to me to prove that the figure was fired solid."

"A reasonable inference," said Thorndyke, "from the particular fact. But, if you look at the sides, you will notice on each a linear mark which suggests that a seam or join had been scraped off. You probably observed similar marks on Broomhill's copy, which were evidently the remains of the seam from the mould. But the question of solidity will be best determined by the weight. Let us try that."

He produced from his pocket a portable spring balance and a piece of string. In the latter he made two "running bowlines", and, hitching them over the figure near its middle, hooked the "bight" of the string on to the balance. As he held up the latter, I read off from the index, "Three pounds, nine and a half ounces. If I remember rightly, Broomhill's image weighed three pounds, three and a half ounces, so this one is six ounces heavier. That seems to support the view that this figure was fired in the solid."

"I don't think it does, Jervis," said he. "Broomhill's copy was undoubtedly a pressing with a considerable cavity and not very thick walls. I should say that the solid figure would be at least twice the weight of the pressing."

A moment's reflection showed me that he was right. Six ounces obviously could not account for the difference between a hollow and a solid figure.

"Then," said I, "it must have been excavated. That would probably just account for the difference in weight."

"Yes," Thorndyke agreed, but a little doubtfully, "so far as the weight is concerned, that is quite sound. But there are these marks, which certainly look like the traces of a seam which has been scraped down. What do you say to them?"

"I should say that they are traces of the excavating process. It would be necessary to cut the figure in halves in order to hollow out the interior. I say that these marks are the traces of the join where the two halves were put together."

"The objection to that," said he, "is that the figure would not have been cut in halves. When a clay work, such as a terra-cotta bust, is hollowed out, the usual practice is to cut off the back in as thin a slice as possible, excavate the main mass of the bust, and, when it is as hollow as is safe, to stick the back on with slip and work over the joins until they are invisible. And that is the obvious and reasonable way in which to do it. But these marks are in the middle, just where the seams would be in a pressing, and in the same position as those in Broomhill's copy. So that, in spite of the extra weight, I am disposed to think that this figure is really a pressing, like Broomhill's. And that is, on other grounds, the obvious probability. A mould was certainly made, and it must have been made from the solid figure. But it would have been much more troublesome to excavate the solid model than to make a squeeze from the mould."

As he spoke, he tapped the figure lightly with his knuckle as it hung from the balance, but the dull sound that he elicited gave no information either way, beyond proving – which we knew already from the weight – that the walls of the shell were thick and clumsy. Then he took off the string, and, having offered the image to me for further examination (which I declined), he put it back in the case. Then we went into the curator's room to let Mr Sancroft know that we had finished our inspection, and to thank him for having given us the facilities for making it.

"Well," said he, laying aside his pen, "I suppose that now you know all about Peter Gannet's works, which is more than I do. They are rather over the heads of most of our visitors, and mine, too."

"They are not very popular, then?" Thorndyke ventured.

"I wouldn't say that," Sancroft replied with a faint smile. "The monkey figure seems to afford a good deal of amusement. But that is not quite what we are out for. Our society seeks to instruct and elevate, not to give a comic entertainment. I shan't be sorry when the owner of that figure fetches it away."

"The owner?" Thorndyke repeated. "You mean Mrs Gannet?"

"No," replied Sancroft, "it doesn't belong to her. Gannet sold it, but, as the purchaser was making a trip to America, he got permission to lend it to us until such time as the owner should return and claim it. I am expecting him at any time now; and, as I said, I shall be glad when he does come, for the thing is making the gallery a laughing-stock among the regular visitors. They are not advanced enough for the really extreme modernist sculpture."

"And suppose the owner never does turn up?" Thorndyke asked.

"Then, I suppose, we should hand it back to Mrs Gannet. But I don't anticipate any difficulty of that sort. The purchaser – a Mr Newman, I think – gave fifty pounds for it, so he is not likely to forget to call for it."

"No, indeed," Thorndyke agreed. "It is an enormous price. Did Gannet, himself, tell you what he sold it for?"

"Not Gannet. I never met him. It was Mrs Gannet who told me when she brought it with the pottery."

"I suppose," said Thorndyke, "that the owner, when he comes to claim his property, will produce some evidence of his identity? You would hardly hand over a valuable piece such as this seems to be, to anyone who might come and demand it, unless you happen to know him by sight?"

"I don't," replied Sancroft. "I've never seen the man. But the question of identity is provided for. Mrs Gannet left a couple of letters with me from her husband which will make the transaction quite safe. Would you like to see them? I know you are interested in Mrs Gannet's affairs."

Without waiting for a reply, he unlocked and pulled out a drawer in the writing-table, and, having turned over a number of papers, took out two letters pinned together.

"Here they are," said he, handing them to Thorndyke, who spread them out so that we could both read them. The contents of the first one were as follows:

12, Jacob Street,

13th April, 1931

DEAR MR SANCROFT,

In addition to the collection of pottery for exhibition on loan, I am sending you a stoneware figurine of a monkey. This is no longer my property as I have sold it to a Mr James Newman. But, as he is making a business trip to the United States, he has given me permission to deposit it on loan with you until he returns to England, which he expects to do in about three months' time. He will then call on you and present the letter of introduction of which I attach a copy, and you will then deliver the figurine to him and take a receipt from him which I will ask you kindly to send on to me.

Yours sincerely,

PETER GANNET

The second letter was the copy referred to, and read thus:

DEAR MR SANCROFT,

The bearer of this, Mr James Newman, is the owner of the figurine of a monkey which I deposited on loan with you. Will you kindly deliver it to him, if he wants to have possession of it, or take his instructions as to its disposal. If he wishes to take it away with him, please secure a receipt for it before handing it over to him.

Yours sincerely,

PETER GANNET

"You see," said Sancroft, as Thorndyke returned the letters, "he wrote on the 13th of April, so, as this is the 7th of July, he may turn up at any moment, and, as he will bring the letter of introduction with him, I shall be quite safe in delivering the figure to him. And the sooner the better. I am tired of seeing the people standing in front of that case and sniggering."

"You must be," said Thorndyke. "However, I hope that Mr Newman will come soon and relieve you of the occasion of sniggers. And I must thank you once more for the valuable help that you have given us: and you may take it that I shall not forget my promise to try to find you a deputy so that you can have a little more freedom."

With this, and a cordial handshake, we took our leave; and once more I was surprised and even a little puzzled by Thorndyke's promise to seek a deputy for Mr Sancroft. I could understand his sympathy with that overworked curator; but, really, Mr Sancroft's troubles were no affair of ours. Indeed, so abnormal did Thorndyke's attitude appear that I began to ask myself whether it was possible that some motive other than sympathy might lie behind it. No one, it is true, could be more ready than Thorndyke to do a little act of kindness if the chance came his way, but, on the other hand, experience had taught me that no one's motives could be more difficult to assess than Thorndyke's. For there was always this difficulty – that one never knew what was at the back of his mind.

CHAPTER SEVENTEEN

Mr Snuper

When we arrived at our chambers we were met on the landing by Polton, who had apparently observed our approach from an upper window, and who communicated to us the fact that Mr Linnell was waiting to see us.

"He has been here more than half an hour, so perhaps you will invite him to stay to lunch. I've laid a place for him, and lunch is ready now in the breakfast room."

"Thank you, Polton," said Thorndyke, "we will see what his arrangements are," and, as Polton retired up the stairs, he opened the oak door with his latch-key and we entered the room, where we found Linnell pacing the floor with a distinctly unrestful air.

"I am afraid I have come at an inconvenient time, sir," he began apologetically; but Thorndyke interrupted:

"Not at all. You have come in the very nick of time; for lunch is just ready, and, as Polton has laid a place for you, he will insist on your joining us."

Linnell's rather careworn face brightened up at the invitation, which he accepted gratefully, and we adjourned forthwith to the small room on the laboratory floor which we had recently, for labour-saving reasons, adopted as the place in which meals were served. As we took our places at the table, Thorndyke cast a critical glance at our friend and remarked:

"You are not looking happy, Linnell. Nothing amiss, I hope?"

"There is nothing actually amiss, sir," Linnell replied, "but I am not at all happy about the way things are going. It's that confounded fellow, Blandy. He won't let matters rest. He is still convinced that Mrs Gannet knows, or could guess, where Boles is hiding; whereas I am perfectly sure that she has no more idea where he is than I have. But he won't leave it at that. He thinks that he is being bamboozled and he is getting vicious – politely vicious, you know – and I am afraid he means mischief."

"What sort of mischief?" I asked.

"Well, he keeps letting out obscure hints of a prosecution."

"But," said I, "the decision for or against a prosecution doesn't rest with him. He is just a detective inspector."

"I know," said Linnel. "That's what he keeps rubbing in. For his part, he would be entirely opposed to subjecting this unfortunate lady to the peril and indignity of criminal proceedings – you know his oily way of speaking – but what can he do? He is only a police officer. It is his superiors and the Public Prosecutor who will decide. And then he goes on, in a highly confidential, friend-of-the-family sort of way, to point out the various unfortunate (and, as he thinks, misleading) little circumstances that might influence the judgment of persons unacquainted with the lady. And, after all, he remarked to me in confidence, he found himself compelled to admit that if his superiors should decide (against his advice) to prosecute, they would be able, at least, to make out a *prima facie* case."

"I doubt whether they could," said I, "unless Blandy knows more than we know after attending the inquest."

"That is just the point," said Thorndyke. "Does he? Has he got anything up his sleeve? I don't think he can have; for if he had knowledge of any material facts, he would have to communicate them to his superiors. And, as those superiors have not taken any action so far, we may assume that no such facts have been communicated. I suppose that Blandy's agitations are connected with Boles?"

"Yes," Linnell replied. "He keeps explaining to me, and to Mrs Gannet, how the whole trouble would disappear if only we could get into touch with Boles. I don't see how it would, but I do think that if Blandy could lay his hands on Boles, his interest in Mrs Gannet would cease. All this fuss is to bring pressure on her to make some sort of statement."

"Yes," said Thorndyke, "that seems to be the position. It is not very creditable, and very unlike the ordinary practice of the police. But there is this to remember; Blandy's interest in Boles, and that of the police in general, is not connected with the murder in the studio, but with the murder of the constable at Newingstead. Blandy's idea is, I suspect – assuming that he seriously entertains a prosecution – that if Mrs Gannet were brought to trial, she would have to be put into the witness box, and then some useful information might be extracted from her in cross-examination. He is not likely to have made any such suggestions to his superiors, but, seeing how anxious the police naturally are to find the murderer of the constable, they might be ready to give a sympathetic consideration to Blandy's view if he could make out a really plausible case. And that is the question. What sort of case could he make out? Have you any ideas on that subject, Linnell? I take it that he would suggest charging Mrs Gannet as an accessory after the fact."

"Yes, he has made that clear to both of us. If the Public Prosecutor decided to take action, the charge would be that she, knowing that a felony had been committed, subsequently sheltered or relieved the felon in such a way as to enable him to evade justice. Of course, it is the only charge that would be possible."

"So it would seem," said I. "But what facts has he got to support it? He can't prove that she knows where Boles is hiding."

"No," Linnell agreed, "at least, I suppose he can't. But there is that rather unfortunate circumstance that, when her husband was missing, she was – as she has admitted – afraid to enter the studio to see if he was there. Blandy fears that her behaviour might be interpreted as proving that she had some knowledge of what had happened."

"There isn't much in that," said I. "What are the other points?"

"Well, Blandy professes to think that the relations between Boles and Mrs Gannet would tend to support the charge. No one suggests that their relations were in any way improper, but they were, admittedly, on affectionate terms."

"There is still less in that," said I. "The suggestion of a possible motive for doing a certain act is no evidence that the act was done. If Blandy has nothing better than what you have mentioned, he would never persuade a magistrate to commit her for trial. What do you say, Thorndyke?"

"It certainly looks as if Blandy held a remarkably weak hand," he replied. "Of course we have to take all the facts together; but even so, assuming that he has nothing unknown to us in reserve, I don't see how he could make out a *prima facie* case."

"He has also," said Linnell, "dropped some obscure hints about that affair of the arsenic poisoning."

"That," said Thorndyke, "is pure bluff. He would not be allowed to mention it, and he knows he wouldn't. He said so, explicitly, to Oldfield. It looks as if the threat of a prosecution were being made to exert pressure on Mrs Gannet to make some revelation. Still, it is possible that he may manage to work up a case sufficiently plausible to induce the authorities to launch proceedings. Blandy is a remarkably ingenious and resourceful man, and none too scrupulous. He is a man whom one has to take seriously."

"And suppose he does manage to get a prosecution started," said Linnell, "what do you advice me to do?"

"Well, Linnell," Thorndyke replied, "you know the ordinary routine. We are agreed that the lady is innocent and you will act accordingly. As to bail, we will settle the details of that later, but we can manage any amount that may be required."

"Do you think that she might be admitted to bail?"

"But why not?" said Thorndyke. "She will be charged only as an accessory after the fact. That is not a very grave crime. The maximum penalty is only two years' imprisonment, and, in practice, the sentences are usually quite lenient. You will certainly ask for bail, and I don't see any grounds on which the police could oppose it.

"And now as to the general conduct of the case; I advise you very strongly to play for time. Delay the proceedings as much as you can. Find excuses to ask for remands, and, in all possible ways keep the pot boiling as slowly as you can contrive. The longer the date of the final hearing can be postponed, the better will be the chance of finding a conclusive answer to the charge. I will tell you why, following Blandy's excellent example by taking you into my confidence.

"I have been examining this case in considerable detail, partly in Mrs Gannet's interests and partly for the other reasons; and I have got a clear and consistent theory of the crime, both as to its motive and approximate procedure. But at present it is only a theory. I can prove nothing. The one crucial fact which will tell me whether my theory is right or wrong is still lacking. I cannot test the truth of it until certain things have happened. I hope that they may happen quite soon, but still, I have to wait on events. If those events turn out as I expect, I shall know that my construction of the crime has been correct; and then I shall be able to show that Mrs Gannet could not possibly have been an accessory to it. But I can give no date because I cannot control the course of events."

Linnell was visibly impressed, and so was I – though less visibly. I was still in the same state of bewilderment as to Thorndyke's proceedings. Still I failed to understand why he was busying himself in a case which did not seem to concern him – apart from his sympathy with Mrs Gannet. Nor could I yet see that there was anything to discover beyond what we already knew.

Of course, I had realized all along that I must have missed some essential point of the case, and now this was confirmed. Thorndyke had got a consistent theory of the crime, which, indeed, might be right or wrong. But long experience of Thorndyke told me that it was pretty certainly right, though what sort of theory it might be

I was totally unable to imagine. I could only, like Thorndyke, wait on events.

The rest of the conversation concerned itself with the question of bail. Oldfield we knew could be depended on for one surety, and, by a little manoeuvring, it was arranged that Thorndyke should finance the other without appearing in the transaction. Eventually Linnell took his departure in greatly improved spirits, cheered by Thorndyke's encouragement and all the better for a good lunch and one or two glasses of sound claret.

Thorndyke's "confidence", if it mystified rather than enlightened me, had at least the good effect of arousing my interest in Mrs Gannet and her affairs. From time to time during the next few days I turned them over in my mind, though with little result beyond the beneficial mental exercise. But in another direction I had better luck, for I did make an actual discovery. It came about in this way.

A few days after Linnell's visit, I had occasion to go to the London Hospital to confer with one of the surgeons concerning a patient in whom I was interested. When I had finished my business there and came out into the Whitechapel Road, the appearance of the neighbourhood recalled our expedition to the People's Museum, and I suddenly realized that I was within a few minutes' walk of that shrine of the fine arts. Now, I had occasionally speculated on Thorndyke's object in making that visit of inspection and on his reasons for interesting himself in Sancroft's difficulties. Was it pure benevolence or was there something behind it? And there was the further question, had his benevolent intentions taken effect? The probability was that they had. He had given Sancroft a very definite promise, and it was quite unlike him to leave a promise unfulfilled.

These questions recurred to me as I turned westward along the Whitechapel Road, and I decided that some, at least, of them should be answered forthwith. I could now ascertain whether any deputy for Mr Sancroft had been found, and if so, who that deputy might be. Accordingly, I turned up Commercial Street and presently struck the junction of Norton Folgate and Shoreditch; and, traversing the length of the latter, came into Kingsland Road and so to the People's Museum.

One of my questions was answered as soon as I entered. There was no sign of Mr Sancroft, but the priceless collection was being watched over by a gentleman of studious aspect who was seated in an armchair – a representative specimen of Curtain Road Chippendale – reading a book with the aid of a pair of horn-framed spectacles. So engrossed was he with his studies that he appeared to be unaware of my entrance, though, as I was the only visitor, I must have been a rather conspicuous object and worthy of some slight notice.

Taking advantage of his preoccupation, I observed him narrowly; and though I could not place him or give him a name, I had the distinct impression that I had seen him before. Continuing a strategic advance in his direction under cover of the glass cases, and still observing him as unobtrusively as I could, I had a growing sense of familiarity until, coming within a few yards of him, I suddenly realized who he was.

"Why," I exclaimed, "it is Mr Snuper!"

He lowered his book and smiled blandly. "Mr Snuper it is," he admitted. "And why not? You seem surprised."

"So I am," I replied. "What on earth are you doing here?"

"To tell the truth," said he, "I am doing very little. You see me here, taking my ease and spending my very acceptable leisure profitably in reading books that I usually have not time to read."

I glanced at the book which he was holding and was not a little surprised to discover that it was Bell's *British Stalk-eyed Crustacea*. Observing my astonishment, he explained, apologetically:

"I am a collector of British crustacea in a small way – a very small way. The beginnings were made during a seaside holiday, and now I occasionally secure small additions from the fishmongers' shops."

"I shouldn't have thought," said I, "that the fishmongers' shops would have yielded many rare specimens."

"No," he agreed, "you wouldn't. But it is surprising how many curious and interesting forms of life you may discover among the heaps of shellfish on a fishmonger's slab, especially the mussels and winkles. Only the day before yesterday I obtained a nearly perfect specimen of *Stenorhynchus phalangium* from a winkle stall in the Mile End Road."

Now this was very interesting. I have often noticed how the discovery of some unlikely hobby throws most unexpected light on a man's character and personality. And so it was now. The enthusiastic pursuit of this comparatively erudite study presented a feature of Mr Snuper's rather elusive personality that was quite new to me, and somewhat surprising. But I had not come here to study Mr Snuper; and it suddenly occurred to me that that very discreet gentleman might be making this conversation expressly to divert my attention from other topics. Accordingly, I returned to my muttons with a direct question.

"But how do you come to be here?"

"It was Dr Thorndyke's idea," he replied. "You see, there was nothing doing in my line at the moment, and Mr Sancroft was badly in need of someone who could look after the place while he went about his business, so the Doctor suggested that I might as well spend my leisure here as at home, and do a kindness to Mr Sancroft at the same time."

This answer left me nothing to say. The general question that I had asked was all that was admissible. I could not pursue the matter further, for that would have been a discourtesy to Thorndyke, to say nothing of the certainty that the discreet Snuper would keep his own counsel if there were any counsel to keep. So I brought the conversation gracefully to an end with a few irrelevant observations, and, having wished my friend good day, went forth and set a course for Shoreditch Station.

But, if it was not admissible for me to question Snuper, I was at liberty to turn the matter over in my mind. But that process had the effect rather of raising questions than of disposing of them. Snuper's account of his presence at the gallery was perfectly reasonable and plausible. Thorndyke had no use for him at the moment and Sancroft had. That seemed quite simple. But was it the whole explanation? I had my doubts; and they were based principally on what I knew of Mr Snuper.

Now, Mr Snuper was a very remarkable man. Originally he had been a private inquiry agent whom Thorndyke had employed occasionally to carry out certain observation duties which could not be discharged by either of us. But Snuper had proved so valuable – so dependable, so discreet, and so quick in the uptake – that Thorndyke had taken him on as a regular member of our staff. For, apart from his other good qualities, he had a most extraordinary gift of inconspicuousness. Not only was he, at all times, exactly the kind of person whom you would pass in the street without a second glance, but, in some mysterious way he was able to keep his visible personality in a state of constant change. Whenever you met him, you found him a little different from the man whom you had met before, with the natural result that you were constantly failing to recognize him. That was my experience, as it had been on this very occasion. I never discovered how he did it. He seemed to use no actual disguise (though I believe that he was a master of the art of make-up), but he appeared to be able, in some subtle way, to manage to look like a different person.

But whatever his methods may have been, the results made him invaluable to Thorndyke, for he could keep up a continuous observation on persons or places with practically no risk of being recognized.

Reflecting on these facts: on Mr Snuper's remarkable personality, his peculiar gifts, and the purposes to which they were commonly applied, I asked myself once more, could there be anything behind his presence at the People's Museum of Modern Art? And – so far as I was concerned – answer there was none. My discovery had simply landed me with one more problem to which I could find no solution.

CHAPTER EIGHTEEN

Mr Newman

The premonitory rumblings which had so disturbed Linnell continued for some days, warning him to make all necessary preparations for the defence; and in spite of the scepticism which we all felt as to the practicability of a prosecution, the tension increased from day to day.

And then the bomb-shell exploded. The alarming fact was communicated to us in a hurried note from Linnell which informed us that a summons had been served on Mrs Gannet that very morning citing her to appear at the Police Court on the third day after that on which it was issued to answer to the charge of having, as an accessory after the fact of the murder of Peter Gannet, harboured, sheltered, or otherwise aided the accused person to evade justice.

Thorndyke appeared to be as surprised as I was, and a good deal more concerned. He read Linnell's note with a grave face and reflected on it with what seemed to me to be un-called-for anxiety.

"I can't imagine," said I, "what sort of evidence Blandy could produce. He can't know where Boles is, or he would have arrested him. And, if he doesn't, he couldn't have discovered any evidence of any communications between Boles and Mrs Gannet."

"No," Thorndyke agreed, "that seems quite clear. There can have been no intercepted letters from her, for the obvious reason that such letters would have had to be addressed in such a way as to reach him and thus reveal his whereabouts. And yet one feels that the police would not have taken action unless Blandy had produced enough facts to enable them to make out a *prima facie* case. Blandy might have been ready to gamble on his powers of persuasion, but the responsible authorities would not risk having the case dismissed by the magistrate. It is very mysterious. On my theory of the crime, it is practically certain that Mrs Gannet could not have been an accessory either before or after the fact."

Those observations gave me some clue to Thorndyke's anxiety; for they conveyed to me that Blandy's case, if he really had one, would not fit Thorndyke's theory. I put the suggestion to him in so many words, and he agreed, frankly.

"The trouble is," said he, "that my scheme of the crime is purely hypothetical. It is based on a train of deductive reasoning from the facts which are known to us all. I am in possession of no knowledge other than that which is possessed equally by Blandy and by you. The reasoning by which I reached my conclusions seems to me perfectly sound. But I may have fallen into some fallacy, or it may be that there are some material facts which are not known to me, but which are known to Blandy. One of us is mistaken. Naturally, I hope that the mistake is Blandy's; but it may be mine. However, we shall see when the prosecution opens the case."

"I assume," said I, "that you will attend at the hearing."

"Undoubtedly," he replied. "We must be there to hear what Blandy has to say, if he gives evidence, and what sort of case the prosecution propose to make out; and then we have to give Linnell any help that he may require. I suppose you will lend us the support of your presence?"

"Of course I shall come," I replied. "I am as curious as you are to hear what the prosecution have to say. I shall make a very special point of being there."

But that visit to the police court was never to take place. For, on that very night, the "events" on which Thorndyke had been waiting began to loom up on our horizon. They were ushered in by the appearance at our chambers of a young man of Jewish aspect and secretive bearing who, having been interviewed by Polton, had demanded personal audience of Thorndyke and had refused to indicate his name or business to any other person. Accordingly, he was introduced to us by Polton, who, having conducted him into the presence, stood by and kept him under observation until he was satisfied that the visitor had no unlawful or improper designs, when he retired and shut the door.

As the door closed, the stranger produced from an inner pocket a small packet wrapped in newspaper, which he proceeded to open; and, having extracted from it a letter in a sealed envelope, silently handed the latter to Thorndyke, who broke the seal and read through the evidently short note which it contained.

"If you will wait a few minutes," said he, placing a chair for the messenger, "I will give you a note to take with you. Are you going straight back?"

"Yes," was the reply. "He's waiting for me."

Thereupon Thorndyke sat down at the writing-table, and, having written a short letter, put it in an envelope, which he sealed with wax, and handed to the messenger, together with a ten-shilling note.

"That," said he, "is the fee for services rendered so far. There will be another at the end of the return journey. I have mentioned the matter in my letter."

The messenger received the note with an appreciative grin and a few words of thanks, and, having disposed of it in some secret receptacle, wrapped the letter in the newspaper which had enclosed the other, stowed it away in an inner pocket and took his departure.

"That," said Thorndyke, when he had gone, "was a communication from Snuper, who is deputizing for Sancroft at the People's Museum. He tells me that the owner of Gannet's masterpiece is going to call tomorrow morning and take possession of his property."

"Is that any concern of ours?" I asked.

"It is a concern of mine," he replied. "I am anxious not to lose sight of that monkey. There are several things about it which interest me, and, if it is to be taken away from the museum, I want to learn, if I can, where it is going to, in case I might wish at some future time to make a further examination of it. So I propose to go to the museum tomorrow morning and try to find out from Mr Newman where he keeps his collection, and how the monkey is to be disposed of. It is possible, for instance, that he may be a dealer, in which case there would be the danger of the monkey's disappearing to some unknown destination."

"I shouldn't think that he is a dealer," said I. "He would never get his money back. Probably he is a sort of Broomhill, but, of course, he may live in the provinces or even abroad. At what time do you propose to turn up at the museum?"

"The place opens at nine o'clock in the morning and Snuper expects Mr Newman to arrive at about that time. I have told him that I shall be there at half-past eight."

Now, on the face of it, the transaction did not promise any very thrilling experiences. But there was something a little anomalous about the affair. Thorndyke's interest in that outrageous monkey was quite incomprehensible to me, and I had the feeling that there was something more in this expedition than was conveyed in the mere statement of Thorndyke's intentions and objects. Accordingly, I threw out a tentative suggestion.

"If I should propose to make one of the party, would my presence be helpful or otherwise?"

"My dear fellow," he replied, "your presence is always helpful. I had, in fact, intended to ask you to accompany me. Up to the present you have not seemed to appreciate the importance of the monkey in this remarkable case; but it is possible that you may gather some fresh ideas on the subject tomorrow morning. So come by all means. And now I must go and make the necessary preparations, and you had better do the same. We shall start from here not later than a quarter to eight."

With this, he went up to the laboratory floor, whence, presently, I heard the distant tinkle of the telephone bell. Apparently he was making some kind of appointment, for shortly afterwards his footsteps were audible on the stairs descending to the entry; and I saw him no more until he came in to smoke the final pipe before going to bed.

On the following morning, Polton, having aroused me by precautionary and (as I thought, premature) thumpings on my door, served a ridiculously early breakfast and then took his stand on the doorstep to keep a look-out for the taxi which had been chartered overnight. Evidently he had been duly impressed with the importance of the occasion, as, apparently, had the taxi man, for he arrived at half-past seven and his advent was triumphantly reported by Polton just as I was pouring out my second cup of tea. But, after all, there was not so very much time to spare, for in Fleet Street, Cornhill, and Bishopsgate, all the wheeled vehicles in London seemed to have been assembled to do us honour and retard our progress; and it was a quarter past eight when we alighted opposite the Geffrye Museum, and, having dismissed the taxi, began to walk at a leisurely pace northward along the Kingsland Road.

When we were a short distance from our destination, I observed a man walking towards us, and, at a second glance, I actually recognized Mr Snuper. As soon as he saw us, he turned about and walked back to the People's Museum, where he unlocked the door and entered. On our arrival, we found the door ajar and Mr Snuper lurking just inside, ready to close and lock the door as soon as we had passed in.

"Well, Snuper," said Thorndyke, as we emerged from the lobby into the main room, "everything seems to have gone according to plan so far. You didn't give any particulars in your letter. How did you manage the adjournment?"

"It didn't require much management, sir," Snuper replied. "The affair came off by itself quite naturally. Mr Sancroft didn't come to the museum yesterday. He had to go out of town on business and, of course, as I was here, there was no reason why he shouldn't go. So I was here all alone when Mr Newman came just before closing time. He told me what he had come for and showed me the letter of introduction and the receipt which he had written out and signed. But I explained to him that I was not the curator and had no authority to allow any of the exhibits to be taken away from the museum. Besides, the case was locked, and Mr Sancroft had the key of the safe in which the other keys were kept, so I could not get the figure out even if I had been authorized to part with it.

"He was very disappointed and inclined to be huffy, but it couldn't be helped, and after all, he had only to wait a few hours. I told him that Mr Sancroft would be here today and would arrive in time to open the museum as usual; so I expect he will be waiting outside when Mr Sancroft comes to let himself in."

This forecast, however, was falsified a few minutes later, for Mr Sancroft arrived before his time and locked the door when he had entered. Naturally, he knew nothing of what had been happening in his absence and was somewhat surprised to find Thorndyke and me in the museum. But whatever explanations were called for must have been given by Snuper, who followed Sancroft into the curator's room and shut the door behind him; and, judging by the length of the interview, I assumed that Sancroft was being put in possession of such facts as it was necessary for him to know.

While this conference was proceeding, Thorndyke reconnoitred the galleries in what seemed to me a very odd way. He appeared to be searching for some place whence he could observe the entrance and the main gallery without being himself visible. Having tried one or two of the higher cases, and, apparently found them unsuitable, owing to his exceptional stature, he turned his attention to the small room which opened from the main gallery and was devoted entirely to water colours. The entrance of this room was exactly opposite the case which contained the "Figurine of a Monkey", and it also faced the main doorway. But it seemed to have a further attraction for Thorndyke; for, on the wall nearly opposite to the entrance, hung a large water colour painting, the glass of which, taken at the proper angle, reflected the whole of the principal room, the main doorway, and the case in which the Monkey was exhibited. I tried it when Thorndyke had finished his experiments, and found that, not only did it reflect a perfectly clear image, owing to the very dark colouring of the picture, but that the observer looking into it was quite invisible from the main gallery, or, indeed, to anyone who did not actually enter the small room.

This was an interesting discovery, in its way. But the most interesting part of it was Thorndyke's motive in seeking this secret point of observation. Once more I decided that things were not quite what they had seemed. As I had understood the programme, Thorndyke was going to introduce himself to Mr Newman and try to ascertain the destination and future whereabouts of the Monkey. But with this purpose, Thorndyke's present proceedings seemed to have no connection.

However, there was not much time for speculation on my part, for, at this point Mr Snuper emerged from the curator's room and, walking up the gallery, unlocked the front door and threw it open; and, as he returned, accompanied by a man who had slipped in as the door opened, I realized that the proceedings, whatever they might be, had begun.

"Keep out of sight for the present," Thorndyke directed me in a whisper; and, forthwith, I flattened myself against the wall and fixed an eager gaze on the picture as well as I could without obstructing Thorndyke's view. In the reflection I could see Snuper and his companion advance until they were within a few yards of the place where we were lurking, and then I heard Snuper say:

"If you will give me the letter and the receipt, I will take them in to Mr Sancroft and get the key of the case, unless he wishes to hand the figure to you himself."

With this, he retired into the curator's room and shut the door; and, as he disappeared, the stranger – presumably Mr Newman – who, I could now see, carried a largish hand-bag, advanced to the case which contained the Monkey and stood peering into it with his back to us, and so near that I could have put out my hand and touched him. As he stood thus, Thorndyke put his head round the jamb of the doorway to examine him by direct vision, and, after a few moments' inspection, stepped out, moving quite silently on the solid parquet floor, and took up a position close behind him. Whereupon I, following his example, came out into the middle of the doorway and stood behind Thorndyke to see what was going to happen next.

For a few moments nothing happened; but, just then I became aware of two men lurking in the lobby of the main entrance, half hidden by the inner door and quite hidden from Newman by the case at which he was standing. Suddenly, Newman seemed to become conscious of the presence of someone behind him, for he turned sharply and faced Thorndyke. And then I knew that something critical was going to happen; and I realized, too, that Thorndyke had got his "one crucial fact". For, as the stranger's eyes met Thorndyke's, he gave one wild stare of horror and amazement and his face blanched to a deathly pallor. But he uttered no word; and, after that one ghastly stare, turned about and appeared to resume his contemplation of the figurine.

Then three things happened in quick succession. First, Thorndyke took off his hat, then the door of the curator's room opened and Snuper and Sancroft emerged; and the two men whom I had noticed came out of the lobby and walked quickly up the museum to the place where Newman and Thorndyke were standing. I looked at them curiously as they approached, and recognized them both. One was Detective-Sergeant Wills of the CID. The other was no less a person than Detective-Inspector Blandy.

By this time Newman seemed, to some extent, to have recovered his self-possession, whereas Blandy, on the contrary, looked nervous and embarrassed. The former, ignoring the police officers, addressed himself to Sancroft, demanding the speedy conclusion of his business. But here Blandy intervened, with little confidence but more than his usual politeness.

"I must ask you to pardon me, sir," he began, "for interrupting your business, but there are one or two questions that I want you to be so kind as to answer."

Newman looked at him in evident alarm but replied gruffly:

"I have no time to answer questions. Besides, you are a stranger to me, and I don't think I have any concern in your affairs."

"I am a police officer," Blandy explained, "and I – "

"Then I am sure I haven't," snapped Newman.

"I wanted to ask you a few questions in connection with a most unfortunate affair that happened at Newingstead last September," Blandy continued, persuasively; but Newman cut him short with the brusque rejoinder:

"Newingstead? I never heard of the place, and, of course, I know nothing about it."

Blandy looked at him with a baffled expression and then turned an appealing face to Thorndyke.

"Can you give us something definite, sir?" he asked.

"I thought I had," Thorndyke replied. "At any rate, I now accuse this man, Newman, as he calls himself, of having murdered Constable Murray at Newingstead on the 19th of last September. That justifies you in making the arrest; and then – well, you know what to do."

But still Blandy seemed undecided. The man's evident terror and the glare of venomous hatred that he cast on Throndyke, proved nothing. Accordingly, the Inspector, apparently puzzled and unconvinced, sought to temporize.

"If you would allow me, Mr Newman," said he, "to take an impression of your left thumb, any mistake that may have been made could be set right in a moment. Now, what do you say?"

"I say that I will see you damned first," Newman replied fiercely, edging away from the Inspector and thereby impinging on the massive form of Sergeant Wills, which occupied the only avenue of escape.

"You've got a definite charge, you know, Inspector," Thorndyke reminded him in a warning tone, still narrowly watching the accused man; and something significant in the way the words were spoken helped Blandy to make up his mind.

"Well, then, Mr Newman," said he, "if you won't give us any assistance, it's your own look-out. I arrest you on the charge of having murdered Police-Constable Murray at Newingstead on the 19th of last September and I caution you that – "

The rest of the caution faded out, for Newman made a sudden movement and was in an instant clasped in the arms of Sergeant Wills, who had skilfully seized the prisoner's wrists from behind and held them immovably pressed against his chest. Almost at the same moment, Blandy sprang forward and grasped the prisoner's ears in order to secure his head and defeat his attempts to bite the sergeant's hands. But Newman was evidently a powerful ruffian, and his struggles were so violent that the two officers had the greatest difficulty in holding him, even when Snuper and I tried to control his arms. In the narrow interval between two glass cases, we all swayed to and fro, gyrating slowly and making uncomfortable contacts with sharp corners. Presently, Blandy turned his streaming face towards Thorndyke and gasped.

"Could you manage the print, Doctor? You see I can't let go. The kit is in my right hand coat pocket."

"I have brought the necessary things, myself," said Thorndyke, producing from his pocket a small metal box. "It is understood," he added as he opened the box, "that I am acting on your instructions."

Without waiting for a reply, he took out of the box a tiny roller which had been fixed by its handle in a clip, and, having run it along the inside of the lid, which formed an inking-plate, he approached the squirming prisoner, and, waiting his opportunity, suddenly seized the left thumb, and holding it steady, ran the little roller over its bulb. Then he produced a small pad of smooth paper, and, again watching for a moment when the thumb was fixed immovably, quickly pressed the pad on the inked surface. The resulting print was not a very perfect impression, but it showed the pattern clearly enough for practical purposes.

"Have you got the photograph with you?" he asked.

"Yes," replied Blandy. "But I can't – could you take hold of his head for a moment?"

Thorndyke laid the pad on the top of the nearest case and then, following Blandy's instructions, grasped the prisoner's head so as to relieve the Inspector; who thereupon stepped back, and, having taken up the pad, thrust his hand into his pocket and brought out a photograph mounted on a card. For a few moments he stood, eagerly glancing from the pad to the photograph and evidently comparing them point by point.

"Is it the right print?" Thorndyke asked.

Blandy did not answer immediately, but continued his scrutiny with evidently growing excitement. At length, he looked up, and, forgetting his usual bland smile, replied, almost in a shout:

"Yes, by God! It's the man himself."

And then came the catastrophe.

Whether it was that the sergeant's attention was for the moment distracted by the absorbing interest of Blandy's proceedings, or that Newman had been watching his opportunity, I cannot say, but, after a brief cessation of his struggles, as if he had become exhausted, he made a sudden and violent effort and twisted himself out of his captors' grasp, darting instantly into the passage between two cases. Thither the sergeant followed, but the prisoner, with incredible quickness and dexterity, delivered a smashing blow on the chest which sent the officer staggering backwards; and the next moment, the prisoner was standing in the narrow space with an automatic pistol covering his pursuers.

I will do Blandy the justice (which I am glad to do, as I never liked the man) to say that he faced the deadly danger without a sign of fear or a moment's hesitation. How he escaped with his life, I have never understood, for he dashed straight at the prisoner, looking into the very muzzle of the pistol. But by some miracle the bullet passed him by; and, before another shot could be fired, he had grabbed the man's wrists and got some sort of control of the weapon. Then the sergeant and Snuper and I came to his assistance, and the old struggle began again, but with the material difference that each and all of us had to keep a wary eye on the barrel of the pistol.

Of the crowded and chaotic events of the next minute I have but the obscurest recollection. There comes back to me a vague idea of violent, strenuous effort; a succession of pistol shots with a sort of infernal *obbligato* accompaniment of shattering glass; the struggles of the sergeant to reach a back pocket without losing his hold on the prisoner; and the manoeuvres of Mr Sancroft, at first ducking at every shot and finally retreating hurriedly – almost on all fours – into his sanctum. Nor, when the end came, am I at all clear as to the exact manner of its happening. I know only that the firing ceased, and that, almost as the last shot was fired, the writhing, struggling body became suddenly still and began limply to sag towards the floor; and that I then noticed in the man's right temple a small hole from which issued a little trickle of blood.

Blandy rose, and, looking down gloomily at the prostrate body, cursed softly under his breath.

"What infernal luck!" he exclaimed. "I suppose he is dead?"

"I am afraid there is no doubt of that," I replied, as the last faint twitchings died away.

"Infernal luck," he repeated, "to have him slip through our fingers just as we had made sure of him."

"It was the making sure of him that did it," growled the sergeant. "I mean the fingerprints. We ought to have waited for them until we had got the darbies on."

"I know," said Blandy. "But, you see, I wasn't sure that we had got the right man. He didn't seem to me to answer to the description at all."

"The description of whom?" asked Thorndyke.

"Of Frederick Boles," replied Blandy. "This is Boles, isn't it?"

"No," replied Thorndyke. "This is Peter Gannet."

Blandy was thunderstruck. "But," he exclaimed, incredulously, "it can't be. We identified Gannet's remains quite conclusively."

"Yes," Thorndyke agreed, blandly, "that is what you were intended to do. The remains were actually those of Boles – with certain additions."

Blandy smiled sourly. "Well," said he, "this is a knock-out. To think that we have been barking up the wrong tree all the time. But you might have given us the tip a bit sooner, Doctor."

"My dear Blandy," Thorndyke protested, "I told you all that I knew as soon as I knew it."

"You didn't tell us who this man, Newman, was."

"But, my dear Inspector," Thorndyke replied, "I didn't know, myself. When I came here today, I suspected that Mr Newman was Peter Gannet. But I didn't know until I had seen the man and recognized him and seen that he recognized me. I told you last night that it was merely a case of suspicion."

"Well, well," said Blandy, "it's no use crying over spilt milk. Is there a telephone in the office? If there is, you had better ring up the Police Station, Sergeant, and tell them to send an ambulance along as quickly as they can."

The tinkle of the telephone bell answered Blandy's question, and, while the message was being sent and answered, Thorndyke and I proceeded to lay out the body in view of the probability of premature *rigor mortis*. Then we adjourned to the curator's room, where Blandy showed a tendency to revert to the topic of the might-have-been. But our stay there was short, for the ambulance arrived in an almost incredibly short time; and, when the body had been carried out by the stretcher-bearers and the outer door shut, the Inspector and the Sergeant made ready to depart.

"There are some other particulars, Doctor," said Blandy, "that we shall want you to give us, if you will; but now I must get back to the Yard and report what has happened. They won't be over pleased; but, at least we have cleared up a rather mysterious case."

With this, he and the Sergeant went forth to their car, being let out by Mr Sancroft, who, having affixed a notice, which he had written out, to the main door, shut it and locked it. Then he came back to the room and gazed round ruefully at the wreck of the People's Museum of Modern Art.

"The Lord knows," said he, "who is going to pay for all this damage. Seven glass cases smashed and the nose knocked off Israel Popoff's Madonna. It has been a shocking business; and there is that damned image – if you will excuse me – which has been the cause of all the trouble, still standing in one of the few undamaged cases. But I will soon have it out of that; only the question is, what on earth is to be done with it? The beastly thing seems to be nobody's property now."

"It is the property of Mrs Gannet," said Thorndyke; "and I think it would be best if I were to take custody of it and hand it over to her. I will give you a receipt for it."

"You need not trouble about a receipt," said Sancroft, hauling out his keys and joyfully unlocking the case. "I accept you as Mrs Gannet's representative, and I am only too delighted to get the thing out of the museum. Shall I make it up into a parcel?"

"There is no need," replied Thorndyke, picking up Gannet's bag from the floor, on which it had been dropped when the struggle began. "This will hold it, and there is probably some packing inside."

He opened the bag, and, finding it lined with a thick woollen scarf, took the figure from the open case and carefully deposited it in the folds of the scarf and shut the bag.

That seemed to conclude our business; and, after a few more words with the still agitated Sancroft and a brief farewell to Mr Snuper, we accompanied the former to the door, whence we were let out into the street.

CHAPTER NINETEEN
The Monkey Reveals his Secret

By lovers of paradox we are assured that it is the unexpected that always happens. But this is, to put it mildly, an exaggeration. Even the expected happens sometimes. It did, for instance, on the present occasion; for when we passed into the entry of our chambers on our return from the museum, and began to ascend the stairs, I expected that Thorndyke would pass by the door of our sitting-room and go straight up to the laboratory floor. And that is precisely what he did. He made directly for the larger workshop, and, having greeted Polton as we entered, laid Gannet's bag on the bench.

"We need not disturb you, Polton," said he, noting that our assistant was busily polishing the pallets of a dead beat escapement appertaining to a "regulator" that he was constructing. But Polton had already fixed an inquisitive eye on the bag, and, coupling its presence with our mysterious expedition, had evidently sniffed something more exciting than clock-work.

"You are not disturbing me, sir," said he, laying the pallets on the table of the polishing lathe and bearing down with a purposeful air on the bag. "The clock is a spare time job. Can I give you any assistance?"

Thorndyke smiled appreciatively, and, opening the bag, carefully took out the figure and stood it up on the bench.

"There, Polton," said he, "what do you think of that for a work of art?"

"My word!" exclaimed Polton, regarding the figure with profound disfavour, "but he is an ugly fellow. Now, what part of the world might he have come from? South Sea Islands he looks like."

Thorndyke lifted the image, and, turning it up to exhibit the base, handed it to Polton, who examined it with fresh astonishment.

"Why," he exclaimed, "it seems to have been made by a civilized man! It's English lettering, though I don't recognize the mark."

"It was made by an Englishman," said Thorndyke. "But do you find anything abnormal about it apart from its ugliness?"

Polton looked long and earnestly at the base, turned the figure over and examined every part of it, finally tapping it with his knuckles and listening attentively to the sound elicited.

"I don't think it is solid," said he, "though it is mighty thick".

"It is not solid," said Thorndyke. "We have ascertained that."

"Then," said Polton, "I don't understand it. The body looks like ordinary stoneware. But it can't be if it's hollow. There is no opening in it anywhere. But it couldn't have been fired without a vent-hole of some kind. It would have blown to pieces."

"Yes," Thorndyke agreed. "That is the problem. But have another look at the base. What do you say to that white glazed slip on which the signature is written?"

Polton inspected it afresh, and finally stuck a watchmaker's eye-glass in his eye to assist in the examination.

"I don't know what to make of it," said he. "It looks a little like a tin glaze, but I don't think it is. I don't see how it could be. What do you think it is, sir?"

"I suspect that it is some kind of hard, white cement – possibly Keene's – covered with a clear varnish."

Polton looked up at him, and his expressive countenance broke out into a characteristic crinkly smile.

"I think you have hit it, sir," said he; "and I think I begin to ogle, as Mr Miller would say. What are we going to do about it?"

"The obvious thing," said Thorndyke, "is to make what surgeons would call an exploratory puncture; drill a small hole in it and see what the base is really made of and what its thickness is."

"Would a drill go into stoneware?" I asked.

"No," replied Thorndyke, "not an ordinary drill. But I do not think that there is any stoneware in the middle of the base. You remember Broomhill's specimen. There was a good-sized elliptical opening in the base, and I imagine that this figure was originally the same, but that the opening has been filled up. What we have to ascertain is, what it has been filled with and how far the filling goes into the cavity."

"We had better do it with a hand-drill," said Polton, "and steady the image on the bench, as it wouldn't be safe to fix it in the vice. Then it will be convenient if we want to enlarge the hole."

He wrapped the "image" in one or two thick dusters and laid it on the bench, when I took charge of it and held it as firmly as I could to resist the pressure of the drill. Then having fitted an eighth-inch Morse into the stock, he began operations, cautiously, and with only a light pressure; but I noticed that, at first, the hard drill-point seemed to make very little impression.

"What do you suppose the filling consists of, sir?" Polton asked as he withdrew the drill to examine the shallow pit that its point had made, "and how far do you suppose it goes in?"

"My idea is," replied Thorndyke, " – but it is only a guess – that there is a comparatively thin layer of Keene's cement and then a plug of plaster, perhaps three or four inches thick. Beyond that, I should expect to come to the cavity. I hope I am right, for, if it should turn out to be Keene's cement all the way, we shall have some trouble in making a hole large enough for our purpose."

"What is our purpose?" I asked. "To see if there is anything in the cavity, I presume."

"Yes," Thorndyke replied, "though it is practically certain that there is. Otherwise, there would have been no object in stopping up the opening."

Here Polton returned to the charge, now sensibly increasing the pressure. Still, for a while, the drill seemed to make little progress. Then, quite suddenly, as if some obstruction had been removed, it began to enter freely and had soon penetrated as far as the chuck would allow it to go.

"You said, three or four inches, I think, sir?" Polton remarked, as he withdrew the drill and examined the white powder in the grooves.

"Yes," Thorndyke replied, "but possibly more. A sixth-inch drill would be best; and you might use a stouter one − say a quarter-inch − to avoid the risk of its bending."

Polton made the necessary change, and resumed operations with the bigger drill, which soon enlarged the opening and then began quickly to penetrate the softer plaster. When it had entered about four inches, even this slight resistance seemed to cease, for it ran in suddenly right up to the chuck.

"Four inches it is, sir," said Polton, with a triumphant crinkle, as he withdrew the drill and inspected the grooves. "How big an opening will you want?"

"An inch might do," replied Thorndyke, "but an inch and a half would be better. I think that is possible without encroaching on the stoneware body. But you will see."

On this, Polton produced a set of reamers and a brace, and, beginning with one which would just enter the hole, turned the brace cautiously while I continued to steady the figure. Meanwhile, Thorndyke, having cut off a piece of stout copper wire about eight inches long, fixed it in the vice, and, with an adjustable die, cut a screw thread about an inch long on one end.

"We may as well see what the conditions are," said he, "before we go any further."

He took the wire out of the vice, and, as Polton withdrew the third reamer − which had enlarged the hole to about half an inch − he passed the wire into the hole and began gently to probe the bottom of the cavity. Then he pressed it in somewhat more firmly and gave it one or two turns, slowly drawing it out while he continued to turn. When it finally emerged, its end held a small knob of cotton wool from which a little twisted strand of the same material extended into the invisible interior. I watched its emergence with profound interest and a certain amount of self-contempt; for, obviously, he had expected to find the interior filled with cotton wool as was demonstrated by the making of the cotton wool holder. And yet I, who knew as much of the essential facts as he did, had never guessed, and, even now, had only a vague suspicion of what its presence suggested.

As the operations with the reamers progressed, it became evident that the larger opening was possible, for the material cut through was still only cement and plaster. When the full inch and a half had been reached, Thorndyke fixed his wire in the chuck of the hand-drill and, passing the former into the wide hole, pressed the screw end into the mass of cotton wool and began to turn the handle, slowly withdrawing it as he turned. When the end of the wire appeared at the opening, it bore a ball of cotton wool from which a thick strand, twisted by the rapid rotation of the wire into a firm cord, extended to the mass inside; and as Thorndyke slowly stepped back, still turning the handle, the cord grew longer and longer until, at last, its end slipped out of the opening, showing that the whole of the cotton wool had been extracted.

"Now," said Thorndyke, "let us see what all that cotton wool enclosed."

He laid aside the drill, and, carefully lifting the figure, held it upright over the bench, when there dropped out a small, white paper packet tied up with thread. Having cut the thread, he laid the packet on the bench and opened it, while Polton and I craned forward inquisitively. I suppose we both knew approximately what to expect, and I was better able to guess than Polton; but the reality was quite beyond my expectations, and, as for Polton, he was, for the moment, struck dumb. Only for the moment, however; for, recovering himself, he exclaimed, impressively, with his eyes fixed on the packet:

"Never in all my life have I seen the like of this. Fifteen diamonds and every one of them a specimen stone. And look at the size of them! Why that little lot must be worth a king's ransom!"

"I understand," said Thorndyke, "that they represent about ten thousand pounds. That will be their market price; and you can add to that three human lives – not as their value, which it is not, but as their cost."

"I take it," said I, "that you are assuming these to be Kempster's diamonds?"

"It is hardly a case of assuming," he replied. "The facts seem to admit of no other interpretation. This was an experiment to test the correctness of my theory of the crime. I expected to find in this figure fifteen large diamonds. Well, we have opened the figure and here are the fifteen large diamonds. This figure belonged to Peter Gannet, and whatever was in it was put in by him, as is shown by the sealing on the base, which bears his signature. But Peter Gannet has been proved to be the murderer of the constable, and that murderer was undoubtedly the man who stole Kempster's diamonds; and these diamonds correspond in number and appearance with the diamonds which were stolen. However, we won't leave it at a mere matter of appearance. Kempster gave me the full particulars of the diamonds, including the weight of each stone, and, of course, the total weight of the whole parcel. We need hardly take the weight of each stone separately, but, if we weigh the whole fifteen together and we find that the total weight agrees with that given by Kempster, even my learned and sceptical friend will admit that the identity is proved sufficiently for our present purposes."

I ventured mildly to repudiate the alleged scepticism but agreed that the verification was worth while; and, when Thorndyke had carefully closed the packet, we all adjourned to the chemical laboratory, where Polton slid up the glass front of the balance and went through the formality of testing the truth of the latter with empty pans.

"What weight shall I put on, sir?" he asked.

"Mr Kempster put the total weight at 380.4 grains. Let us try that."

Polton selected the appropriate weights, and, when they had been checked by Thorndyke, they were placed in the pan and the necessary "rider" put on the beam to make up the fraction. Then Polton solemnly closed the glass front and slowly depressed the lever; and, as the balance rose, the index deviated barely a hair's breadth from the zero mark.

"I think that is near enough," said Thorndyke, "to justify us in deciding that these are the diamonds that were stolen from Kempster."

"Yes," I agreed; "at any rate, it is conclusive enough for me. What do you propose to do with them? Shall you hand them to Kempster?"

"No." he replied. "I don't think that would be quite in order. Stolen property should be delivered to the police, even if its ownership is known. I shall hand these diamonds to the Commissioner of Police, explain the circumstances, and take his receipt for them. Then I shall notify Kempster and leave him to collect them. He will have no difficulty in recovering them as the police have a complete description of the stones. And that will finish the business, so far as I am concerned. I have more than fulfilled my obligations to Kempster and I have proved that Mrs Gannet could not possibly have been an accessory to the murder of her husband. Those were the ostensible objects of my investigation, apart from the intrinsic interest of the case, and, now that they have both been achieved, it remains only to sing *nunc dimittis* and celebrate our success with a modest festivity of some kind."

"There is one other little matter that remains," said I. "Today's events have proved that your theory of the crime was correct, but they haven't shown how you arrived at that theory, and I have only the dimmest ideas on the subject. But perhaps the festivity will include a reasoned exposition of the evidence."

"I see nothing against that," he replied. "It would be quite interesting to me to retrace the course of the investigation; and if it would also interest you and Oldfield – who must certainly be one of the party – then we shall all be pleased."

He paused for a few moments, having, I think, detected a certain wistfulness in Polton's face, for he continued:

"A restaurant dinner would hardly meet the case, if a prolonged and necessarily confidential pow-wow is contemplated. What do you think, Polton?"

"I think, sir," Polton replied promptly and with emphasis, "that you would be much more comfortable and more private in your own dining-room, and you'd get a better dinner, too. If you will leave the arrangements to me, I will see that the entertainment does you credit."

I chuckled inwardly at Polton's eagerness. Not but that he would, at any time, have delighted in ministering, in our own chambers, to Thorndyke's comfort and that of his friends. But, apart from these altruistic considerations, I felt sure that, on this present occasion, the "arrangements" would include some very effective ones for enabling him to enjoy the exposition.

"Very well, Polton," said Thorndyke. "I will leave the affair in your hands. You had better see Dr Oldfield and find out what date will suit him, and then we will wind up the Gannet case with a flourish."

CHAPTER TWENTY

Thorndyke Reviews the Evidence

Our invitaion to Oldfield came very opportunely, for he was just preparing for his holiday and had already got a *locum tenens* installed. So when, on the appointed evening, he turned up in buoyant spirits, it was as a free man, immune from the haunting fear of an urgent call.

Polton's artful arrangements for unostentatious eavesdropping had come to nought; for Thorndyke and I had insisted on his laying a place for himself at the table and joining us as the colleague that he had actually become in late years, rather than the servant that he still proclaimed himself to be. For the gradual change of status from servant to friend had occurred quite smoothly and naturally. Polton was a man in whom perfect manners were inborn; and, as for his intellect, well, I would gladly have swapped my brain for his.

"This is very pleasant," said Oldfield, as he took his seat and cast an appreciative glance round the table, "and it is most kind of you, sir, to have invited me to the celebration, especially when you consider what a fool I have been and what a mess I made of my part of the business."

"You didn't make a mess of it, at all," said Thorndyke.

"Well, sir," Oldfield chuckled, "I made every mistake that was humanly possible, and no man can do more than that."

"You are doing yourself a great injustice, Oldfield," Thorndyke protested. "Apparently you don't realize that you were the actual discoverer of the crime."

Oldfield laid down his knife and fork to gaze at Thorndyke.

"I, the discoverer!" he exclaimed; and then, "Oh, you mean that I discovered the ashes. But any other fool could have done that. There they were, plainly in sight, and it just happened that I was the first person to go into the studio."

"I am not so sure even of that," said Thorndyke. "There was some truth in what Blandy said to you. It was the expert eye that saw, at once, that something strange had happened. Most persons, going into the studio, would have failed to observe anything abnormal. But that is not what I am referring to. I mean that it was you who made the discovery that exposed the real nature of the crime and led to the identification of the criminal."

Oldfield shook his head incredulously and looked at Thorndyke as if demanding further enlightenment.

"What I mean," the latter explained, "is that here we had a crime, carefully and subtly planned and prepared in detail with admirable foresight and imagination. There was only a single mistake; and, but for you, that mistake would have passed unnoticed and the scheme would have worked according to plan. It very nearly did, as you know."

Oldfield still looked puzzled, as well he might; for he knew, as I did, that all his conclusions had been wrong; and I was as far as he was from understanding what Thorndyke meant.

"Perhaps," Oldfield suggested, "you would explain in a little more detail what my discovery was."

"Not now," replied Thorndyke. "Presently, we are going to have a reasoned analysis of the case. You will see plainly enough then."

"I suppose I shall," Oldfield agreed, doubtfully, "but I should have said that the entire discovery was your own, sir. I know that it came as a thunderbolt to me, and so, I expect, it did to Blandy. And he must have been pretty sick at losing his prisoner, after all."

"Yes," said I, "he was. And it *was* unfortunate. Gannet ought to have been brought to trial and hanged."

"I am not sorry that he wasn't, all the same," said Oldfield. "It would have been horrible for poor Mrs Gannet."

"Yes," Thorndyke agreed, "a trial and a hanging would have ruined her life. I am inclined to feel that the suicide, or accident, was all for the best, especially as there are signs that very warm and sympathetic relations are growing up between her and our good friend Linnell. One likes to feel that the future holds out to her the promise of some compensation for all the trials and troubles that she has had to endure."

"Still," I persisted, "the fellow was a villain and ought to have been hanged."

"He wasn't the worst kind of villain," said Thorndyke. "The murder of the constable was, if not properly accidental, at least rather in the nature of 'chance medley'. There could have been no intention to kill. And, as to Boles, he probably offered considerable provocation."

From this point the conversation tended to peter out, the company's jaws being otherwise engaged. What there was ranged over a variety of topics – including Polton's *magnum opus,* the regulator, now in a fair way of being completed – and kept us entertained until the last of the dishes had been dealt with and removed and the port and the dessert had been set on the table. Then, when Oldfield and I had filled our pipes (Polton did not smoke but took an occasional, furtive pinch of snuff), Thorndyke, in response to our insistent demands, put down his empty pipe and proceeded to the promised analysis.

"In order," he began, "to appreciate the subtlety and imagination with which this crime was planned, it is necessary to recall the whole sequence of events and to note how naturally and logically it evolved. It begins with a case of arsenic poisoning, a perfectly simple and ordinary case with all the familiar features. A man is poisoned by arsenic in his food. That food is prepared by his wife. The wife has a male friend to whom she is rather devoted, and she is not very devoted to her husband. Taken at its face value, there is no mystery at all. It appears to be just the old, old story.

"The poisoning is detected, the man recovers, and he returns home and resumes his ordinary habits. But any observer, noting the facts, must feel that this is not the end. There will surely be a sequel. A murder has been attempted and has failed; but the will to murder has been proved, and it, presumably, still exists, awaiting a fresh opportunity. Anyone, knowing what has happened, will naturally be on the look-out for some further attempt.

"Then, during his wife's absence at the seaside, the man disappears. She comes home and finds that he is missing. He has not gone away in any ordinary sense, for he has taken nothing with him, not even a hat. In her alarm, she naturally seeks the advice of the doctor. But the doctor, recalling the poisoning incident, at once suspects a tragedy, and the more so since he knows of the violent enmity existing between the husband and the wife's friend. But he does not merely suspect a tragedy in the abstract. His suspicions take a definite shape. The idea of murder comes into his mind, and when it does, it is associated, naturally enough, with the man who was suspected of having administered the poison. He is not, perhaps, fully conscious of his suspicions; but he is in such a state of mind that, in the instant when the fact of the murder becomes evident, he confidently fills in the picture and identifies not only the victim but the murderer, too.

"Thus you see how perfectly the stage had been set for the events that were to follow; how admirably the minds of all who knew the facts had been prepared to follow out a particular line of thought. There is the preliminary crime with Boles as the obvious suspect. There is the expectation that, since the motive remains, there will be a further attempt – by Boles. Then comes the expected sequel; and instantly, by the most natural and reasonable association, the *dramatis personae* of the first crime are transferred, in the same rôles, to the second crime. It is all quite plain and consistent. Taking things at their face value, it seemed obvious that the murdered man must be Peter Gannet, and his murderer,

Frederick Boles. I think that I should have been prepared to accept that view myself, if there had been nothing to suggest a different conclusion.

"But it was just at this point that Oldfield made his valuable contribution to the evidence. Providence inspired him to take a sample of the bone ash and test it for arsenic; and, to his surprise, and still more to mine, he proved that the ash did contain arsenic. Moreover, the metal was present, not as a mere trace but in measurable quantities. And there could be no doubt about it. Oldfield's analysis was carried out skilfully and with every precaution against error, and I repeated the experiment with the remainder of the sample and confirmed his results.

"Now, here was a definite anomaly, a something which did not seem to fit in with the rest of the facts; and I am astonished that neither Blandy nor the other investigators appreciated its possible importance. To me an anomalous fact, a fact which appears unconnected, or even discordant, with the body of known facts, is precisely the one on which attention should be focused. And that is what I did in this present case. The arsenic was undeniably present in these ashes, and its presence had to be accounted for.

"How did it come to be there? Admittedly, it was not in the body before the burning. Then it must have found its way into the ashes after their removal from the kiln. But how? To me there appeared to be only two possible explanations, and I considered each, comparing it with the other in terms of probability.

"First, there was the suggestion made at the inquest that the ashes might have become contaminated with arsenic in the course of grinding or transference to the bin. That, perhaps, sounded plausible if it was only a verbal formula for disposing of a curious but irrelevant fact. But when one tried to imagine how such contamination could have occurred, no reasonable explanation was forthcoming. What possible source of contamination was there? Arsenic is not one of the potter's ordinary materials. It would not have been present in the bin or in the iron mortar or in the grinding mills. It was a foreign substance, so far as the pottery studio was concerned, and the only arsenic known to exist in the place was that which was contained in a stoppered jar in Boles' cupboard.

"Moreover, it had not the character of a mere chance contamination. Not only was it present in a measurable quantity; it appeared to be fairly evenly distributed throughout the ashes, as was proved by the fact that the Home Office chemist obtained results substantially similar to Oldfield's and mine. After a critical examination of this explanation, I felt that it explained nothing, that it did not agree with the facts, and was itself inexplicable.

"Then, if one could not accept the contamination theory, what was the alternative? The only other explanation that could be suggested was that the arsenic had been intentionally mixed with the ashes. At the first glance this did not look very probable. But, if it was not the true explanation, it was at least intelligible. There was no impossibility; and, in fact, the more I considered it, the less improbable did it appear.

"When this hypothesis was adopted, provisionally, two further questions at once arose: if the arsenic was intentionally put into the ashes, who put it there and for what purpose? Taking the latter question first, a reasonable answer immediately suggested itself. The most obvious purpose would be that of establishing a connection between the present crime and the previous poisoning; and when I asked myself what could be the object of trying to establish such a connection, again a perfectly reasonable answer was forthcoming. In the poisoning crime, the victim was Peter Gannet, and the would-be murderer was almost certainly Frederick Boles. Then the introduction of the arsenic as a common factor linking together the two crimes would have the purpose of suggesting a repetition of the characters of victim and murderer. That is to say, that the ultimate object of putting the arsenic into the ashes would be to create the conviction that the ashes were the remains of Peter Gannet, that he had been murdered by means of arsenic, and that the murderer was Frederick Boles.

"But who would wish to create this conviction? Remember that our picture contains only three figures: Gannet, his wife, and Boles. If the arsenic had been planted, it must have been planted by one of these three. But by which of them? By Mrs Gannet? Certainly not, seeing that she was under some suspicion of having been an accessory to the poisoning. And, obviously, Boles would not wish to create the belief that he was the murderer.

"Thus, of the three possible agents of this imposture, we had excluded two. There remained only Gannet. The suggestion was that he was dead and, therefore, could not have planted the arsenic. But could we accept that suggestion? The arsenic was (by the hypothesis) admittedly an imposture. But with the evidence of imposture, we could no longer take the appearances at their face value. The only direct evidence that the remains were those of Gannet was the tooth that was found in the ashes. It was, however, only a porcelain tooth and no more an integral part of Gannet's body than his shirt button or his collar stud. If the arsenic had been planted to produce a particular belief, it was conceivable that the tooth might have been planted for the very same purpose. It was, in fact, conceivable that the ashes were not those of Gannet and that, consequently, Gannet was not dead.

"But if Gannet had not been the victim of this murder, then he was almost certainly the murderer; and if Boles had not been the murderer, then he must almost certainly have been the victim. Both men had disappeared and the ashes were undoubtedly the remains of one of them. Suppose the remains to be those of Boles and the murderer to be Peter Gannet; how does that affect our question as to the planting of the arsenic?

"At a glance we can see that Gannet would have had the strongest reasons for creating the belief that the remains were those of his own body. So long as that belief prevailed, he was absolutely safe. The police would have written him off as dead and would be engaged in an endless, and fruitless, search for Boles. With only a trifling change in his appearance – such as the shaving off of his beard and moustache – he could go his ways in perfect security.

Nobody would be looking for him; nobody would even believe in his existence. He would have made the perfect escape.

"This result appeared to me very impressive. The presence of the arsenic was a fact. The hypothesis that it had been planted was the only intelligible explanation of that fact. The acceptance of that hypothesis was conditional on the discovery of some motive for planting it. Such a motive we had discovered; but the acceptance of that motive was conditional on the assumption that Peter Gannet was still alive.

"Was such an assumption unreasonable? Not at all. Gannet's death had rather been taken for granted. He had disappeared mysteriously, and certain unrecognizable human remains had been found on his premises. At once it had been assumed that the remains were his. The actual identification rested on a single porcelain tooth; but as that tooth was no part of his body and could, therefore, have been purposely planted in the ashes, the evidence that it afforded as to the identity of the remains was not conclusive. If any grounds existed for suspecting imposture, it had no evidential value at all. But, apart from that tooth, there was not, and never had been, any positive reasons for believing that these ashes were the remains of Peter Gannet.

"The completeness and consistency of the results thus arrived at by reasoning from the hypothesis that the arsenic had been planted impressed me profoundly. It really looked as if that hypothesis might be the true one, and I decided to pursue the argument and see whither it led; and especially to examine one or two other slight anomalies that I had noticed.

"I began with the crime itself. The picture presented (and accepted by the police) was this: Boles had murdered Gannet and cremated his body in the kiln, after dismembering it, if necessary, to get it into the cavity. He had then pounded the incinerated bones and deposited the fragments in the bone-ash bin. Then, after having done all this, he was suddenly overcome by panic and fled.

"But why had he fled? There was no reason whatever for him to flee. He was in no danger. He was alone in the studio and could lock himself in. There was no fear of interruption, since Mrs Gannet was away at the seaside; and even if any chance visitor should have come, there was nothing visible to excite suspicion. He had done the difficult and dangerous part of the work and all that remained was the few finishing touches. If he had cleaned up the kiln and put it into its usual condition, the place would have looked quite normal, even to Oldfield; and, as to the bone fragments, there was not only the grog-mill but also a powerful edge-runner mill in which they could have been ground to fine powder. If this powder had been put into the bone-ash bin – the ordinary contents of which were powdered bone-ash – every trace of the crime would have been destroyed. Then Boles could have gone about his work in the ordinary way or taken a holiday if he had pleased. There would have been nothing to suggest that any abnormal events had occurred in the studio or that Gannet was not still alive.

"Contrast this with the actual conditions that were found. The kiln had been left in a state that would instantly attract the attention of anyone who knew anything about the working of a pottery studio. The incinerated bones had been pounded into fragments, just too small to be recognizable as parts of any known person, but large enough to be recognized, not only as bones, but as human bones. After all the risk and labour of cremating the body and pounding the bones, there had still been left clear evidence that a man had been murdered.

"I think you will agree that the suggested behaviour of Boles is quite unaccountable; is entirely at variance with reasonable probabilities. On the other hand, if you consider critically the conditions that were found, they will convey to you, as they did to me, the impression of a carefully arranged tableau. Certain facts, such as the murder and the cremation, were to be made plain and obvious, and certain issues, such as the identities of victim and murderer, were to be confused. But, furthermore, they conveyed to me a very interesting suggestion; which was that the tableau had been set for a particular spectator. Let us consider this suggestion.

"The crime was discovered by Oldfield, and it is possible that he was the only person who would have discovered it. His potter's eye, glancing at the kiln, noted its abnormal state and saw that something was wrong. Probably there was a good deal of truth, as well as politeness, in Blandy's remark that if he had come to the studio without his expert guide and adviser, though he would have seen the visible objects, he would have failed to interpret their meaning. But Oldfield had just the right knowledge. He knew all about the kiln, he knew the various bins and what was in them, and what the mills were for. So, too, with the little finger-bone. Most persons would not have known what it was; but Oldfield, the anatomist, recognizes it at once as the ungual phalanx of a human index finger. He would seem to have been the preappointed discoverer.

"The suggestion is strengthened by what we know of the previous events; of Gannet's eagerness to cultivate the Doctor's friendship, to induct him into all the mysteries of the studio and all the routine of the work that was carried on there. There is an appearance of Oldfield's being prepared to play the part of discoverer – a part that would naturally fall to him, since it was certain that when the blow fell, Mrs Gannet would seek the help and advice of the doctor.

"The suggestion of preparation applies also to the arsenic in the ashes. If that arsenic was planted, the planting of it must have been a mere gamble, for it was most unlikely that anyone would think of testing the ashes for arsenic. But if there was any person in the world who would think of doing so, that person was most assuredly Oldfield. Any young doctor who has the misfortune to miss a case of arsenic poisoning is pretty certain thereafter to develop what the psychological jargonists would call 'an arsenic complex'. When any abnormal death occurs, he is sure to think first of arsenic.

"The whole group of appearances, then, suggested that Oldfield had been prepared to take a particular view and to form certain suspicions. But did not that suggestion carry us back still farther?

What of the poisoning affair, itself? If all the other appearances were false appearances, was it not possible that the poisoning was an imposture, too? When I came to consider that question, I recalled certain anomalies in the case which I had observed at the time. I did not attach great importance to them, since arsenic is a very erratic poison, but I noted them and I advised Oldfield to keep full notes of the case; and now that the question of imposture had arisen, it was necessary to reconsider them, and to review the whole case critically.

"We had to begin our review by reminding ourselves that practically the whole of our information was derived from the patient's statements. The phenomena were virtually all subjective. Excepting the redness of the eyes, which could easily have been produced artificially, there were no objective signs; for the appearance of the tongue was not characteristic. Of the subjective symptoms we were told; we did not observe them for ourselves. The abdominal pain was felt by the patient, not by us. So with the numbness, the loss of tactile sensibility, the tingling, the cramps and the inability to stand; we learned of their existence from the patient and we could not check his statements. We accepted those statements as there appeared to be no reason for doubting them; but it was quite possible for them all to have been false. To an intelligent malingerer who had carefully studied the symptoms of arsenic poisoning, there would have been little difficulty in making up a quite convincing set of symptoms."

"But," Oldfield objected, "there really was arsenic in the body. You were not forgetting that?"

"Not at all," replied Thorndyke. "That was the first of the anomalies. You will remember my remarking to you that the quantity of arsenic obtained by analysis of the secretions was less than I had expected. Woodfield and I were both surprised at the smallness of the amount; which was, in fact, not much greater than might have been found in a patient who was taking arsenic medicinally. But it was not an extreme discrepancy, since arsenic is rapidly eliminated, though the symptoms persist, and we explained it by assuming that no considerable dose had been taken quite recently. Nevertheless, it was rather remarkable, as the severity of the symptoms would have led us to expect a considerable quantity of the poison.

"The next anomaly was the rapidity and completeness of Gannet's recovery. Usually, in severe cases, recovery is slow and is followed by a somewhat long period of ill-health. But Gannet began to recover almost immediately, and when he left the hospital he seemed to be quite well.

"The third anomaly – not a very striking one, perhaps – was his state of mind on leaving the hospital. He went back home quite happily and confidently, though his would-be murderer was still there; and he would not entertain any sort of inquiry or any measures to ascertain that murderer's identity. He seemed to assume that the affair was finished and that there was nothing more to fear.

"Now, looking at the case as a whole with the idea of a possible imposture in our minds, what did it suggest? Was there not the possibility that all the symptoms were simulated? That Gannet just took enough arsenic to supply the means of chemical demonstration (a fairly full daily dose of Fowler's solution would do) and, on the appropriate occasion, put a substantial quantity of arsenic into the barley-water? In short, was it not possible that the poisoning affair was a deception from beginning to end?

"The answer to this question obviously was that it was quite possible, and the next question was as to its probability. But the answer to this also appeared to be affirmative; for, on our hypothesis, the appearances in the studio were false appearances deliberately produced to create a certain erroneous belief. But those appearances were strongly supported by the previous poisoning crime and obviously connected with it. The reasonable conclusion seemed to be that the poisoning affair was a deception calculated to create this same erroneous belief (that an attempt had been made to murder Gannet) and to lead on naturally to the second crime.

"Now let us pause for a moment to see where we stand. Our hypothesis started with the assumption that the arsenic had been put into the ashes for a definite purpose. But we found that the only person who could have had a motive for planting it was Peter Gannet. Thus we had to conclude that Gannet was the murderer and Boles the victim. We have examined this conclusion, point by point, and we have found that it agrees with all the known facts and that it yields a complete, consistent, and reasonable scheme of the studio crime. Accordingly, we adopt that conclusion – provisionally, of course; for we are still in the region of hypothesis and have, as yet, actually proved nothing.

"But assuming that Gannet had committed this murder, it was evident that it must have been a very deliberate crime; long premeditated, carefully planned, and carried out with extraordinary foresight and infinite patience. A crime of this kind implies a proportionate motive; a deep-seated, permanent and intense motive. What could it have been? Was there anything known to us in Gannet's circumstances that might seem to account for his entertaining murder as a considered policy? Taking the usual motives for planned and premeditated murder, I asked myself whether any of them could apply to him. We may put them roughly into five categories: jealousy, revenge, cupidity, escape and fear. Was there any suggestion that Gannet might have been affected by any of them?

"As to jealousy, there was the undeniable fact that Mrs Gannet's relations with Boles were unusual and perhaps indiscreet. But there was no evidence of any impropriety and no sign that the friendship was resented by Gannet. It did not appear to me that jealousy as a motive could be entertained.

"As to revenge. This is a common motive among Mediterranean peoples but very rare in the case of Englishmen. Boles and Gannet disliked each other to the point of open enmity. An unpremeditated murder might easily have occurred, but there was nothing in their mere mutual dislike to suggest a motive for a deliberately planned murder. So, too, with the motive of cupidity;

there was nothing to show that either stood to gain any material benefit by the death of the other. But when I came to consider the last two motives – escape and fear – I saw that there was a positive suggestion which invited further examination; and the more it was examined, the more definite did it become."

"What, exactly, do you mean by escape?" I asked.

"I mean," he replied, "the desire to escape from some intolerable position. A man, for instance, whose life is being made unbearable by the conduct of an impossible wife, may contemplate getting rid of her, especially if he sees the opportunity of making a happy and desirable marriage; or who is haunted by a blackmailer who will never leave him to live in peace. In either case, murder offers the only means of escape, and the motive to adopt that means will tend to develop gradually. From a mere desirable possibility, it will grow into a definite intention; and then there will be careful consideration of practicable and safe methods of procedure. Now, in the present case, as I have said, it appeared to me that such a motive might have existed; and when I considered the circumstances, that impression became strongly confirmed. The possible motive came into view in connection with certain facts which were disclosed by Inspector Blandy's activities, and which were communicated to me by Oldfield when he consulted me about Mrs Gannet's difficulties.

"It appeared that Blandy, having finished with the bone fragments, proceeded to turn out Boles' cupboard. There he found fairly conclusive evidence that Boles was a common receiver – which was not our concern. But he also found a piece of gold plate on which were some very distinct fingerprints. They were the prints from a left hand, and there was a particularly fine and clear impression of a left thumb. Of this plate Blandy took possession with the expressed intention of taking it to the Fingerprint Department at Scotland Yard to see if Boles happened to be a known criminal. Presumably he did so, and we may judge of the result by what followed. Two days later he called on Mrs Gannet and subjected her to a searching interrogation, asking a number of leading questions, among which were two of very remarkable significance. He wanted to know where Boles was on the 19th of last September, and when it was that his friendship with Gannet suddenly turned to enmity. Both these questions she was able to answer; and the questions and the answers were highly illuminating.

"First, as to the questions. The 19th of September was the date of the Newingstead murder; and the murdered constable's truncheon bore a very distinct print of a left thumb – evidently that of the murderer. At a glance it appeared to me obvious that the thumbprint on the gold plate had been found to correspond with the thumbprint on the truncheon and that Boles had been identified thereby as the murderer of the constable. That was the only possible explanation of Blandy's question. And this assumption was confirmed by the answer; by which it transpired that Boles was at Newingstead on that fatal day and that, incidentally, Gannet was with him, the two men apparently staying at the house of Boles' aunt.

"Blandy's other question and Mrs Gannet's answer were also profoundly significant; for she recalled, clearly, that the sudden change in the relations of the two men was first observed by her when she met them after their return from Newingstead. They went there friends; they came back enemies. She knew of no reason for the change; but those were the facts.

"Here we may pause to fill in, as I did, the picture thus presented to us in outline. There are two men (whom we may conveniently call A and B) staying together at a house in Newingstead. On the 19th of September, one of them, A, goes forth alone. Between eight and nine in the evening he commits the robbery. At about nine o'clock he kills the constable. Then he finds Oldfield's bicycle and on it he pedals away some four miles along the London Road. Having thus got away from the scene of the crime, he dismounts and seeks a place in which to hide the bicycle. He finds a cart shed, and, having concealed the bicycle in it, sets out to return to Newingstead. Obviously, he would not go back by the same route, with the chance of encountering the police, for he probably suspects that he has killed a man, and, at any rate, he has the stolen diamonds on his person. He must necessarily make a detour so as to approach Newingstead from a different direction, and his progress would not be rapid, as he would probably try to avoid being seen. The cart shed was over four miles from Newingstead along the main road, and his detour would have added considerably to that distance. By the time that he arrived at his lodgings it would be getting late; at least eleven o'clock and probably later. Quite a late hour by village standards.

"The time of his arrival home would probably be noted by B. But there is something else that he would note. A had been engaged in a violent encounter with the constable and could hardly fail to bear some traces of it on his person. The constable was by no means passive. He had drawn his truncheon and was using it when it was snatched away from him. We may safely assume that A's appearance, when he sneaked home and let himself into the house, must have been somewhat unusual.

"By the next morning the hue and cry was out. All the village knew of the robbery and the murder, and it would be inevitable that B should connect the crime with A's late homecoming and disordered condition. Not only did the times agree, but the man robbed, Arthur Kempster, was known to them both, and known personally at least by one of them. Then came the inquest with full details of the crime and the vitally important fact that a clear fingerprint, left by the murderer, was in the possession of the police. Both the men must have known what was proved at the inquest, for a very full report of it was published in the local paper, as I know from having read a copy that Kempster gave me. Both men knew of the existence of the thumbprint; and one knew, and the other was convinced, that it was A's thumbprint.

"From these facts it was easy to infer what must have followed. For it appears that it was just at this time that the sudden change from mutual friendship to mutual enmity occurred. What did that change (considered in connection with the aforesaid facts) imply?

To me it suggested the beginning of a course of blackmail. B was convinced that A was the robber and he demanded a share of the proceeds as the price of his silence. But A could not admit the robbery without also admitting the murder. Consequently, he denied all knowledge of either.

"Then began the familiar train of events that is characteristic of blackmail, that so commonly leads to its natural end in either suicide or murder. B felt sure that A had in his possession loot to the value of ten thousand pounds and he demanded, with menaces, his share of that loot – demands that A met with stubborn denials. And so it went on with recurring threats and recriminations and violent quarrels.

"But it could not go on for ever. To A, the conditions were becoming intolerable. A constant menace hung over him. He lived in the shadow of the gallows. A word from B could put the rope round his neck; a mere denunciation without need of proof. For there was the deadly thumbprint, and they both knew it. To A a simple accusation showed the way directly to the execution shed.

"Was there no escape? Obviously, mere payment was of no use. It never is of use in the case of blackmail. For the blackmailer may sell his silence, but he retains his knowledge. If A had surrendered the whole of the loot to B he would still not have been safe. Still B would have held him in the hollow of his hand, ready to blackmail again when the occasion should arise. Clearly, there was no escape that way. As long as B remained alive, the life of A hung upon a thread.

"From this conclusion the corollary was obvious. If B's existence was incompatible with the safe and peaceful existence of A, then B must be eliminated. It was the only way of escape. And having come to this decision, A could give his attention, quietly and without hurry, to the question of ways and means, to the devising of a plan whereby B could be eliminated without leaving a trace, or, at any rate, a trace that would lead in the direction of A. And thus came into being the elaborate, ingeniously devised scheme which I had been examining and which looked, at that time, so much like a successful one.

"The next problem was to give a name to each of the two men. A and B represented Boles and Gannet; but which was which? Was Boles, for instance, A the murderer, or B the blackmailer? By Blandy, Boles was confidently identified as the Newingstead murderer. But then Blandy accepted all the appearances at their face value. In his view Gannet was not in the picture. He was not a person; he was a mere basketful of ashes. The thumbprint had been found in Boles' cupboard on Boles' own material. Therefore, it was Boles' thumbprint.

"But was this conclusion in accordance with ordinary probabilities? From Blandy's point of view it may have been, but from mine it certainly was not. So great was the improbability that it presented that, even if I had known nothing of the other facts, I should have approached it with profound scepticism. Consider the position. Here is a man whose thumbprint is filed at Scotland Yard. That print is capable of hanging him, and he knows it. Then is it conceivable that, if he were not an abject fool – which Boles was not – he would be dabbing that print on surfaces that anyone might see? Would he not studiously avoid making that print on anything? Would he not, when working alone, wear a glove on his left hand? And if by chance he should mark some object with that print, would he not be careful to wipe it off? Above all, if he were absconding as he was assumed to have absconded, would he leave a perfect specimen of that incriminating print in the very place which the police would be quite certain to search for the express purpose of discovering fingerprints? The thing was incredible. The very blatancy of it was enough to raise a suspicion of imposture.

"That, as I have said, is taking the thumbprint apart from any other facts or deductions. But now let us consider it in connection with what we have deduced. If we suggest that the thumbprint was Gannet's and that he had planted it where it was certain to be found by the police, at once we exchange a wild improbability for a very striking probability. For thus he would have contrived to kill an additional, very important bird with the same stone. He has got rid of Boles, the blackmailer. But now he has also got rid of the Newingstead murderer. He has attached the incriminating thumbprint to the person of Boles, and, as Boles has ceased to exist, the fraud can never be discovered. He has made himself absolutely safe; for the police have an exact description of Boles – who was, at least, three inches taller than Gannet and had brown eyes. So that even if, by some infinitely remote chance, Gannet should leave his thumbprint on some object and it should be found by the police, still he would be in no danger. They would assume as a certainty that it had been made by a tall, brown-eyed man, and they would search for that man – and never find him.

"Here, then, is a fresh agreement; and you notice that our deductions are mounting up, and that they conform to the great rule of circumstantial evidence; that all the facts shall point to the same conclusion. Our hypothesis is very largely confirmed, and we are justified in believing it to be the true one. That, at least, was my feeling at this stage. But still there remained another matter that had to be considered; an important matter, too, since it might admit of an actual experimental test. Accordingly I gave it my attention.

"I had concluded (provisionally) that Gannet was the Newingstead murderer. If he were, he had in his possession fifteen large diamonds of the aggregate value of about ten thousand pounds. How would he have disposed of those diamonds? He could not carry them on his person, for, apart from their great value, they were highly incriminating. Merely putting them under lock and key would hardly be sufficient, for Boles was still frequenting the house and he probably knew all about the methods of opening drawers and cupboards. Something more secure would be needed; something in the nature of an actual hiding-place. But he was planning to dispose of Boles and then to disappear; and, naturally, when the time should come for him to disappear, he would want to take the diamonds with him. But still he might be unwilling to have them on his person. How was this difficulty to be met?

"Here, once more, enlightenment came from the invaluable Oldfield. In the course of his search of the deserted house he observed that the pottery which had been on the mantelpiece of Gannet's bedroom had disappeared. Now, this was a rather remarkable circumstance. The disappearance of the pottery seemed to coincide with the disappearance of Gannet, and one naturally asked oneself whether there could be any connection between the two events, and, if so, what the nature of that connection might be. The pottery consisted, as I remembered, of a number of bowls and jars and a particularly hideous stoneware figure. The pots seemed to be of no special interest. But the figure invited inquiry. A pottery figure is necessarily made hollow, for lightness and to allow of even shrinkage during the firing; and the cavity inside would furnish a possible hiding-place, though not, perhaps, a very good one, if the figure were of the ordinary type.

"But this figure was not of the ordinary type. I ascertained the fact from Oldfield, who had examined it and who gave me an exact description of it. And a most astonishing description it was; for it seemed to involve a physical impossibility. The figure, he informed me, had a flat base covered with some sort of white enamel on which was the artist's signature. There was no opening in it, nor was there any opening either at the back or the top. That was according to his recollection, and he could hardly have been mistaken, for he had examined the figure all over and he was certain that there was no hole in it anywhere.

"Now, here was a most significant fact. What could be the explanation? There were only two possibilities, and one of them could be confidently rejected. Either the figure was solid or an opening in it had been filled up. But it could not be solid, for there must be some cavity in a pottery figure to allow of shrinkage without cracking. But if it was hollow, there must have been some opening in it originally. For a hollow figure in which there was no opening would be blown to pieces by the expansion of the imprisoned air during the firing. The only possible conclusion was that an opening originally existing had been filled up; and this conclusion was supported by the condition of base. It is there that the opening is usually placed, as it is hidden when the figure is standing; and there it had apparently been in this case; for the white, glazed enamel looked all wrong, seeing that the figure itself was salt-glazed, and, in any case, it was certainly an addition. Moreover, as it must have been added after the firing, it could hardly have been a ceramic enamel but was more probably some kind of hydraulic cement such as Keene's. But whatever the material may have been, the essential fact was that the opening had been filled up and concealed, and the open cavity converted into a sealed cavity.

"Here, then, was an absolutely perfect hiding-place, which had the additional virtue of being portable. But if it contained the diamonds, as I had no doubt that it did, it was necessary to find out without delay what had become of it. For wherever the diamonds were, there, sooner or later, Gannet would be found. In short, it seemed that the stoneware monkey might supply the crucial fact which would tell us whether our hypothesis was true or false.

"There was no difficulty in tracing the monkey, for Oldfield had learned that it had been sent, with the other pottery, to a loan exhibition at a museum in Hoxton. But before going there to examine it and check Oldfield's description, I had to acquire a few preliminary data. From Mr Kempster of the Bond Street gallery I obtained the name and address of the owner of a replica of the figure; and as the question of weight might arise, I took the opportunity to weigh and measure one of Gannet's bowls.

"The owner of the replica, a Mr Broomhill, gave us every facility for examining it and even weighing it. We found that it was hollow, and, judging by the weight, that it had a considerable interior cavity. There was an oval opening in the base about an inch and a half in the longer diameter, through which we could see the marks of a thumb, showing that the figure was a squeeze from a mould; and it was a little significant that all the impressions appeared to be those of a right thumb.

"Armed with these data, we went to the museum, where we were able to examine, handle, and weigh Gannet's figure. It corresponded completely with Oldfield's description, for there was no opening in any part of it. The appearance of the base suggested that the original opening had been filled with Keene's cement and glazed with cellulose varnish. That the figure was hollow was proved by its weight, but this was about six ounces greater than that of Broomhill's replica; a difference that would represent, roughly, the weight of the diamonds, the packing, and the cement stopping. Thus the observed facts were in complete agreement with the hypothesis that the diamonds had been concealed in the figure; and you will notice that they were inexplicable on any other supposition.

"We now went into the office and made a few inquiries; and the answers to these – quite freely and frankly given by the curator, Mr Sancroft – disclosed a most remarkable and significant group of facts. It appeared that the figure had been sold a short time before it had been sent to the museum. The purchaser, Mr James Newman, had then gone abroad but expected to return in about three months, when he proposed to call at the museum and claim his property. The arrangements to enable him to do so were very simple but very interesting. As Mr Newman was not known, personally, to Mr Sancroft (who also, by the way, had never met Peter Gannet), he would produce a letter of introduction and a written order to Mr Sancroft to deliver the figurine to Newman, who would then give a receipt for it.

"These arrangements presented a rather striking peculiarity. They involved the very minimum of contacts. There was no correspondence by which an address would have had to be disclosed. Mr Newman, a stranger to Sancroft, would appear in person, would present his order, receive his figurine, and then disappear, leaving no clue as to whence he had come or whither he had gone. The appearances were entirely consistent with the possibility that Mr Newman and Peter Gannet were one and the same person. And this I felt convinced was the fact.

"But if Newman was Gannet, what might we predict as to his personal appearance? He would almost certainly be clean shaved and there might be a certain amount of disguise. But the possibilities of disguise, off the stage, are very limited, and the essential personal characteristics remain. Stature cannot be appreciably disguised, and eye-colour not at all. Gannet's height was about five feet eight and his eyes were of a pale grey. He had a scar across his left eyebrow, and the middle finger of his right hand had an ankylosed joint. Neither the scar nor the stiff joint could be disguised, and it would be difficult to keep them out of sight.

"We learned from Sancroft that the three months had expired and that Mr Newman might be expected at any moment. Evidently, then, whatever was to be done must be done at once. But what was to be done? The final test was the identity of Newman, and that test could be applied only by me. I had to contrive, if possible, to be present when Newman arrived, for no subsequent shadowing of him was practicable. Until he was identified as Gannet he could not be stopped or prevented from leaving the country.

"It looked, at first, almost like an impossible problem, but certain peculiar circumstances made it comparatively easy. I was able to install my man, Snuper, at the museum to hold the fort in my absence. I gave him the description of Gannet and certain instructions, which I need not repeat in detail as it never became necessary to act on them. By good luck it happened that Newman arrived in the evening when Snuper was in charge alone. He had no authority to deliver up the figure so he made an appointment for the following morning. Then he sent me a message stating what had happened and that Mr Newman seemed to answer my description; whereupon I got into communication with Blandy and advised him to come to the museum on the chance that

Newman might be the man whom he wanted for the Newingstead affair.

"You know the rest. Jervis and I were at the museum when Newman arrived and Blandy was lurking in the entry. But, even then, the case was still only a train of hypothetical reasoning. Nothing had really been proved. Even when I stood behind Newman waiting for him to discover my presence, it was still possible that he might turn and reveal himself as a perfectly innocent stranger. Only at the very last moment, when he turned to face me and I recognized him as Gannet and saw that he recognized me, did I know that there had been no flaw in my reasoning. It was a dramatic moment; and a more unpleasant one I hope never to experience."

"It *was* rather horrible," I agreed. "The expression on the poor devil's face when he saw you haunts me to this day. I was almost sorry for him."

"Yes," said Thorndyke, "it was a disagreeable duty. The pursuit had been full of interest, but the capture I would gladly have left to the police, if that had been possible. But it was not. Our mutual recognition was the crucial fact.

"And now, after all this logic-chopping, perhaps a glass of wine would not come amiss. Let us pledge our colleague, Oldfield, who set our feet on the right track. And I may remark, Polton, that one fluid drachm is not a glass of wine within the meaning of the act."

The abstemious Polton crinkled guiltily and poured another thirty minims into the bottom of his glass. Then we solemnly pledged our friend, who received the tribute with a rather sheepish smile.

"It is very good of you, sir," said he, "to give me so much undeserved credit, and most kind of you all to drink my health. I realize my limitations, but it is a satisfaction to me to know that, if my wits are none of the most brilliant, I have, at least, been the occasion of wit in others."

There is little more to tell. The repentant Blandy, by way of making amends to his late victim (and possibly of casting a discreet veil over his own mistakes) so arranged matters with the coroner that the inquest on "a man who called himself James Newman" was conducted with the utmost tact and the minimum of publicity; whereby the future of Mrs Gannet was left unclouded and the susceptibilities of our friend, Linnell, unfounded.

As to the monkey, it experienced various vicissitudes before it came finally to rest in appropriate surroundings. First, by Mrs Gannet, it was presented to Thorndyke "as a memorial". But we agreed that it was too ugly even for a memorial, and I secretly took possession of it and conveyed it to Oldfield; who accepted it gleefully with a cryptic grin which I did not, at the time, understand. But I understood it later when he informed me – with a grin which was not at all cryptic – that he had presented it to Mr Bunderby.

R Austin Freeman

The D'Arblay Mystery
A Dr Thorndyke Mystery

When a man is found floating beneath the skin of a green-skimmed pond one morning, Dr Thorndyke becomes embroiled in an astonishing case. This wickedly entertaining detective fiction reveals that the victim was murdered through a lethal injection and someone out there is trying a cover-up.

Dr Thorndyke Intervenes
A Dr Thorndyke Mystery

What would you do if you opened a package to find a man's head? What would you do if the headless corpse had been swapped for a case of bullion? What would you do if you knew a brutal murderer was out there, somewhere, and waiting for you? Some people would run. Dr Thorndyke intervenes.

R Austin Freeman

Felo De Se
A Dr Thorndyke Mystery

John Gillam was a gambler. John Gillam faced financial ruin and was the victim of a sinister blackmail attempt. John Gillam is now dead. In this exceptional mystery, Dr Thorndyke is brought in to untangle the secrecy surrounding the death of John Gillam, a man not known for insanity and thoughts of suicide.

Flighty Phyllis

Chronicling the adventures and misadventures of Phyllis Dudley, Richard Austin Freeman brings to life a charming character always getting into scrapes. From impersonating a man to discovering mysterious trapdoors, *Flighty Phyllis* is an entertaining glimpse at the times and trials of a wayward woman.

R Austin Freeman

Helen Vardon's Confession
A Dr Thorndyke Mystery

Through the open door of a library, Helen Vardon hears an argument that changes her life forever. Helen's father and a man called Otway argue over missing funds in a trust one night. Otway proposes a marriage between him and Helen in exchange for his co-operation and silence. What transpires is a captivating tale of blackmail, fraud and death. Dr Thorndyke is left to piece together the clues in this enticing mystery.

Mr Pottermack's Oversight

Mr Pottermack is a law-abiding, settled homebody who has nothing to hide until the appearance of the shadowy Lewison, a gambler and blackmailer with an incredible story. It appears that Pottermack is in fact a runaway prisoner, convicted of fraud, and Lewison is about to spill the beans unless he receives a large bribe in return for his silence. But Pottermack protests his innocence, and resolves to shut Lewison up once and for all. Will he do it? And if he does, will he get away with it?

2313073R00144

Printed in Great Britain
by Amazon.co.uk, Ltd.,
Marston Gate.